David Alvarez
Austin, TX 146

CO-AUS-673

# MIKE NICOL

# HORSEMAN

Born in Cape Town in 1951, Mike Nicol is the
author of two previous novels, *The Powers
That Be* and *This Day and Age*, and a work of
nonfiction, *A Good-Looking Corpse*. He lives in
Muizenberg, South Africa.

GRAND VALLEY STATE UNIVERSITY LIBRARIES

VINTAGE

INTERNATIONAL

BOOKS BY MIKE NICOL

*The Powers That Be*

*A Good-Looking Corpse*

*This Day and Age*

*Horseman*

# HORSEMAN

# MIKE NICOL

# HORSEMAN

ILLUSTRATED BY DAVID JACKSON

VINTAGE INTERNATIONAL

VINTAGE BOOKS

A DIVISION OF RANDOM HOUSE, INC.

NEW YORK

FIRST VINTAGE INTERNATIONAL EDITION, OCTOBER 1996

*Copyright © 1994 by Tortuga Publishing Limited*

All rights reserved under International and Pan-American Copyright Conventions. Published in the United States by Vintage Books, a division of Random House, Inc., New York, and distributed in Canada by Random House of Canada Limited, Toronto. Originally published in Great Britain by Bloomsbury Publishing Ltd., London, in 1994. First published in the United States in hardcover by Alfred A. Knopf, Inc., New York, in 1995.

The Library of Congress has cataloged the Knopf edition as follows:
Nicol, Mike, [date]
Horseman / Mike Nicol: illustrations by David Jackson.—1st ed.
p. cm.
ISBN 0-679-43766-5
I. Title.
PR9369.3.N54H67 1995
823—dc20
95-5841
CIP
Vintage ISBN: 0-679-76039-3

Author photograph © Jerry Bauer

Random House Web address: http://www.randomhouse.com/

Printed in the United States of America
10  9  8  7  6  5  4  3  2  1

*For Jill, in appreciation*

My sincere thanks to the Authors' Foundation
for financial assistance during the writing of this book.

# HORSEMAN

# CHAPTER ONE

*A bailiff arrives to arrest the youth's father on a charge of murder. The youth seeks refuge in the forest where, from the schoolteacher and the woodsman, Madach, he learns of people's duplicity, and of the nature of betrayal and revenge. He is visited by dreams of dark foreboding.*

## The arrest

THEY WERE DRUNK WHEN THE BAILIFF CAME: the man unconscious among the hens; the youth in the house. It was the sisters who took the bailiff to the man. They stood about him in the heat and the bailiff nudged the man with his boot until he stirred and blinked up at the sun and the grinning face beside his sisters.

It has taken you a long time, he said.

Perhaps, replied the bailiff. But now I am here.

He dangled a length of chain and the fetters, and held a warrant charging murder.

It is time to go.

From where he lay in the dirt the man considered the irons. The drink was powerfully in him and his words were slow to form.

I do not need those, he said.

I say you do.

The man struggled to his feet, knelt for a time to steady himself, then groped upwards, leaning upon a chair. He waited until the blood had quieted in his head.

Nor will you take me like this.

He pushed past the bailiff.

I'll take you drunk or with the soberness beaten into you, said the bailiff, reaching out to grapple with the man, wielding the chain like a whip.

As they circled in the yard the youth came down and stood in the kitchen doorway. The thinness of him leant against the architrave and he was almost its height, beaked and fix-eyed as a stork. He squinted into the brightness at the forms he could barely see. His eyes were hard with liquor. He heard his father call for clean clothes and stumbled away to find them. In the darkness of the chest he found too a rifle wrapped in its cloths, smelling of linseed and powder. He took it out and laid it across his knees and for long moments was lost in wonder at the weapon. Then the man's shouts came through the drink and broke his mood. He took the rifle to his room and concealed it.

When the youth brought out the clothes his father stood naked in the yard, dripping with water. The man's hair was stuck to his head which now seemed too small for the thickness of the body that carried it.

The youth gave him the clothes and the man dressed. Twice he fell and was helped up by his son. Yet they both staggered in their drunkenness. The bailiff waited in the shade; the shackles swung from his hand like a pendulum. The sisters were nowhere in sight.

A drink, said the man, and the youth took him over to the bottle.

No, ordered the bailiff, moving without earnestness to intervene.

The man clasped the bottle like a club, threatening.

We'll drink, he said.

2

The bailiff shrugged. Then get on with it.

The man drank first while the youth watched him. When he was finished he gave the liquor to his son who took it and drank with a capacity beyond his adolescence. The man watched his son. The youth swallowed twice quickly and his father smiled. Neither spoke.

Then they went out of the house to the road where the bailiff's cart stood. The youth helped his father into the cart and waited while the manacles were locked. The bailiff climbed to his seat; the horse pulled forward. They went through the village where men put down their work and women came out of the houses. The schoolteacher bowed his head; the beekeeper raised a hand in salute. The youth walked behind the cart until it started up the hill. There he stopped: uncouth as any before maturity, hair curling on his jaws like chicken fluff, his skin erupted in pustules, his size that of any man but unmuscled. Only his eyes suggested an adult age, the gaze black. He watched the cart pull slowly away until the road was empty.

### The refuge of the forest

Before dawn the youth took his coat and the gun and went up the hill into the woods. His aunts did not hear him leave the house; nor was anyone in the fields to see him go. No dogs barked and the grey light held on because the clouds were down and raining. The youth was still addled by the drink but there was in him too a violence that drove his legs against the slope without pause. He punished himself with the going; his chest heaving at the effort and from his anger. But he fought it and it quietened and he went on more easily, angling away from the path towards the trees. The ground he crossed was spongy with the night's rain but the clay had not yet dampened in the soil to turn it slippery. He went bowed against the drizzle, the rifle clasped tightly under his coat.

All night he had drunk and tossed upon his bed. Whenever he woke he took wine until he passed again into an uneasy sleep. He dreamt, and his dreams were troubled for in them a dark figure lurked which soon would throw him back to wakefulness and the image of his father chained in the cart. With the first lighting he had left the house.

On the uplands the rain turned to mist. The youth hurried into the trees and sheltered beneath the canopy, shivering as the liquor left him. It was no drier here but his exhaustion after the restless night gave him sleep. All day he took refuge in the forest, only venturing out with dark.

Now hunger and thirst drove him back to the village. He circled the houses like a lame wolf but neither the dogs nor the geese paid attention to his passing. At his aunts' house he stood long at the window watching them at their knitting and mending until desperation forced him in. He came in at a barge and they shrieked at the sight of him, cowered as the rifle waved across them, fled before his menacing. He found food and ate. Above him he could hear the sisters locking themselves from his enmity. But he thought no more of it than that. When he was done he put bread and cheese and meat and the last of his father's wine in a sack and took all the cartridges and a blanket and went out into the night.

The youth did not go down to the village again for three nights. When he did he waited in the darkness until the last lamp had gone out in the aunts' house. Then he came off the lower slopes. The doors were bolted against him, yet he prised them open. He emptied the larder and a cupboard. Filled two sacks and searched for drink, but there was nothing. This raised his ire. He hauled aside a chest, scavenged among empty bottles heedless of the clatter, threw out pots and pans until he found the bottle he knew would be there: the brandy they kept for fevers. He pulled the cork and drank. When his own noise stopped and the sound of swallowing had gone from his ears he heard the screams and cries of his aunts. Near by dogs yelped; lights flared in the closer cottages.

He took the sacks and ran, struggling under the clumsiness of their weight, glancing back to see if he was followed. At first he was not: the women still howled for help from the upper windows and more voices were added to their confusion. Lanterns juggled in the dark before the house, then lamps went on inside and the youth saw others appear at the back. He was not yet far enough off to be safe so he ran harder when a light detached itself from the circle and started up the hill. The pursuer gained on him because the sacks hampered his flight. He discarded one, knowing he could return in the early light to fetch it. Unburdened he pressed on faster. But the man giving chase was soon winded and stopped. He called out the youth's name. The youth heard it and knew it was the schoolteacher, but he did not pause.

From the forest edge he watched the village return to darkness, except for a lamp which burnt all night in the sisters' house. He dozed sometimes, but mostly he worried about the sack lying unprotected on the slope. It was there for any passing fox or lynx to ravage. He strained eyes and ears to sense the smallest movement on the hill; out there nothing seemed to stir. About him the forest was alive but he had grown accustomed to its sounds: the quick rustle of mice or the sigh of trees settling their roots in deeper after the rains. An owl came into the branches above him with a rush of wings that brought a long silence on the ground. The youth noticed this, even though he concentrated elsewhere.

With the first greying of the dark he went out on the slope but could not see the sack. He found where it had been discarded and saw how the footsteps of another had crossed his and, heavier now, went on along the hill. He followed the prints into the trees yet lost them: as if the person had ceased to tread upon the ground. He gripped harder on the rifle and saw in the shadows all that could menace him: the forest now savage, offering no refuge. He went cold and crept away.

Weary and unslept, the youth retreated farther into the woods. All day he walked until he was in regions he had never been before, descending into glades and tangled parts concealing a river and pools, then up again into a belt of firs. Here were no traces that others had been: not litter from a meal, skins, bones, nor charcoal and ashes. Those who had travelled through had done so without stopping. He rested once between the roots of an elm, lay hidden beneath a blanket, pensive until he was sure no one followed him, then slept. When he woke the sun was well over, its beams slanting down. He ate quickly from the bread and the cheese then hurried on until the light failed.

And so he lived in the deep reaches of the forest. Kept on the move, favouring the dense bracken in the gullies to the upland woods where the oaks were sparse and the soft ground deadened all approach; never stopping until the day was gone and none could see the bed he chose. He lived as though hunted, yet he heard no one; caught not even a distant glimpse of a woodsman. But sometimes his skin would crawl with the sense that he was watched. Then he spun suddenly, or dropped, or dodged into a thicket and waited hour upon hour, but there was nothing. And he took to the boughs of the greater trees and found some solace there. From a height he watched the movement of the forest: how moles came up through the roots and earth, a passage of weasels, deer, and even boar.

When he chewed on roots to assuage his hunger he considered the ease of a hunt but would not waste cartridges for the sake of a stomach of wood-dove or three nights of venison. Instead he rooted through the undergrowth for mushrooms and in the bramble for berries, finding nothing. The hunger churned in him. And he went back through the forest to the hill above the village.

The youth waited out the time until he could slip down in the quiet hours. Before going he fitted a cartridge and when the gun was ready moved out of his cover. A thin moon low in the sky cast no light to bother him. He entered the yard of his aunts' house and took a hen from the fowl-run and snapped its neck before it could chatter in surprise. The birds shifted at his presence and for long moments he listened, but the night about him was undisturbed. He let the dead one drop into the sack. Behind the run he found the traps his father had made for catching foxes and with them too a length of wire that could be shaped into snares. These he placed beside the sack. As he laid them down the iron jingled; the youth crouched, watchful, ready. Far off there sounded a noise like laughter that could have been the crying of some animal and then it was still again. In the corner of the yard stood the bench where his father had kept tools and here, as carefully as a blind man and as silent as a stoat, he felt through the pieces until he found a hunting knife which he drew out. The weight was comfortable and the blade ground to a fine edge.

In the next days the youth set the traps and his snares in the woods and on the edge of the fields, but caught nothing. The traps he rebaited; the snares he moved to other runs where rabbits or quail had been recently. This yielded a pheasant, and a hare that wriggled from his grasp even as he pulled off the noose. One bird was not enough.

Once more the hunger clawed at him; once more he went down to his aunts' house, but now the fowl-run was locked against him. The youth's hands trembled at this injustice. Inside him there rose that which was terrible and urgent. He gripped the lock and it sheared at his wrenching. He went in. His left hand found the hens and his right went over their heads in a clamp. He twisted. Their necks broke with a soft plopping. He killed two birds for himself and left three dead on their roosts. Then he tried the kitchen door and it was bolted. The windows were barred. The youth did not rant at this but he levelled the rifle and destroyed the hinges to the door with a single blast. Dogs began barking in the village and frightened voices called out. None of it distracted the youth. According to method he broke the gun, lifted out the spent cartridge and laid in another. At an upstairs window a lamp flared. The shutters opened; a face looked down. The movement caught the youth's eye. He turned, raised the gun, fired. There came a cry, a shattering of glass, and the light went out.

### The schoolteacher's pronouncements

In the afternoon the schoolteacher came alone up the hill. The youth watched him all the way, puzzled by his intentions. The man carried a bag, the one that usually held his books, which he changed from hand to hand every few yards as if it were too heavy to hold on one side. He walked at a slow pace, stopping occasionally to scan the treeline, then coming on again with what seemed like a greater reluctance. At the point where the road headed left along the crest of the hill a faint path led off across the wheat and into the trees. Here the schoolteacher put down his bag. He glanced back at the village: there were people in the sisters' yard and a group on the road but they were too distant for him to be sure they followed his progress. He raised an arm and someone waved back. Then he looked at the trees, a black wall of shadow in the bright afternoon, and picked up the bag.

From his vantage the youth watched the schoolteacher take the path then snoop towards him along the forest's foot, swishing through the stalks with the exaggeration of someone searching for a quail's nest. The youth drew deeper into his hide. The schoolteacher came on. When he was so close the youth could smell the mustiness of his jacket, the man reached into the grass and pulled up a snare. He clicked his tongue as he examined the expertise that had fashioned the wire, and carefully returned it to the ground. Then, shielding his face from low branches, he entered the silence of the woods.

At first the schoolteacher moved stealthily, peering into the shade, slipping from tree to tree. He was quiet, cunning, displaying an ability the youth had not accorded him. But the youth was a match for this and better. Now the forest was his home he had become it: could disappear in its shadows, could assume its shapes; hear in its breathing the messages of warning, feel the textures of comfort in its bark.

As animals stalk, the youth went after his prey, kept him in sight, noted every pause and action, and dreaded the man's capacity. For the schoolteacher was clever in his scouting: from the lie of fallen leaves determined a place where the youth had slept, picked from the bracken a feather that told of a hen's plucking, found ashes the youth had strewn, came close to where the slaughtered fowls were hidden. And with each discovery he triumphed, gave up his wiles, and began calling for the youth.

In a clearing he sat down against a tree and took wine and pickles from the bag. He drank in long draughts. When he had taken half he held up the bottle for the youth's inspection and said, Come out. You have nothing to fear from me. And there is news of your father.

Then he put the bottle to his lips once more, swallowed and wiped the back of his hand across his mouth.

Come out. I have pickles and bread. Do you hear me, lad: pickles and bread. You want wine? There is wine here too.

Again he held up the bottle.

Tokay. Noble tokay.

The schoolteacher stared about, expecting the youth to appear.

It's good wine, shouted the schoolteacher again. Good wine, my lad. Come hear the news I have of your father. I have seen him. I swear I have talked with him.

And the youth was of every intent to go out, yet even as he would a hand smothered his mouth, jerked his head up, exposing his neck to a sharp and ready knife. The youth gagged on the rankness of his attacker's sweat and the sourness of his breath but he did not struggle for the blade held a serious motive. Thus tightly locked and invisible, assailant and victim watched the schoolteacher in the clearing.

You're there, lad, I know it. I have found you out where you have been, but that's no business of mine.

The schoolteacher ate pickles and drank more wine. After each mouthful he called out for the youth, but less confidently.

See, I can do you no harm.

He held up his arms clutching the bottle in one hand.

Trust me, lad. You can trust me, I am the only friend to your father. And to you. The only one who has been troubled by this. Such I will swear on the Book.

He brought his arms down but lifted the bottle to drink. He finished the wine.

I came only to bring you news ... To warn you ...

He waited, glancing about.

Do you hear me, lad? To warn you. There's people down there who think the mark's on you, what with your violence. They've long held it was you that crucified the shepherd's dog and hung that pig from the chestnut bough. And that it's you who has done the other things too: drawn in blood upon their doors and dug for bones in the churchyard. They whisper these things about you. Even to your father they said it. Mark me, there are those who have always considered it and more so now. Now they'll gossip you into some worse and truly evil fiend with their superstitious talk. Some diabolical. Some fright to answer for those horrors and your silence and your forest living. They'll have you hounded, lad, if you continue thus. Do you hear me? They'll have you hounded.

For a long while the schoolteacher sat with his head bowed, the bottle dangling between his fingers. At last he dropped it and rose unsteadily to his feet. He clutched at a branch in support and spoke again.

You cannot blame them. Your ways are devilish and threatening to them. They are afraid of you. Heed me in this.

The schoolteacher took from his bag two more bottles which he laid

8

against the tree and then other provisions: bread, cheese, potatoes, turnips, a head of cabbage. All these he left.

See, lad, he shouted, these are from your father's friend. If you would trust me, I could be your friend too.

Again he waited, expecting a response. The quiet of the forest settled about him because neither birds nor small creatures stirred after his shouting.

All right. All right, he complained, picking up the empty bag. There is nothing for it.

He moved off, then paused for a last time: If you want food, come to me. There is always food for you in my house. But leave the old women, just leave the old women.

He shrugged finally, and left.

### Madach

The youth's captor did not talk until the schoolteacher's footsteps had been long silent. Then he whispered: This knife's quicker than you'n and will go just where I want it 'fore you'n can raise anything. Remember that.

He jerked the youth's head.

Answer me! It's only manners to answer me.

The youth did so with a muffled noise, and the man grinned to himself.

Now'n this is how it will be, he said. First I'm going to take this knife from your throat and lay it along your spine. And you'n not going to move even to draw breath. Hear that?

The youth nodded against the arm that bound his face.

Smart fellow, 'cause there's a lot of damage I can do if you'n move badly. A lot of organs I can hurt with a quick poke. Just think on these things while we're dancing. They're wise things to think on. And then . . . And then we're going to walk slower'n a snail to that tree where your friendly visitor sat and you'n going to hug the trunk like it was your mother. What're you'n say to that?

He paused.

Come on tell me 'cause it's your'n help in this.

The youth nodded again.

Fine. That's fine. It's fine to get along with such co-operation. Then there's no cause for unnecessary bloodshed. And I wouldn't want that between us at this early stage. Nor would you'n 'cause it would be your blood splashing on the leaves, no doubt about it.

The youth felt a weakening of the pressure that squeezed his head and moved with this advantage. But the grip pinned him closely once more: Easy, came the warning. Easy if it's wine you'n rather have in your throat than blood.

The hunched man let the lesson take hold in the youth before he spoke again.

Now 'fore we go journeying there's this little necklace for you'n just to make sure all the untowards are accounted for.

In one movement he had a rope noose over the youth's head pulled so tautly it bit into the skin, and the knife jabbing his backbone, getting him on. Slowly they shuffled towards the tree.

Carefully, cautioned the man, carefully to mind the roots and creepers for this is no time to trip.

A short length from the tree the man pushed the youth sprawling against it and had the rope around the trunk and bound tightly to the youth's ankle so he was half bent and could move neither head nor leg. It was that swift, that quickly done.

Yet the man was shouting even as the youth struggled to keep his balance: Hug her! Hug her the way I told you'n so's there's no trouble between us.

The youth did, and his wrists were tied.

The man, well pleased with this procedure, stepped back and smiled at his captive.

There now, he said, we can do formal introductions. I know who you'n are but you'n wouldn't know me. I'm called Madach by those who call me anything at all.

The youth stared at his tormentor but made no response.

Ah those are hellish eyes you'n giving me, sighed Madach, but they're not worth a bird's shit in your condition.

The youth spat.

Madach jumped back at the insult.

Well, if you'n can get gob out of your throat then the rope's not keeping your words in. But be warned, my peacock, in your way manners would be a handy thing.

He considered the youth.

Perhaps you'n should know this before we go further. You'n have been the object of my watching for days now. I could've put this knife through you'n every time you'n went to sleep. But I didn't. And if I've done you'n any injustice then maybe it was picking up your sack but even that's no crime 'cause it was lying there for anybody.

He edged closer again.

I saw the bailiff fetch your father. So I know why you'n here. Only thing I don't know exactly is what's in your head. But that's your property. All I'm saying is don't hold this action against me 'cause you'n tied up like that for your own sake.

Let me go, the youth got out although the noose pinched his sounds.

So you'n have words inside, smiled Madach. But there's nothing I can do about those particular words until we've come to an understanding. And that understanding, my peacock, is all up to you'n and your good common sense.

Let me go, said the youth.

Not yet, said Madach. There's things you'n will learn more easily in your present way than if you'n had the run of the place. But we'll get to those subjects in their own time. First there is the matter of sustenance demanding our attention.

And Madach winked, his face creasing into laughter.

He disappeared from the youth's sight and stood contemplating the wine and the food.

Now this is a feast, he said, the likes of which Mr Madach hasn't seen in a long while.

The youth heard him pull a wine cork and the gurgle of the wine as it went out the bottle's neck.

Ah, yes, this is a good harvest, he called out. And these are fine pickles, what few your friendly visitor left. Oh yes, my peacock, we could eat well here.

And he appeared again before the youth with the measure of wine well down. He offered the bottle.

I know you've a notion for this, and I'm not one to enjoy a drink alone.

The youth's eyes dodged from the wine to Madach's face.

Nor'm I a withholder, not when I know a man's got a taste for liquor. T'only problem as I see it is how're you'n going to take this in with your face all squashed up against the bark.

Madach stepped forward and twisted the youth's head.

Perhaps if you'n just turn yourself like this we can get the bottle in your mouth and then you'n have got all the wine you'n ever wanted.

As the wine came in the youth swallowed, and again, but there was too much and he was drowning with wine in his nose and in the passages behind his eyes. He choked and gagged fighting to draw breath until the tears ran and the liquor washed out his nostrils.

Madach looked on.

It's not an easy way to drink, he said. Maybe until our understanding it's best you'n stay dry.

11

Then he collected food and sat down facing the youth. He was silent for some time before speaking.

There's things, my peacock, which you'n should know about the world, he said, not important things, but things which offer a cause. Or should I say a likely explanation because from what I've seen there's a hundred ways of making sense of events and each one is right according to who argues it. Now let's consider your friendly visitor, that schoolteacher. He was a good man to your father wouldn't you'n say! And to you'n. Here he's been bringing wine and food and saying he's got news of your interests. Warning you'n, too, of the malice some bear. Not without cause, it would seem. Surely you'n would have sat down here and listened to his wiles if I hadn't put a knife at your throat. And then, my peacock, he'd've lured you'n to the village with him to drink more wine until you'n couldn't stand. In itself there's no harm in that. But when you'n woke up you'n would've been tied like a sheep in the back of a cart jolting off to the monastery. Just think of that!

Madach stuck out his chin in triumph.

Not a pleasant thought, my peacock. Not a pleasant thought, is it? But that's the truth of what's going on.

He took a draught from the bottle, filling up his cheeks, and then drinking slowly from the store in his mouth.

Eventually he said, Or that's my truth. It's up to you'nself to pick which truth you'n would put your faith in. And right now – he leered up – right now there's not the slightest doubt you'n think I'm a wicked liar.

And he laughed: Not that I could blame you'n. 'Cause all I seem to've done is treated you'n badly, drunk your wine, and stopped you'n hearing about the thing that probably most worries you'n. At least that'd be the case from where you'n standing clapped round the tree. To you'n and any outsider that's an awful injustice. Then again, the way I see it, you'n should be licking my boots with gratitude. Let me tell you'n, my peacock, if you'n were this moment a fly on the schoolteacher's jacket you'n would be hearing things you'n wouldn't believe. 'Cause right now he's telling those villagers that he had a talk with you'n and soon he'll get you'n down and then the monks can have you'n. Because that is best for the likes of you'n that shun the normal ways and attributes. Let the monks use you'n, he's saying. They can teach you'n prayers and due subservience and keep what's mad in you'n well caged. For what better place could you'n be? Except in a bedlam! Or a jail! And they will nod their heads, fearing you'n every bit the devil they believe.

Madach yawned: All this is a lot for you'n to think about, my

12

peacock, but neither of us is in much hurry and, in the end, you'n will truly see the logic of my reasoning.

He propped himself on his arms and stared at the youth for a long time.

N'while you'n thinking about those things, think about why I didn't just cut your throat.

Then he lay down and closed his eyes.

The youth waited until he was sure the man was asleep before he strained against the knots, but they were firmly tied. He ached from the distortion of his bindings where they cut and where there was no slack to give him relief. Yet he would not moan. After some hours his water hurt and he let it go and felt how it filled his boot. Then the damp on his trousers turned cold where it stuck along the skin. He shivered as the light went down and it grew darker among the trees.

Sometime the youth must have slept because the leg that took his weight gave under him and he slid down until he half hung from his arms and half rested on the bent leg. Such is how Madach found him. The humped man lit a brand and held it near the youth's face until the heat woke him.

Come, my peacock, he soothed, you'n and me have still got talking to do.

The youth pulled back from the fire by turning on the tree. But the leg beneath him had knotted its muscles: he could neither stand again nor move any way. His struggles gave up a stink of urine. Madach wrinkled his nose.

Ah, pissed yourself have you'n! There was no need of that. I'm not a hard man when it comes to these functions. If you'n would of asked we could have worked out ways to have you'n wetting free.

The youth kept his face turned from the fire and clenched his teeth at the numbing pain of the blood going back into the veins and arteries of his cramp. All he said was: Let me go.

Maybe, said Madach, but that would depend. The way I see it you'n couldn't have done enough thinking just yet or you'n would have other words to say to me. But as you'n haven't it would seem I'll have to set to explanations.

He slipped round the tree bringing them face to face and trapped the youth's head beneath his hand. Their eyes met and neither wavered. Madach came in close.

First then, he said, if it was me squirming like a weasel in a wire trap, I'd want to know what proof there was of the schoolteacher's motives. To which, the only answer your captor could give is to say, Trust me; and then he might add, 'cause I know, 'cause Madach's a man of the night and at night people lay their plots and plans never thinking there's an ear at the window. Which is a fair enough reply although it brings another question begging: and that is why should a man-o'-the-woods with skin like tree bark and a way quieter than animals give a pigeon's fart for what happens to the likes of you'n? Now that's a deep question with some answers that not even the woodsman wants to hear 'cause they would be prying into mysterious ways. Rather he'd just leave it at the simple truth that he's concerned for the fellow. Concerned, do you'n hear, not sorry, or pitying or anything like that because we all have to make choices in this world according to events, and those choices, good or bad, shouldn't carry praise or blame from others ... Anycause, my peacock, that's his explanation: he's concerned. But then, too, he's seen the fellow shoot in the days you'n hunted with your father and knows that few are better taught, and seen how he gets on in the forest and thinks that with this fellow there's things that two could do which one can't. Like there'd be no waste of a killed deer; and as one was checking traps another could be picking berries. Getting along in such a way would ease things. So what he's proposing is a partnership. Him and the fellow.

Madach's face was so close the youth could feel the long hairs of his beard. He came nearer yet until they were cheek to cheek.

Now this means the fellow's got to trust, he whispered. And trust's a thing that usually takes its time. Only the fellow's got no time.

At this Madach sprang backwards seeming to keep on the air with his lightness as he danced about the clearing in a shower of sparks from the brand. The youth saw his antics: the jumping and the quickness of them, as if the man's crabbed body had renounced its flesh and blood; then he leapt in and squatted beside the youth again and said, Let me tell you'n more aspects about matters, my peacock.

He was breathing heavily from the dance yet he spoke when his lungs exhaled, riding the speech out on this air.

Listen carefully 'cause as you'n have not much value for words, I have. When there's no one to talk to but yourself you'n soon appreciate their rate. Now, do you'n know this one? You'n should. You'n have felt its edge, the sheer injustice of it, the puzzle. Yet despite the weight it carries, it's easily hired. Some once set it at thirty pieces but it's gone for less and it's gone for more and it'll find a price every time. It's betrayal. A treacherous word with more agony locked in it than a quick glib saying can ever express. Wouldn't you'n agree? And from what I've just told you'n its doubt and its hurt must be working round your heart even now.

14

He stopped to look intently at the youth, bringing the torch in ١
the youth shut his eyes against the glare of the flames. Madach noducu.
As it is. As it is.

He settled back on his haunches; planted the brand firmly in the
ground.

There's no helping it, he said at last. No way out but to be wounded
by every thrust – and then, brightening: But listen to this, my peacock,
'cause in my knowledge the word following betrayal is a sweet one,
one that brings hours of content, that works the imagination to a
pitch with images of pleasure and delight, that can bring a laugh
or a smile or a happiness better than spring mornings, indeed, that
promises everything. This is a priceless word, my peacock. Oh it's been
traded again and again to mercenaries but that doesn't matter 'cause a
monetary exchange is no reflection of its true worth. Its true worth lies
only with one person. Only he will know the beauty of it; only he will
treasure its comfort. The word I mean is vengeance. Consider it, as
I'm sure you'n have. Vengeance on those who betrayed your father.
Vengeance on those who betrayed you'n, as they surely do who won't
have you'n in their village. Vengeance on all those who threaten us.
Vengeance. Bloody and merciless vengeance.

The last words Madach spat out in his fury.

Endless, red gushing vengeance. That is what you'n want and that
is what you'n will have.

He considered the youth for a moment: There is truth in this, he
said, slowly, deliberately, but there is also deception. You'n see it is
a tricky word as well. It fools by its substance and its meaning, it
goads, it irritates, it won't be put aside until the deed is done. And
then instantly it is an illusion, an emptiness, a nothingness. It carries
no satisfaction, no triumph. Again you'n have been betrayed. Again
you'n must have vengeance.

Madach turned away from the youth and stood up.

I tell you'n this not as a warning but 'cause it is what I
have found.

For a length of silence, he stood over the youth looking down. Then
he walked into the dark and the youth heard his voice drifting back
and forth across the clearing. There was no sound of movement, just
his voice now here, now there.

You'n should know I've had revenge on one who was once a soldier,
he said. 'Cause that's when I learnt the nature of revenge. When I
came for him I learnt it . . . but he did not continue and the sentence
faded into the communication of leaves that rustled over the man's
quiet. The youth strained into the gloom behind the torch, sensing,

listening, until he was convinced the man Madach had abandoned him. He sank upon the tree. And then the voice came suddenly from behind him: I've had revenge, my peacock. Once. A hundred times. These things cannot be counted. Nor'n can they overpower the first moment. It has its purity, its simple justice.

Once more Madach fell silent and then his voice sounded from another direction yet the youth had not heard his passing.

He was a soldier, my peacock, when I first saw him but when I came for him he was a worn man who could no longer walk. No matter, I tell you'n, no matter at all: not today nor tomorrow nor in all the time of the universe because you'n see it was his face, the face I'd kept stored against such a day, never expecting to find it, always hoping right would prevail. Always hoping. And there he was: him, the actual man in flesh and blood. Him who'd taken my father and my brothers; him who'd led off my mother and my sisters. Him who'd kicked my buckled body into a ditch and made me, me who'd not asked for it, nor'n wanted it, yet was made the witness of his deeds. Tender witness. Child witness to the acts of himself and his comrades. Witness who couldn't close his eyes, or cry, but had to watch every moment, I tell you'n, my peacock, every single moment of their bloody doings. Know that, my peacock, know that. Everything. All destroyed. Love, kindness, kisses all killed, even the blueness of the sky made ugly 'cause how could the sky keep its colour on a day when such deeds're done? How? How? How? You'n think you'n know! You'n can't tell the beer from cow's piss! Destroyed. Everything. 'Cause on this morning our houses that couldn't keep those soldiers out betrayed us, as did those men who should've defended us, as did whoever my father called Lord and made his prayers to. The great God in heaven! Let me tell you'n that afterwards the birds betrayed us with their song and the cows never bellowed. Not once. Not ever. They just went on chewing and chewing.

Madach was unexpectedly close again yet the youth still could not see him.

But I kept the image of his face, my peacock, I kept that safe inside my head and crept into the woods. The woods've never betrayed me. They know the value of these memories and how to preserve them. They know what happened. And when the time is right they exact their vengeance. 'Cause it was while I wandered along the edge of the woods, going nowhere in particular except where the forest knew, I saw him. D'you'n know what that means? Can you'n guess? Hey! Huh! Huh-huh!

Madach was at the youth's ear but even as the youth wrenched his head in alarm, mouth gaping for a scream never howled, the woodsman was gone.

Then let me tell you'n, my peacock: it was joy; it was savage. There he sat on the edge of a field mumbling at the men and women as they worked the crops. And it was him. Him, the very same him who'd lived in my mind against this day. I went closer. Quieter than a fox I went closer. And loud my heart beat with it, my peacock, louder and louder as I watched him. None paid any attention to him, except me. He just sat there complaining, but none paid any attention. All the hours they worked I watched him. Forgot about thirst and hunger, forgot about all the world but him. Come the end of the day they picked him up and took him home. And there sat Madach among the leaves watching where they left him 'cause when night came he was intent on visiting.

Madach paused and each heard the other's breathing.

That night I did it, my peacock, that same night. You'n must know that I went visiting. Visiting, without a knock, without a kindly call. It's the truth you'n hearing, my peacock, the actual truth of Madach's revenge. And the real truth is this: I gagged him; I sat him in a chair and told him of what he'd done on that blue day. He was frightened. Oh yes he was frightened at it. Shivered and shook and even tried on tears of pity. But they were wasted. Light rain, I tell you'n, light rain that doesn't even wet the earth. Still I told it to him again just to be sure he'd heard me right. And thought on it; and recalled the day. Then I told him of other things: of the burnt houses that're ruins now almost hidden in grass and bracken. Of how I'd stand among the stones that'd made our rooms and listen for the voices of my mother, my father, any one of the people who'd lived there. Listen and listen and listen. But you'n and I know not one of them could make a sound again. So I told him there was no trace of the horror he'd done. It was gone, I said, and if any one found the ruins they'd not be able to say what'd happened there. Oh some might guess that the people'd moved on when the land turned sour, or they'd gone to work in the factories, reasons like that which are common enough. Don't you'n think, my peacock, those are the reasons some might think of? 'Cause who would dare imagine the truth? No one, my peacock, no one. Not you'n or a thousand others. 'Cause the real actual truth is not what we can think of. Just as him before me, snivelling, pissing, shitting, never once, never once in all the years he lived thought this was how it'd end. Him, as frightened as a pig before the knife. You'n know, my peacock, what I wondered then? I wondered would anyone ever know of his barbarity, and if they did how would they see it? Would they say it's history? Or it's war? Would they say it's in us all. In you'n and me. In priests and nuns. In children. D'you'n think they'd say this? 'Cause it's my belief, my peacock. It's my belief that's how it is. None would see the way my father died, or how my mother crawled towards him at the last. None would see it. Which is why I had no other way, no choice except to make it right in only this one way. Which likewise I explained being a man given to explanations as you'n know. Carefully, detail for detail I told him how it had to be. How it had to be the same death they died 'cause otherwise there was no point to his dying. That which is done unto others has to be done unto the doer. 'Tis a true expression, my peacock, common to all those of us gathered under the name of vengeance. Which, too, I explained to him. Yet he shook his head to deny me as no man should when Madach's boiled up. 'Cause it was at that I hauled him from the chair on to the floor. Oh how he squirmed away. Twisting this side and that like a frightened worm. Yet I came on. Still he shook his head. But I came on. It was the face, my peacock. It was his face. Him, there before me was guilty. Guilty as if the blood was still on him. I struck. I stuck the bayonet into him just as he'd done it to others years ago. When I pulled the steel clear he curled around the wound like a hedgehog. No, I said to him, that's just one. The worst is still to come. D'you'n think he heard me? D'you'n think he heard any of it? Perhaps they do that are receiving the equal of what they did. Now I kicked him. And whenever he moved I put the bayonet in, sometimes twisting it as I remembered him doing. Sometimes just stabbing short and quick. 'Cause I was witness. 'Cause I was avenger. Growing madder and madder, stabbing and stabbing and slashing and crazy with the frenzy just as he'd been. And so he died.

Madach came out of the dark and lifted the brand. He held it so that he and the youth were within its light and the youth saw how he was laughing without a sound.

Isn't that what we dream of, my peacock? he said when the spasm had passed. Isn't that what you'n have conjured for all those who've done you'n badly? Is it? It must be. It's still my dream. And yet, my peacock, and yet. I can tell you'n, there came a moment in the killing, a short doubting moment, when his face wasn't the face I'd preserved but a face I didn't know. Clear as a frost morning he was a stranger. Which stayed my hand. Which held back one strike against his possible innocence. Yet who's innocent, I ask you'n? Not him, not anyone out there. Even if it wasn't his hand that plunged the bayonet, he was guilty anycause 'cause it'd happened in his time and worse, he'd let it go untold.

In the quiet at the end of these words Madach brought down the brand and the forest clustered its darkness about them, and if they had listened they would have heard an owl not far off and a hunting fox that was distant, and outside the trees the calls of a man who was never answered except in the groaning of the woods. But they had no attention for what was beyond them. The youth leant splayed about the tree and had given up struggling to find accommodation with his bonds; the other, the torch forgotten in his hand, the youth invisible before him, twitched and jerked to the charge in his muscles. He neither tried to control it nor seemed to notice his condition yet his face twisted from mask to mask and his shoulders rode at their affairs. Now the fire went out and the dark came in completely.

The youth felt the blackness creep along his skin like a moth, and shivered. It was damp, both light and damp where it touched and flew around him. Yet he could not wave it off, as he could not defend himself from Madach's knife which he awaited because surely it would cut between his ribs because this was how and where he expected to die. Even as the minutes lengthened and the knife never came and he could not hear Madach nor sense where he might be, he expected it.

### Foreboding and freedom

Towards morning the youth woke with a terror in him. The image was large and the face invisible. He sensed that the mouth would be slewed in a smile both thin and hard. The figure did not advance but kept its distance: a single shape without flesh that stood as he had seen monks stand at prayer in the churches. Then it was quickly gone with his waking, but the foreboding lingered thicker than the fear of Madach's knife. He did not sleep again. His body hung from the trunk as it had done all night, twisted in a pain he no longer acknowledged.

When Madach cut him down he sprawled helpless and in agony. He could neither crawl nor shrug the gun from his shoulder where it had been slung like a dead weight throughout his capture. He lay fearing his weakness. Madach sat by and watched him and said nothing during this time or into the afternoon when the youth, who had sometimes slept from exhaustion, sometimes writhed with the ache of returning blood, at last hauled himself up against a tree. Madach pushed wine and food at him and he took it. Afterwards he shifted the gun from his shoulder and placed it on the ground beneath his hand. He drank more of the wine until the bottle was half finished. Madach never took his eyes off the youth and the youth regained his anger with his strength. He lifted the rifle and broke it and loaded it, going slowly through the motions, alert to any movement Madach made. But the crooked man did not stir. When the gun was cocked the youth steadied it at his adversary. Madach shrugged.

You'n can go or you'n can stay, he said. I have told all you'n need to know.

*Madach instructs the youth in the lore of survival but the winter proves too harsh for their resources. They resort to desperate ways. In this activity the youth confronts the grim figure of his dreams, and grows restless.*

**Madach's instruction**
THE YOUTH STAYED WITH THE HUMPED MAN CALLED MADACH. Both accepted it and both understood it could be no other way.

In the last warm weeks before the start of winter, they ranged widely in the forest, sometimes stealing from villages if their traps were short, but mostly content to hunt and gather. It was then the youth learnt the shriek of a caught fawn or the dread of a hare quivering in his hands before the killing. And how the blood spat when the jugular was severed and how the rush of air whistled in the slit gullet. He saw that each was a necessary condition to dying, each a final protest against such order and its perversity. Then, quickly, sharply, he would cut down between the vertebrae.

And after the hard shudder he slipped in the knife as Madach showed and flayed from the throat to the anus taking care not to break the muscle or puncture the stomach. Again from the brisket he worked to the right leg and then to the left and did the same with the back legs to the hocks. At the chest Madach had him tear free from the body enough skin to bunch in his hand which slowly he pulled away using his knuckles to squeeze down the muscle underneath, or his knife to slice clear the flesh when the skin stuck, until it was all peeled away and lay either side of the carcass like an open coat. Then he knifed through the muscles to expose the gut and cleaned it out not breaking the stomach or the gall and guarding carefully the liver. Madach nodded at his progress and told him where to nick the windpipe and how to rip that clear. Finally he flayed the skin from the backbone, and butchered the animal. They ate where they killed but stored the skins in a hollow tree-trunk for the times when Madach got the taste for liquor.

Then from these pelt sales they were gin-sodden for days. Often the youth was useless: fouled himself, stank, lay drunk wherever Madach could hide him in ditch or graveyard until it was slept off and he would return of single purpose, taking no pleasure in the liquor, silent compared to Madach's verbosity, unsmiling, drinking into the next oblivion. And sometimes there were fights which Madach began for no cause but malevolence, bringing the youth in too until they were both struck down or chased off. In this way they went: the youth pulling the man, who never ceased his invective, struggled to break free, demanded vengeance against them all. Like this they returned to the forest, for days too bruised to mind their traps or the animals dying in them.

The cold came on. With it came the damp mists which settled among the trees until nothing was dry. The leaves dripped; fungus sprouted in the thicker bark. Then Madach moved them to his winter quarters: a hollowed chamber dug into a mat of roots beneath an oak. The cavern walls were lined with stone; the roof was of rough-hewn planks yet even on the days of worst weather they did not leak. But if there was comfort in this then that was all. Because there were nights now when they went hungry having failed in the hunt and found the traps unsprung. Alone the youth went after deer and boar but saw neither, nor even their tracks. In desperation they stole more often from the villages, going down after dark to take a hen or a clutch of eggs or to scavenge amongst what offal had been discarded in the pits. Once they found money, which worked at them when they lay unfed in the burrow bringing to mind the possibility of drink and the heat of beerhalls. They imagined the laughter and the women, the men raising toasts, the dense smoke from pipes, the smell of warmed grog and fire, the desirability of it, until their fantasies demanded satisfaction. And so they went into the nearest place and drank pints of brew but the money was insufficient for their wants. The youth could have left and gone back to the woods with his head light and a warmth in his stomach but Madach needed yet another because he was gripped and the liquor had him in its power. He pulled the youth to him and laid a plan in his ear.

Smile, my peacock, smile, said Madach laughing now, courageous with his scheme.

The youth shrugged his acceptance.

They went outside as men do who need relief.

The first man to do likewise the youth clubbed down. The victim sank grunting to his knees but did not succumb; the youth swung at him again and this time he dropped. Together they pulled the man along a ditch into the blackness beyond the lights. Madach went quickly through the villager's pockets but there was not enough to give him comfort.

Again, he whispered to the youth. Quickly now, quickly.

They went back, stumbling from the drink and breathing heavily. Near the beer-room a man called out in greeting and they heard the splash of his urine on the fallen leaves. Madach answered, going up to stand beside the man. The youth crept near silently. This time he felled their victim with a single blow. The man collapsed but his water carried on, wetting Madach. He, too, they dragged along the ditch and robbed. With this Madach was content.

That's it, he whistled, that's justice for you'n, my peacock, 'cause that's a rich man lying there who's given you'n me enough to drink with for days to come. Thank you'n, sir – and he bowed mockingly towards the prone figure – and for that reason I'll even forgive the pissing of my trousers. Come – and Madach took the youth's arm and hurried them back inside.

Now the liquor circled through them and the whole company in the room was drunk such as the youth had never seen before. But there had been a child born that day who gave the villagers cause for celebration. They named it and praised it and called on the saints to bless it and raised their glasses to its health and life. As did Madach and the youth, drinking its good fortune whenever someone demanded it. And Madach even more often, stealing others' jugs when his own was empty. Then men took out their fiddles, and the chairs and tables were cleared back against the walls in a rush that left splintered pieces which were kicked aside even as the landlord tried to stop the damage. The music started fast with the fiddlers in accord, grinning at each other while they worked the tempo to a pitch no one could resist and the floor that had stood so briefly empty soon thundered to the dancers. The youth, caught up in this gaiety, laughing from the beer and antics, sat on a window-sill where he could watch undisturbed. He saw Madach, bent yet nimble, taking a woman through the movements who afterwards would never have guessed his deformity. He saw a dog trampled beneath the feet until it was hauled out. He saw the lecherous with their hands squeezing at women's breasts and he saw a woman who sent a man howling with a slap in the face. Yet the music did not stop. The people danced and drank and the music did not stop. Even when the man the youth had clubbed twice stood like the dead returned swaying in the doorway, the music did not stop.

The youth saw him first: this man with his mouth broken and his right ear bloody and the blood matted in his hair and runnels of dried blood streaking his face and his neck. There were flecks of blood, too, on his shirt. And his hands were red with it where he had tried to staunch the flow at his ear. The youth watched him leave the open doorway, lurching forward, his arms stretched out like a blind man in search of support. At first the dancers skipped round him and the music did not stop. He went on step by step until his hands found the fabric of a woman's dress and he gripped hard. The woman turned at this violation, tearing her dress, ready with abuse but not prepared for the battered face that swam towards her through the haze and dim light. The music did not stop. Neither at her first shriek nor at her second did the music stop. Then the man too screamed, showing where his teeth were broken and one had driven up into the cheek. The music did not stop but the dancers turned their heads and went out of step and gasped at the horror of this man. Only then did the music end suddenly, the fiddles screeching in discord.

Madach glanced up at the youth in the window. In the pandemonium each went out as best he was able.

In the next days they drank the money in other villages and stole food which they took to the burrow but it was soon finished. And Madach was restless and wanted to rob again. He incited the youth. During the meagre nights when the youth sat cleaning the gun, pulling a rope through the barrel again and again, scraping imaginary powder from the breech, Madach talked of suckling pig and crisp rind. After they had suppered on little more than boiled bones, Madach heightened their misery with dreams of goulash or stewed knuckles of pork. Through all this the youth kept at his gun although his stomach growled and the juices ran in his mouth.

We'n could have hot dumplings and the drink in us every night for no more trouble than it takes to walk and get it, my peacock, enticed Madach. That's what we deserve. It's the least a man deserves considering all circumstances.

The youth lifted his gun and squinted down the barrel at the candle guttering between them.

It's what every villager has and our lives are no softer than theirs.

They have money, said the youth, lowering the gun.

We could have money, said Madach. There are men with more money in their purses than we could count in a lifetime passing through this forest every day and night. We could stop them for the price of a meal and they would be none the lighter.

The youth fastened the rifle, cocked it, fitted it to his shoulder, and sighted. His finger tightened about the trigger. He squeezed it back, and the hammer struck dully.

'Twasn't something I could ever do before, mused Madach. A man by himself's not worth much in that situation, but with two'n of us and that weapon we'd have the wherewithal to make people listen.

### The horseman

After this they did not speak of it again or during the following day, yet as night came on they found themselves heading towards the road which climbed on to the uplands from the youth's village and went off towards the town where his father had been taken. A first snow had fallen in the afternoon but only in places was the ground frozen enough to keep it, and where it had settled on the trees it melted now in a steady drip. Yet it was a cold night with the clouds clearing above them.

They had no plan, neither raised the issue nor thought of how it would be. They waited. In the shadows beside the road, they waited.

The youth huddled into himself, the rifle lying protected across his

25

knees. In this way he half slept but like an animal heard the small noises of the forest about him. Once he woke from a different sound and soon felt Madach's hand on his shoulder.

It was a horse coming slowly at its own pace. Madach moved closer to the road. The youth stalked forward too and crouched among the edging trees. The hooves were loud yet the horse and rider still invisible. In one hand the youth held the rifle, his other fingered the cartridges in the pouch. The horse got nearer but remained part of the night.

When're he comes get him off the horse, said Madach. Or shoot it under him.

The youth did not respond.

D'you'n hear.

Still the youth said nothing.

Suddenly the horseman appeared from the dark. He was hunched in the saddle, more a bulk than any shape that could be called a man. Yet he was large despite the way he held himself tightly against the cold. The youth let them come on until they were almost opposite. Then he sprang out and the horse stopped at his action. The man jerked forward but held his seat easily. He swayed in the saddle and made no movement to coax the horse on or to see what obstructed them. The horse shifted its back legs, skewing slightly at an angle closer to the youth. He stepped away, raising the rifle more directly towards the man. For a moment they were transfixed, except where the muscles pulled and rippled in the horse's shoulder.

Now Madach, armed with a bayonet which the youth had never seen nor knew he carried, slipped out of the forest. He darted into the road, dancing from leg to leg in his agitation, circling the horseman. At this the horse took fright and snorted, but the rider did not stir.

You'n! Get down! shouted Madach.

The horse dropped dung; the horseman sat unchanged.

Get down. We are armed. Get down.

Madach ran in against the horse's flank intent to cut at the man's leg. But in that instant the man kicked backwards, the heel of his boot taking Madach on the shoulder and staggering him. He dropped the bayonet, going down too with the force of the blow.

He screamed at the youth: Shoot the horse. Shoot the horse. This motherbastard. Show him. Shoot the horse.

But the rider raised a hand from under his cloak in a sign forbidding the youth to shoot, and the youth could not disobey.

At the horse's feet Madach scrambled for his bayonet in the dirt, and shouted, Shoot the horse. The motherbastard. Shoot the horse.

The youth did not hear this: he watched the form that had been hunched and hidden in the cloak slowly straighten, the head coming up but the face unseen in the blackness of the hood, until the man sat erect. His hand retained its gesture of authority, and then the fingers folded and the arm went down to the reins that lay loosely over the horse's neck. The rider sat his horse as dark and terrible as a shadow.

At this sight the youth backed off, and the man nudged the horse after him.

Still Madach yelled, Shoot the motherbastard, boy. Vengeance and retribution. Death, motherbastard, death.

The youth could not run. He stopped, but the horse kept on until it stood over him and he looked up into the shadow that hid the man's face and was more fearsome than a death's head.

Again Madach attacked; again the man kicked him away without sparing a glance for his assailant.

The youth and the horseman stared at one another and the youth was too afraid to move.

Then the rider lifted his free hand from the depths of his coat and tossed a purse of coins at the youth. It struck the youth's chest and fell heavily on to the road, the coins jingling.

Heee agh, motherbastard. This'n is vengeance, screamed Madach getting up from the dirt, victorious at the sound of money.

The horseman flipped the reins against the horse's neck; it started forward. They went past the youth into the dark and were quickly gone. The youth listened for the hooves but they made no sound.

Heee agh. Vengeance and justice, cried Madach dancing with delight, swinging the purse above his head. That's it, my peacock. That's what I told you'n we could do. Now let the poor man have his way. We'll drink and eat all winter and half the summer no doubt. Heee agh. Vengeance on all motherbastards.

### The youth's predicament

In the days afterwards the youth kept his unease. He went alone about the forest to clear the traps, staying out until nightfall in a ceaseless wandering. He would take the rifle but he did not hunt. He seldom stopped on his way, except to ensure he was alone. Then he would pause briefly to listen, before moving on again in a new direction quickly. Yet each day's course brought him back to the woodline above his village. From its safety he would scan the distant roads where they joined at the beerhouse: if there were people about they were villagers, women carrying billets or men with

27

dogs. Few travellers used the roads in the winter months. Not once was there a sign of the dark horseman on the roads that led through the forest.

Yet the youth was drawn to the village. If once, in the first days with Madach, he had forgotten it, now the place would not leave him. It was from where the horseman had come and where he knew he must go. He remembered the schoolteacher's words, and they brooded in him. But he lingered. Even when the first snows fell thick and bitter, he stayed in the woodland fringe and would not descend. Each day the tension of what was to come, and what had been, pulled him to the road that led down past his aunts' house, yet he could not take it.

During this time Madach watched the youth and saw the conflict in him. He grew spiteful at the youth's predicament and when they lay warm in the burrow at night chided him with betrayal.

You'n would go, he said. Don't deny it, 'cause I've seen you'n each day hesitating where the road is. I've seen you'n about to walk out yet too weak-minded to take the first step. But you'n will, my peacock, you'n will. And I should've known it would come to this. From the beginning I should've known it. Which maybe I did but still I put my faith against betrayal. 'Cause that's my way. I have faith in those like us. We've been betrayed. We know the misery of it and wouldn't be quick to inflict it yet again. Or so they say.

He struck a match and held it up, but the youth turned his head from the light.

So, you'n won't look at me either. That's an ill omen if ever I saw one. But you'n go off, my peacock. You'n do what you'n have got to do 'cause old Madach can manage in the woods. He's been managing all these years and he can manage some more without help or kindness. Oh you'n go off. Have your way. But while you'n are having it just consider if the morality should be with the living or with the dead. 'Cause that's something you'n have got to face sometime: whether there's right in what you'n are doing?

The match went out and left them with only a faint light coming off the coals. Madach sighed.

All right. All right, he whispered a while later. I know about these things too, these things that ride us. There's no helping them and there's no language to dissuade us against them either. But remember, my peacock, I warned you'n about going down there and I'm doing so again. That way's another story for the likes of you'n me, and not one I'd be inclined to relish.

The youth fell asleep soon afterwards but Madach lay awake until, in the early dawn, he heard him rise. He pretended sleep while the other dressed. Even as the youth left he did not stir; and the youth went without a word.

## The schoolteacher expounds

All day the youth kept hidden on the hill then, late in the afternoon, he took the road down to the village. He passed the house of his aunts but the windows were dark and neither woman was about. Along the street a child recognised him and ran inside crying his name. This brought people to their doors. They stared at the youth, calling their children away. And the youth walked on without looking at them, the rifle slung on his shoulder. He went to the schoolteacher's house, and knocked. The villagers came out of their houses and someone ran back the way the youth had come to tell his aunts. The youth knocked again, louder. The schoolteacher was slow in answering and the youth had to knock twice more. In the distance someone wailed and the youth half turned at this to glimpse two women, his aunts, black as crows, hopping in the road. Then the door opened.

The schoolteacher stood there blinking. He peered closely at the youth and at last he nodded and looked up beyond his visitor at the gathering villagers. He raised his hand in annoyance and waved them off.

This is expected, he shouted out. This was to be expected.

He stood aside for the youth to enter, and closed the door.

You have taken longer than I thought, said the schoolteacher, leading the youth into a dim room lit only by two lamps and a fire. He went to stand against the warmth and the youth stood in the centre of the room. He stared at the youth for a time, then his eyes shifted down to the floor which was almost invisible in the gloom. Eventually he looked up. The youth's eyes were still on him.

He said, I have to tell you that your father is dead. They hanged him some weeks ago.

The youth heard the words and understood them as he had come to over the last days. They were mere words and the reality of them had been lost and no longer mattered. What they described he could not imagine for they told nothing of how his father had gone to his last moments or the fear that had been in him. They did not allow for the place where it had happened or the final sights and sounds. Instead they were close and narrow like a coffin, their meaning confined in an obscurity.

He was dead when he could no longer be seen, said the youth.

The schoolteacher jerked, startled by this comment.

What? What did you say?

The youth did not answer. He turned to go.

Wait! said the schoolteacher. Wait. He paused: I have an obligation. To you. To your father.

He rushed across the room and laid a restraining hand on the youth. The youth shook himself free, and the schoolteacher's hand dropped off. Suddenly the man lost his resolve.

It is what I said I would do.

But he spoke more to himself than to the youth. He turned back to the fireplace; the youth stood just within the room.

It doesn't matter.

The youth waited.

It doesn't matter, the schoolteacher repeated. You have made your decision. What I promised does not matter.

He looked up.

But perhaps at the least I can give you a meal?

He did not wait for a reply. From a cupboard he drew plates and cutlery and glasses which he arranged untidily on the table. Then he went through to another room and returned with bread and fruit. He went again and again, bringing back wine, cold hams, and a pot of stew which still bubbled with heat. He poured two glasses of wine.

Come. Please.

The youth hesitated, but the temptation of food was too great. He sat down. They ate in silence, each keeping his eyes to himself.

Later, when they were drunk, the schoolteacher leant on the mantel over the fire and kicked at the coals and put on more logs. The youth still sat at the table.

It was there, said the schoolteacher, pointing at the youth, that your father often sat. He sat there at the death of your mother, your birth. It was there he forswore his belief. And no priest could persuade him otherwise. Could he have read the work of such as Aquinas or Berkeley, or Augustine or Bonaventura, I doubt even they could have convinced him. He saw her dying as irrefutable proof of godlessness, of chaos.

The schoolteacher drained his glass.

Science has determined that there are laws which order the seasons and keep our feet on the ground but perhaps they are based on an accident, a trivial compatibility in the universe and for all we know possibly a temporary one. Perhaps behind our happenstance and illusory existence are great spirals of chaos without meaning, without end.

For a while he was distracted by his thoughts. The youth nodded with the heaviness of the wine and once his head fell forward. He snapped it back and stared wildly at the schoolteacher. But the man soon drifted out of focus.

I can expound on metaphysics, I understand about the essence of things, the schoolteacher said abruptly. I have followed Aquinas's themes to the existence of God, yet they are no help. I know that it is words, those we speak and those we write, which make us real. I know that without them we would be nothing.

The schoolteacher let go of the mantelpiece and sank into a chair.

There is a truth in that, lad, a truth which I find horrible.

The youth had fallen asleep with his head on the table, the rifle slung over the chair. The schoolteacher mumbled to himself.

To your father you were the cause of his wife's death and the harbinger of his grief and sadness. Yet he could love you. You brought him joy. But it was not something he could understand. It was injustice, indifference, caprice. Truly caprice. That's tonight's goat.

He raised his voice: Hey lad! Was it that which brought you here tonight? Caprice!

The youth did not stir.

He would have said so, your father, if he had known such words. I would have disagreed. As we often did. As we often did.

He was up now, the schoolteacher, and reached for the weapon and lifted it clear and paused in unsteadiness but the youth still slept.

It is my obligation, he whispered.

Then quietly left the house.

# CHAPTER THREE

*In the catacombs below a monastery the hooded monk talks of the savagery of mankind and of the triumph of death. He contracts the youth to wreak revenge on mankind. The youth, tormented, plunges from a high window.*

**The youth is captured**
HERE! HE'S HERE! IN THERE!
Ho demon!
Lo foulsprite!
Murderer come out.

Devil! The devil's spawn!
Padfoot! Barguest!
Satan!
A Satan!
Black Satan!

So they chanted and so they circled the house beating the ground with hoes and sticks: women and children and men. They had waited through the night for this time, whispering in their kitchens until the demon they created rose up in them and they went out into the early morning screaming its fear.

Burn him, they cried. Padfoot. This padfoot, evil padfoot.

And they beat upon the windows and the doors.

The youth woke with the noise and lay unmoving. He was cold because the fire had dampened to a whiteness and the wine in him now ran too thinly. Yet it had left him dull and slow. The rocm was not as he remembered it: it had the smell of cats, pungent and unnerving; it danced about him with its clutter and its objects. Stones rattled against the windowpanes. Shadows flickered across the floor as faces broke the light to leer quickly in. He lay in his unease listening to their violence. He saw that his gun was missing but could feel the shape of the knife in its sheath where it pressed against his thigh. This he released, slipping his hand down to take it with an imperceptible movement, as smooth as a snake over water. In his grasp it gave him comfort. He crept into the dark below the window, and waited the way he had seen animals wait in his traps, agitated yet helpless, dependent on events.

The youth shivered from fear and cold: deep shudders that ran through his skin, raising the down on his arms. The desperation was in his stomach too, and he had to squat to let it go, yet dreaded this vulnerability. His mess was loose and stank, and while he crouched half-naked he was most afraid. When it was out he fastened himself quickly. There were men shouting now and the chants were louder. He knew the knife was not enough. He took the fire poker as a weapon. He lit the lamps as incendiaries. He prepared an arsenal of geological specimens and the flints of ancient hunters. He waited.

A moment came when it all went quiet. The chanting stopped; the villagers crowded at the windows. The room was darker now they had taken up the light. He heard a door open and men enter the house, their boots solid on the wooden floors. They paused. The schoolteacher called his name. Then they came on cautiously to where the youth was waiting.

Hullo, fellow! one sang out.

Hey boy! Come, boy, wherever you are?

Don't fear us!

They'll not harm you, pledged the schoolteacher.

The footsteps continued.

Before they entered the room, the youth lobbed a lamp. It arced over the open door and dropped into the doorway with a shatter of glass and a whoosh as the oil ignited into sudden flame. The men swore and stumbled backwards.

No, lad! No! screamed the schoolteacher at the rise of fire but the oil was fast consumed and the flame died blackly.

The men consulted in whispers: a board creaked and the first one rushed in.

The youth tossed the other lamp into the doorway and it went off in a sheet of flame that caught on a cloth and burnt. Then he turned on the man lunging towards him and hit him once with the poker so that the man cried and ducked away. Two more had come through the fire and leapt at the youth, smothering him in a blanket, his arms trapped and his weapons useless. Yet he pushed out with his knife and it cut flesh but he had no further reach to work it in. He heard the man scream. A side of the blanket flapped free and the youth rolled out. He stood up into the blow of a long handle that took him in the face and dropped him without a sound.

The men trussed the youth and dragged him outside. He lay in the snow, blood dripping from his nose, stained too by the blood of his victim. About him the villagers gathered and his aunts came screaming.

Do you see, they yelled, there's death in him. There's been death in him since the instant of his birth. Murderer. Satan. Devil's spawn.

They kicked at the bound form, beat at the youth with sticks until the schoolteacher and the monks pushed them back.

Lock him up, this evil. Take him off.

Leave him, shouted the schoolteacher, there would have been none of this if you'd been decent women.

At this they howled, shrieked at his accusations, but he turned away and knelt to staunch the youth's bleeding with lumps of snow. The stabbed monk did the same where he bled and one of the others tore strips of cloth to bandage the wound.

He'll need the whip to have this wildness abated, said the injured monk.

Yes, screamed the aunts. Give him the whip. The whip and salt's all he's good for.

It's your business, friar, said the schoolteacher, but consider the way it's been for him.

34

The monk winced as the bandage was pulled tight.

Even so, he said, there's some who need more than prayers to save them. But we've turned worse men from their ways.

The schoolteacher made no comment: he dabbed at the youth's face and felt how the nose was broken beneath the skin.

Perhaps prayers would be the better start.

Perhaps, said the monk, though from what I've seen he'll need more than most.

He pointed at the youth: Get him ready. We have a difficult road back.

Take him, screeched the aunts. There's none who want to see him here again.

The monk stepped towards the women.

Go home! Go!

He waved them off.

The villagers fell back before him; some muttered, but the excitement had gone out of them. The sight of the youth helpless and bloody was not the demon they had imagined. Half ashamed they edged away, but none went home.

From a distance they watched the schoolteacher scrape snow from the ground, pack it into ice and hold the lumps against the youth's swellings. The cold brought the youth to consciousness and he groaned and opened his eyes on the schoolteacher's concern. For a moment he struggled at the bonds, his breathing hard, his face contorted with the effort. Then he lay still, averting his face.

It is my vow, said the schoolteacher. My obligation.

The youth looked at him.

My father would not have wanted this.

No.

The schoolteacher shook his head.

No. Your father would not have wanted this. But it is the best that I can do.

Let me go, said the youth. He grimaced with the pain of speech.

You will die out there, said the schoolteacher. I cannot let you die out there.

He pulled at his beard in consternation.

Or worse, die as your father died, for some worthless violent reason. This is my obligation. It is the best that I can do.

He stood up.

At some time you will come to thank me for it.

Never, said the youth.

Never! repeated the schoolteacher, blinking; stunned by the venom of the word.

Never.

Then crouching down again: Do not hate me. I am your friend. Truly, I am your friend.

The youth's nose was bleeding again and the schoolteacher reached out to stem the flow.

Leave me, said the youth. And he shouted it: Leave me – bringing all his pain and grievance into the cry.

The schoolteacher staggered back.

It is my obligation, he mumbled. My obligation to your father. That you would be cared for. It is what I promised him. At the end it was what I promised him.

But no one listened to the schoolteacher. For a while he stood lost in his repetitions, then stared at the youth being manhandled into the cart as if he could not remember what had happened or comprehend what transpired. Finally he went indoors, even before the monks had lashed their horses into motion.

### The compassion of water and philosophy

In the afternoon the monastery stood above them on its crags, roofed in white and stark against a dismal sky. The youth could not see it for he was prone upon the cart planks, face down and aching from the fracture. Even so he knew they had come out of the forest because the monks relaxed, put down the weapons they had held in readiness since leaving the village.

You can forget about rescue now, scoffed the monk who had been cut by the youth. He forced a laugh and nudged at the youth's ribs with his boot.

Nor're your cohorts bound by loyalty or brave men either, it seems, if they'll let three monks have you away.

At this they all gave snorting laughs.

Though in times to come when the fear of God's put in you, you'll wish they'd tried.

Again they snorted, grinning at the joke.

But better to face it in this world than the next, hey boy!

Oh, much better. Much wiser, agreed one.

The monk dug at the youth again and bent closer to him: Think of it, friend, what's a few months' penance compared to an eternity of torture?

He paused to wink at his companions.

I'll tell you, it's nothing at all.

They laughed, but ignored the youth thereafter, returning to their own reveries.

Slowly the tree-edge receded as the cart pulled closer to the abbey. But the gradient across the pasture approaches was steepening and the horses laboured, their breath coming as thick as smoke. Two monks swung down to ease the burden and hurried forward, taking up the horses' reins and urging them on. The pace did not falter.

Under the snow the country was silent and empty, the only noise being the creaking of the cart and the steady tread of the horses' hooves; and the only creatures about being this group drawing their tracks into the purity of the landscape. And from this distance the presence before them showed no lights or smoke or any sign of habitation.

But closer could be seen the traces of human activity: splinters of wood, the drag-marks and faded vermilion of shot game. And from here the monks called out and their shouts were answered and the great doors opened to swallow them.

In the court the horses were unharnessed but the youth was left bound. He made no movement, lay as one dead and of that moment believed he was gone to some hell unique to himself. He could hear the monks taking sustenance, their grunts of satisfaction and relish and the tinker of mugs on stone. He craved water but he would not plead. And they ignored him, offered him neither a glance nor nourishment, left him in the cart even when the bells rang for mass. Alone, the youth struggled and eventually turned on his back and looked up at the walls that boxed him. He could see nothing but stone and sky and each was as formless and as lacking in substance as the other. It was a place of fear.

Only then did he notice the gatekeeper who stared at his discomfort without empathy. The man approached, his head shaking from side to side while he moved, and even when he stopped before the youth his head kept its jerking. For some time he eyed the youth and the youth eyed him back.

I-i-it's n-no-no g-good strug-strug-struggling against those r-ropes, he said at last. I-i-if they were m-m-m-meant to-to come lose th-th-they w-would have done so at the f-fir-first test-ing and you-you could have ss-ss-skipped f-free. But they didn't, and y-y-you're still bound as tightly as a ba-ba-bale.

He cleared his throat and spat.

Whi-whi-whi-which would seem to-to sh-show this was how it wa-wa-was meant.

The man leant against the side of the cart. His head was still moved

37

by its affliction, jiggling across his shoulders like a marionette's. His lips trembled with the formation of speech.

But my o-op-opinions are of n-n-no account. M-my words have n-n-never c-caused attention or stopped one man in his t-tra-tracks because I-I-I spoke a ra-rare truth. My words are c-c-crumbs: u-use-less, stale bread. Which is why I-I watch at th-the gate or am ca-called to empty n-n-ni-night buckets. B-b-but once I r-read-read the great th-th-thinkers, so my words ca-carry their authority. I know wha-wha-what the Greeks said of your c-con-condition, or Vol-taire. The-the-they ta-ta-talk of destiny, of im-immut-able laws which tie us all a-and f-f-from whi-which there is no escape. A-a-and, and so it is.

He spat again then bent into the cart until his face was close to the youth's.

Wh-why you're here-here-here, or who-who you are is n-n-n-no concern of mine. Y-you could be thief, even m-mur-murderer for all I n-n-know or ca-care, b-b-but we're all of us in ad-adversity with not much com-comfort to be ha-had from others, so-so I'll-I'll tell you this, son: th-th-there's n-n-n-no better world than the w-w-one you've got, e-e-eve-n if you could im-imagine a thou-thousand others.

The man stood up out of the youth's sight and walked back to his shelter beside the gate where a brazier burnt. The youth heard him stoke it and the crackle of bark catching fire. Then the man reappeared with a mug of melted snow which he held close over the youth's mouth before he tilted it so that the liquid ran out slowly and the youth could swallow without choking. When the mug was empty the man withdrew; the youth was left to stare at the walls and the sky that towered above them.

At dusk two came who pulled him like a carcass from the cart. They cut free his bonds and gave him a drink which was sour and which spun the world and dropped him into darkness.

### Requiem

At some time the youth heard singing and leapt off the pallet to pound at the door. Even above his own noise it continued to swell in his head beyond forbearance. When it stopped he collapsed. At the next mealtime they found him on the floor curled tightly into himself like a frightened animal. They hefted him back on to the pallet and he was made to swallow a bitter decoction. He coughed and spat but the liquid went down and the monks leaning over him grew bigger, their faces horrible and leering. He screamed. The men showed no pity, nor was there caring in their faces. When the youth had quieted they went, leaving water and food that was eaten by the rats before he woke again.

Once more there was singing. A singing unaccompanied by any instrument, that was only the cadence of voices, those of men and those of boys. A singing scored with the vastness of cellars and halls, that echoed in the corridors and in the cells, that was both lonely and sad, distant and close. A singing of stone, a chant of supplication. Madly, the youth shook his head. He beat his fists against the door that was unyielding in its solidity. He rolled on the stone floor among the shit of birds and rats and his own defecations. He retched with the terror that churned in him until the gall stung his throat. Then like a dog baying at the agony of other hounds he leapt at the small window, clutched the ledge and hauled himself up until he could see into the void, and he howled. Again and again he howled. Now he crouched on the pallet all through the night, whimpering. He could hear the shrieks of rats and the scratch of their claws on the stone. A cold wind tore at the window driving in the snow. Towards morning he sensed the singing. Even before there was light he sensed it, a moan heavier than wind through the architecture, a vibration deep and powerful in its resonance.

*Merso sole chaos*

He listened with his ear pressed against the door as the great domed ceilings, the vaults, the chapels, the crypts filled with it, low and harmonious, swelling, booming, until the full voices rose through the cloister and the hymns came at him.

*Merso sole chaos*
*irruit horridum*

When they visited the youth again he was smeared with his own blood because the wound had broken open in his flailings. They doused him, forced more potion into him, and went away. He lay in this stupor with the hurt of his face excluding all other sensations. Far off he heard the soprano of the boys rising through the granite:

*Merso sole chaos*
*irruit horridum,*
*lumen redde tuis*

and he saw this place in the vast emptiness of the country at night:

39

the black forests thrown across the hills; the whiteness of fields, with no human light except where one dully glimmered in the steep and towering walls of the monastery. And the hymns went out in their sacred language, out into the sky that was dark with depth between the stars:

*Merso sole chaos*
*irruit horridum,*
*lumen redde tuis*
*Christe, fidelibus*

### In the kitchens

When the youth was weak with dysentery and his eyes lacklustre, two monks came for him. They hauled him from the pallet where he lay covered with straw and the shreds of a blanket torn in his hallucinations. He offered no resistance, neither shrank from them nor hit out as he had done in the first days, but collapsed on the stone, too weak to keep his feet at the withdrawal of their support. The men circled in annoyance, pulled him up again, only now they did not let go, and he stood between them although his reality had no foundation. They held him: one gripped his neck as he would have lifted a dead dog to hurl it aside, while the other tied the youth's hands. Neither spoke. Nor did they answer the youth's plea for water, a plea so faint it was inaudible above the rustle of straw on a sudden draught. Water, he said once more, yet his lips did not move and the words were dust on his tongue. And then he lost interest or no longer cared. His eyes were dead again.

The monk worked slowly at the knot with fingers numbed by the cold. When it was complete he jerked the rope as he would have done to a cow and led the youth into the corridor that was dim even at midday, its walls cold and green. Behind them came the second monk. They went cautiously, feeling their way over the flags.

The youth was held in a high cell in a part where once mendicants had taken shelter but was now seldom used. It was given to the elements which wreaked havoc, loosening the mortar between the stones, splitting the wood of the architraves and the doors, and to owls and bats and recalcitrant novices whose reflections found new meaning in its gloom. As a consequence the descent was a narrow spiral of stairs lit only by loopholes. Twice the youth fell because of his weakness and because the stones were wet from the squalls driven through the fenestration. He would stumble against the monk before him and they would both go down without words, grunting at their bruising. And the monk would lash him until he was on his feet and able to continue. Which is how they descended.

They came out of the tower into a great hall empty except for starlings high up in its rafters and old dung on the floor where donkeys had been tethered, and the remains of their bales. They crossed its length to a low door and entered a passage that was lit at half its length by a candle. The leading monk slung the rope over his shoulders so that the youth's hands were raised in an attitude of prayer and pulled him almost at a run to the farther end. He opened a door and dragged the youth into a kitchen that was as light and as noisy and as warm as the parts they had left had been the opposite.

Lanterns flared in every corner yet the light was diffuse: smoke issued from the doors of the ovens yawning crimson, and steam rose from the kettles and the pots, obscuring the activity where the men shifted, their voices disembodied, their appearances transient in that atmosphere. One was seen honing knives, then was gone; another stood with a long spade waiting to bring out the bread, then was gone; here men kneaded dough, or butchered, or sat skinning a mound of potatoes, and they were glimpsed and lost again in the vapour. The group's entrance went unremarked: a few looked up without curiosity, their faces illuminated briefly like moons passing through cloud, then they returned to their work and the clatter and the powerful aroma of ox stew cooking. The youth was led to a corner beside an oven where the monks forced him to the floor and tied him to a metal ring as goats were fastened before slaughter. He went meekly; even when they kicked him to forewarn of trouble, he did not rise in protest but merely pressed himself closer against the bricks to absorb their warmth. Here he was left and the monks went off to take food and wine, and their laughter rose above the clamour.

Out of the density approached an older monk who crouched beside the youth and studied the wasted form and the nose that had reset itself coarsely on the narrow face. He noted the lice and the scabs of bedbugs that pocked the youth's body where it was exposed. The youth's eyes were shut, nor did he open them although he sensed the stranger's presence and expected more torment. He held himself tense for that moment. The monk saw this and spoke gently, his hands reaching out to stroke the youth's cheeks. At his touch the youth looked up and was reviled by the tongue protruding between the old man's lips and the drool wet on his chin. The youth backed away, but the old man came after him with his words and his hands until the youth was trapped against the oven. The hands found him: fondled, played, went into his hair like toads leaving a trail of slime across his brow. The youth could bring nothing to his defence for he was caught and tied. In his desperation he begged for water and the man drew back, grinning. His mouth held not a single tooth.

The old monk fetched water and soup. He moistened the youth's lips with a damp cloth that had been wetted in brandy, then he held up the cup of water so that the youth could drink, who complied swallowing quickly but never ceasing his search of the man's face for the next path of lechery. When the youth had drunk, the man put down the cup and took up the soup. He fished in the broth with his fingers for a lump of meat which he first cooled with his breath before offering it. He held the flesh close to the youth's face and although the youth opened his mouth to receive it, the monk withheld the morsel. Instead he stuck out his own tongue to indicate how the food should be taken. At first the youth would not, but the monk taunted him with the meat, with the smell of it, with the texture of it against his lips, until the youth obeyed. He put out his tongue and the monk put on it the meat, his fingers sliding over the youth's chin and throat before returning to dredge the soup once more. In this manner he fed the youth until there was no meat or vegetable left in the bowl and they were stained with the process. Then he raised the bowl for the youth to drink the broth but tilted it so sharply that liquid dribbled from the edges and wet the youth's smock. The old monk eyed these patches and put out his hand to wipe them but instead groped for the youth's testicles and found them beneath the fabric and squeezed them into his grasp. The youth yelled, as much from the pain of it as from the fear, and the monk released him, falling backwards in his own fright and scuttling off.

At this disturbance the kitchen laughed and the monks made lewd gestures towards both the youth and the fleeing man. But as quickly the moment passed and each one returned to his doing. The youth was forgotten. He slept, comforted by the food and the warmth, until the monks who had brought him down prodded him awake with a bar as they would a dog. He stirred sluggishly even at their rough handling, not caring about the knife the one held, or the assault of the other. They cut free the rope bonds and fettered him by his leg to the iron ring and left him there like a chained exotic. The youth paid no attention to his new condition nor was he able to. He slept again as those do near death. In time the noise and the smoke subsided in the kitchen and for a few hours there was quiet.

Thus the youth was kept: at dawn and at dusk he was unlocked and led to the latrines by the old monk who had molested him and now did penance for his crime. While the youth shat and while he pissed, the man watched, tormented by lust and the desires of sodomy, praying to God for mercy and beseeching the youth's forgiveness, yet shuffling for a better view when the youth obscured his parts. Until a time came when the youth saw that the man was weak. Then he no longer feared him, demanded privacy in the stall and mocked the man for his predilection. The monk was overcome with shame, and they would return to the kitchen with the youth going before.

The kitchen monks fed the youth like an animal: threw raw scraps or charred bones, gave no utensils and seldom plates. Yet he did not question this but ate as the food was presented even to licking its grease from the floor. And like an animal he was gnawed by constant hunger, which the monks knew and had sport with his cravings. Outside his reach they placed roasted ribs and gambled on his resolve, gathering round, revising the odds, calling encouragement even as the youth stretched for it beyond the elasticity of his muscles, and the manacle cut at his ankle to the bone. And they cheered his triumphs and marvelled at his capacity.

Yet he was a dog to them still, no more a part of the kitchen than the bricks and mortar, without history or prospects. None spoke with him or offered him straw to sleep on or the cover of a blanket: they did not consider him of their kind with needs and wants except to eat and defecate. Nor did he seem to expect it: he lay where he was chained and only his eyes had substance.

## The lessons of the catacombs

There came a day when those who had brought him from the tower fetched him again. This time he resisted and was beaten for his insolence while the kitchen monks circled around, laughing, jeering, at the struggle. But the youth was soon tamed. And the men tied his arms and kept him so closely manacled he could not move a step but had to shuffle like a servant. He was taken away with new blood on his smock.

They led him by the chain down a deep spiral of stairs into the crypts and tunnels of the monastery where the air had hardly stirred for a thousand years and was cold and sweet with putrefaction. In these wet depths they threaded a labyrinth, taking sometimes the wrong passage until fallen rock blocked their way or the going ended in a tomb, but entered at last a vaulted chamber darker than any they had passed through, where the light of the candles was circumscribed by the blackness and had no penetration. Here they paused, expecting another, but there was no light to indicate that anyone waited. So they took the youth to the walls and the monks held up their candles to show him the beautiful symmetry of femur and tibia and humerus and skull stacked in an arrangement: a lattice of mortality with the bones interlocking and the whole construction standing against the stone from floor to ceiling. In that light it seemed to weave and warp, more an image than the reality of hundreds dead, yet it was solid. The youth cried out and fought to flee from the sight but the monks held him to it while his fear echoed and echoed in the catacombs going down until it was less than a whisper. In the silence he stared at the fretwork and the trellis: hard yellow bones arranged in order.

They moved along this memorial to where the patterning stopped and in their small light were suddenly heaped skeletons, chaotic and broken up, which told of how the dead had been dumped without ceremony or concern, the adult and the child, thrown here in increasing numbers until no more could be accommodated. And while they stood struck by this sight a figure drew out of the darkness behind them, a shape that was black and huge with not a vestige of body showing, being only the outline of a habit. This emanation approached to where he could have reached out and touched them before he said, Look thoroughly, friends, and consider how they died.

When he spoke the two monks stiffened, gasped at this unexpectedness, and the youth trembled. They made to turn but the voice commanded them otherwise.

No, look on, look on, you have not come to see me, but these. Reflect on them.

The men obeyed but the youth struggled to glance back, yet no movement or shape in the uniform darkness behind them caught his eye. He strained harder against the monks, spitting with the desperation of his act, and they retaliated with a force that knocked him to his knees. A candle went out and the gloom settled heavily on them.

We did not notice you, said the one monk.

We have brought the youth, said the other.

They waited for an answer.

Of course, said the figure at last. But now make him look at them and let us all meditate on this tableau.

Which they did in the silence of the chamber.

Then he spoke: These are the plague dead. The objects of divine wrath.

Once more he fell silent and for long moments he did not speak. The youth began to heave in fear and the monks shifted uneasily.

44

Again came the voice: This is our lot, for the imagination of man's heart is evil and he will always be plagued.

The words were spoken softly, yet with menace and disgust.

Look, he shouted, these died a wretched death, black-spotted, their bodies swollen in tumours, feared because their very touch brought death, abandoned: mothers with no love for their sick children, husbands with no care for their afflicted wives, the diseased put out, the elderly left to ail and rot, forsaken by all and their God. They lay in the streets and in the fields, unmourned by the piteous laments and tears of their relatives, waiting for the porters to dump them in some mass grave in a hillside or to bring them here to this ignoble but consecrated place. Day on day the biers brought them. When the porters went out to collect one they came back with eight; having been called to fetch a husband they returned carrying his wife and children also. The dead. Always the dead. A multitude of corpses in this time of great misfortune. More bodies than even this whole chamber could contain.

He paused.

The plague dead, left in here to become dust and bones. To us they are dust and bones. Not people, just these brittle remains. Such is God's revenge on our violence. And yet it is not enough. We continue with our murder and our rape, our torture and our malevolence. Even a time like this that killed more than did any war or starvation does not change our hearts. For we are evil.

And then his presence leant past them and a long arm dug into the pile of bones, discarding rib, scapula and clavicle until it withdrew holding a femur blackened with tissue at its end. He was turned towards them yet his face was invisible in the cowl where no light reached and the only evidence of his being flesh and blood was a hand of metacarpal fingers, strong-sinewed, blue, and yellow-nailed, that reached at them, displaying the bone. They, all three, retreated as if warding off a horror.

Stop! he commanded. Stop. Hold the light closer. See this!

Which the monk carrying the candle did, stretching out his arm so that the flame burnt beneath the hand, illuminating how the fingers lay closed about the artefact like lizards; and it was the only thing visible in that pitch cavern, disembodied, a truth.

Almost sadly he spoke more to himself than to them: For centuries they have rotted here. One collapsing into another: the ribs of women mixing with the ribs of men, one man's legs entangled with his friend's, the liar and the thief swapping parts with the righteous. Yet what can we say of them now? We do not know who was man, who was woman, let alone their dispositions. All we can say is that they are dead, struck down by plague.

The bone shook in the light: dancing from right to left and left to right, pointing in accusation at each one, ending with the youth.

Take it, he was ordered.

The youth was freed and his hand came into the light and clutched the bone. For a moment his action was resisted: he felt the strength of the other hand, how it refused him, gave no knowledge of his hold, denied his existence. Then the bone was released, and the hand that had held it curled into a claw and withdrew.

Here is chaos, said the figure abruptly, taking the candle. Here is nothing but rubbish and waste.

He swept the light over the bones so suddenly it guttered but caught again, flickering on the bald skulls, the ceaseless grins.

What respect is this? What acknowledgement of God's justice? What sort of memorial?

He held the candle closely towards the three.

It speaks only of indifference: a disregard for history, a mockery of death, yet we all will be longer dead than we ever were alive. And this – he kicked at the bones – our feeble architecture, is our only monument. It should stand in testament to our briefness and our natures: here were men who lived in violence and died by plague.

He moved away from them, the tiny flame floating in mid-air.

What do you say?

The question boomed among those corridors. Neither the monks nor the youth could answer, nor was one expected.

The voice continued: Before the fact of these there are no words. Here language ends. This is beyond our logic and our reasoning: here the guilty are punished, those who betrayed have been cut down. And all heaped into this chaos.

Then he hid the flame in the folds of his habit, casting the chamber into darkness.

As it should be.

In the darkness each was aware of his breathing and the loudness of his heart and knew that the difference between himself and the dead was the pulsation of that muscle. Also they heard the small sounds of matter settling that could have been echoes from another time but were now indistinguishable from the movement of insects or the seep of water coming through the rock. Although they heard such minutiae, none heard the figure treading back towards them. Again he stopped within reach and even in the blackness discerned how the monks sweated and the youth waited, the bone still clasped

46

tightly in his fist. From out of his cloak he brought the candle and thrust it towards the group. The two monks screamed; the youth cowered away.

From these, he said, gesturing towards the skeletons, we must re-create order. The humerus has its place as does the femur, the one fits with the other as was possibly intended. And that is how the youth must proceed until the structure is complete.

He offered the candle for the monks to take it and the one nearest him did.

I shall be about, he said. Then withdrew.

Nor did they see him again that day. Although the monks brought enough lamps to uncover every corner of the chamber and the tunnels were better lit, neither his presence nor his shadow crossed them then or in the immediate days.

But the monks were constantly troubled: pacing nervously about the vault, lashing the youth when the edge of their fear loomed, or starting at any noise, especially if the youth cracked a bone. For they expected his appearance every moment and knew he would come. Nor did their tension ease outside the catacombs. At night they were drunk, and in the morning before going down took brandy with their meat. Towards the youth they were savage: accused him of their misfortune and exacted a revenge.

And the youth, who at first had fought to refuse the task and been beaten into it, now worked quietly although he stung when they whipped him in their hate. Yet he did not retaliate or show animosity. Instead he was absorbed: separating those bones that were material for the structure from the useless accumulation of ribs and knuckles and vertebrae that littered the floor; selecting the perfect specimens, neither flaked nor chipped; arranging each piece with the precision of those who had begun the sculpture. He learnt the value of the femur as a base and support, and how the delicacy of the humerus gave an illusion of flight. He learnt to place the skulls of adults at the foundations and in the rising parts, leaving the higher reaches for those of children where the effect was incorporeal. He crafted with a sure expertise, lacing each into the wall, their monument. Yet he worked slowly, and incurred the monks' anger for each day they anticipated the cowled overseer, and dreaded his return.

## The contract

It came as surely as if it had been appointed. On a morning he was there before them, a massive presence hooded and writing, his hand now circling above the text like a vulture, now drifting down to the page as those birds do that wait in trees above a kill, before taking up again his exegesis. Jointed and stretched the fingers moved with each word quickly across the book. So he wrote throughout the day without addressing them or even looking up. The next morning he was absent but they heard his pacing in the labyrinth and how he recited lamentations until the place sounded with his cacophony. The youth worked through this, but the monks were too agitated to bear it and pulled the youth away after a few hours. On the third day the monks feared to return and drank excessively in preparation. Even when they went down one kept a bottle. In the vault he awaited them. He sat where he had done before but did not write. The book was closed on his knee and his hands folded across it as rigid as crabs. He faced their entrance yet his features were obscured. At the sight of him the monks cowered back; he raised a hand and beckoned them in.

Nor could they refuse and approached to where he indicated a few steps from his stool. He waved the youth back to the bones; he gestured to the monks to sit upon the floor. The youth began his building although now it neared completion the pieces were scarce and he had to ferret more thoroughly among the discarded parts. His search made a dry noise of vertebrae scraping over stone. For a time it was the only sound in the vault; then the figure spoke.

He asked if they had heard tell of an anonymous monk who wandered about appearing in the camps of soldiers before a battle or in villages before a slaughter. A figure that had been seen in the time of Charlemagne and in that of Bonaparte, who was recorded at the Crusades both in the documents and in the tapestries, and shown always in the background, sometimes as witness, sometimes at work on a ledger. Who, in medieval art, was depicted green-faced and trumpeting among those with the heads of fish and deer, leading the damned to their tortures. It was said he had been seen as an owl during catastrophes when rivers flooded or fires laid villages and towns to waste. And as a bat at the assassination of kings and chiefs. His shape was described in the Americas, in the art of the Aztecs and told in the lore of the tribes even before Columbus. Likewise could he be traced in other parts of the south, in African sculpture and the beliefs of Aborigines, in rock art and in the shamans' depictions. He was feared by rulers as much as by peasants because he found nothing to distinguish the blood of the one from the blood of the other. Had they heard of this man?

He looked at each one from the depths of his darkness and they shook their heads in answer, even the youth who no longer worked at the sculpture but had crept up to crouch behind the monks.

Without any movement the figure contemplated them: he had become a statue.

Very well, he said, follow this. Imagine how a hard and jagged landscape, strewn with rocks that cut and thorns that impale every movement, gives on to a beach and endless sea. Imagine how a ground crawling with snakes, pierced by the shrill of beetles, ends in this vision. Yet the sand is cast with the bones of leviathans and turtle shells and mounds of jelly quivering where the water runs out. Beyond waves thunder. On to this whiteness staggers one blistered by the sun, pierced, and bleeding from wounds. Here he collapses. Know that there is nothing living in this landscape except the scavengers: those of the air and those of the sand; and both are shifting in their elements towards him. He lies there on this southern extremity, hopeless. Imagine how a figure, dark with the distance, approaches. He comes on slowly, picking his way between the huge rib cages and the jaws, skirting the unclean carcasses that hum with flies until he stands eventually over the prone body. He wipes off the sea snails that already infest the dying one's skin and offers water from a flask. It is taken. Then the two sit out the afternoon. Until death. He that is dying does so alone, without love, without pity, in pain, groaning. And he that sits beside him is unconcerned, waits to the end. Now see them move off into the hinterland: pass between the rocks and thorns, over black mountains on to plains turned vast and silver by the moon where their way parts and they go separately into the world. Then understand one thing: it is always like this, a triumph and a revenge.

He turned to the youth.

For you, he said, is all this told. To this you have been contracted. And there can be no undoing. No other way. For such is the imagination of men's hearts that this is demanded. Do not resent it, come to hate those that make it so. Now go, until the day I have described.

With that he was finished and spoke no more: silence consumed the chamber. First the youth edged back in terror, never looking away from the hooded figure. In the cowl's shadow he could determine as much a death's head as a face, the dividing nose and the sockets of the eyes, but no other detail. He knew their gaze was on him and he could not escape. He reached the end of the chain that manacled him to the monks and would have pulled them after him, but now they also withdrew, going on their knees almost until they had reached the chamber door. Then they ran and he with them into the labyrinth, taking tunnels they had not been through before, coming again and again into blocked passages, turning wherever an opening showed until, bruised and gasping, they found the spiral stairs and went up in a rush, slipping, falling, tripped by the chain, scrabbling on hands and knees with ragged breath before they reached the upper door and broke into the courtyard. Yet even here they would not pause but headed for another entrance scattering livestock in their plunge, and dragged the youth higher to a cell much like the one he had known. Now in haste and agitation they released him from the chains, threw him down, then fled, fearing him as much as the presence below.

### The lessons of the father

Again the youth was imprisoned, having neither straw nor blanket, nor a bucket for his excrement. He was brought no food; and heard no movement in the corridor. In the stillness he huddled in a corner, and there he kept throughout the singing of the choirs and for some hours into the night. At times he slept. There came to him the image of his father taken to the edge of death by a wound that would allow him neither sleep nor unconsciousness with its painful intensity. Instead it held him unrelenting, exquisite, as clean as flames. The youth watched every breath, every movement. Heard his father curse the life that refused to let him go and the death that remained so distant.

Hear this, said his father. There is only one way for this thing to end. We are each alone.

And the bailiff appeared, saying to the man, You will hang.

Such is the world, said his father, and held out a rifle. He offered it towards the youth: There is not much I can teach you, except the working of this.

He began the naming of the parts: hammer; sights, fore and barrel; trigger; trigger guard; breech. Then he broke the gun to hinge down the barrel exposing pin and loading device. From a pouch tied to the stock he took a cartridge, clipped it into the breech, snapped closed the barrel. He gave the weapon to the youth.

Cock it, he said.

The youth slid back the hammer with his thumb.

These are beautiful things, said his father, it is killing that makes them such. With killing we understand death. We follow the ducks, see each beat of their wings and know when we shoot all that will stop. This lead will churn feathers, smash bones, release blood through those bodies. They will fall from the sky with no more grace than a stone. Or it will go into the heart of a deer shredding a path because we willed it. One moment there was a life proud and shapely, the next we have brought death.

The youth sat up: of wild demeanour, casting about in a frenzy. His hair wet, lying stuck against his neck.

Come, said his father.

The youth shook his head, shrinking foetus-like against the wall.

Come.

They went out towards the hill that would bring them to the upland fields and the woods. It was a pale morning: the sky pulled over with high cloud, the air warm, the grass laced with dew. The youth walked ahead with the gun slung over his shoulder. They climbed without resting, pushing up the slope. The deer, a doe and its fawn, were stopped in a clearing. The youth crouched and brought the gun to his shoulder. The doe was nervous, her head raised in anticipation of a strange smell or sudden movement. The youth waited. The doe returned to her grazing, and the youth fired. He saw the animal go down, spring up, collapse again. He saw the fawn prancing in agitation. He reloaded. Raised the gun once more. The fawn stood beside the fallen doe. With the shot it was lifted into the bracken.

You did not have to shoot it, said his father.

The youth looked down the gloom at the distant carcass.

It would have died soon, he answered.

His father did not reply but beckoned him on.

They were five. Two of them were merry and passed a bottle from one to the other. The father and his son tried to join in their carousing, even called up through the greyness, taunting the men ahead of them, goading, mocking, derisive. Then they all fell silent expecting a response. But none came.

By now it was lighter and they could see the three men walking before them. Behind, the village was still hidden in the valley mist and everywhere the quiet continued deep and unsullied. The youth shivered despite the heavy coat he wore which was too long in the sleeves so that his hands were hidden and too long in the length so that it swept over the snow and was wet at its tails.

I will kill him, said the youth's father.

Above them the first group walked in silence. They strode determinedly side by side, breathing so deeply that ice quickly formed on the scarves wrapped around their mouths and noses. The hill was steep and the going difficult but none was winded. At the top they paused. The tall man brought a hand out from the depths of his coat and pulled the scarf from his face. Yet his features were still invisible. When he spoke his words vaporised upon the air.

Has your man gone into the woods?

The other two nodded.

Good, said the tall man, good.

His teeth showed suddenly, then he covered his face again and the three continued along the hilltop towards the field.

During the night a snow had fallen on the uplands and left an unbroken purity that stretched from the road to the black foot of the forest. Neither fox nor badger nor rabbit had ventured across it in the hours before morning when the field shone with its own brilliance and the only sound was the shifting of snow as it settled and thickened on the branches of the elms. This place waited now in the cold unmoving air.

This is not what I want, said the father. This is not how I imagined it.

The man a step in front of him shrugged: What we want is of little importance. What matters is what happens. There is no amount of imagining can change the way it is going to be.

The youth looked ahead at the silhouettes that stood in the road and watched their approach.

The two men and the youth came up to the three who waited. The youth cowered at the size of the tallest. He knew the man smiled from the shadow of his hood and that his eyes stared upon him.

Two pistols were offered. The youth's father chose one and the tall man took the other. He did not lift it, or judge it, or get the feel of it the way the youth's father did, but held it in his hand, carelessly.

Then he and his protagonist broke the sanctity of the field where the snow covered their boots and reached up to the hems of their coats and walked out into the whiteness scuffing up mud with each footstep until they reached a point that was mutually agreed upon where the man turned to his right and measured eight paces while the youth's father went left and did the same.

Each turned and aimed. And from the blackness of the forest there was a flash which no one noticed because their eyes were on the men preparing to shoot. Yet the bullet tore into its victim. The youth saw his father knocked by the impact, how he staggered, how his arm came down but his hand did not release the pistol. At first there was no blood; what had happened seemed all a charade without the colour of mortality: the bright, vital parts of life being punched from their functions and sprayed about the world. Or the anger of this injustice being howled. But as the man wheeled through the shock the first drops came away and went red on to the snow. He continued his gyration, never losing his feet, coming up with his coat stained and torn about the area of his kidneys and straightening, both hands taking the pistol, his knees bending for balance in the short slide, the barrel glued to the tall man at the end of his vision. The youth's father fired and the tall man's head shattered into bone and blood and lead, and was even as they witnessed it reconstituted. Then they saw his face unhooded, and it was the face of the youth.

### Revelation and choice

He woke at his own screaming to the cold cell and the odour of fear. He clutched his arms about his chest, shivering. His teeth chattered. He hurt in every joint, a pain as sharp as pins inserted there. Slowly he sat, bent forward, and saw a dish of food uneaten and a mug of black fluid. These wavered and reeled about the room and disappeared. He fell back yet the walls still buckled. Pressed down. He shut his eyes, lay curled, tight-mouthed to fight the spasms driving upwards from his stomach. His mind pictured a host of feathered devils that danced as they danced in hell upon the skulls of the damned. And they would not leave. Abruptly he spoke, saying, Kill with sword, and with hunger, and with death, and with the beasts.

He laughed, a shriek like the flighted nightjar.

He stared into the faint rectangle of the unglassed window in the dark. It brought the only light into the cell, a greying of the blackness without stars or any discernible object. Yet it offered a relief from the night's monotony. In the later hours he went to stand below the high window. A draught came in bringing with it light drops of rain and the smell of churned snow mixed with mud and dung. He stood in this coldness estimating the height of the window, preparing himself to reach it. Suddenly he sprang and his hands caught the stone edge. So he hung, straining in his fingers and his arms, until his feet took purchase on the wall and he could haul himself on to the ledge. It was small and rough with no space to manoeuvre but there was no pause in his actions: he went over it into the dark and fell without hesitation.

# CHAPTER FOUR

*The youth is nursed to health by a gypsy woman who divines the meaning and purpose of his life. He knows he is contracted but still attempts to flee. From the schoolteacher he hears of wild continents in the south; from Madach he is given sustenance.*

## The fall

THE YOUTH FELL SOUNDLESSLY.

Fell head down, arms thrust out, hands splayed against the coming ground.

Fell.

Into that blackness; into that wet.

Fell a long fall with the rain and the wind and a noise like screaming in his ears.

Fell.

And it was as if the night beat with wings and as if their leather lashed about his face.

Fell.

And was illuminated in the jags of lightning: a figure tumbling, then gone.

The night drove on with its howling and its thunder.

## Flight

Thus he plunged, and thus he was saved by the high-stacked summer hay which still stood against the walls. He went into it, yet the impact rode the air from his lungs, slammed his bones, tossed him, slid him crumpled and gasping to the ground where he lay and did not move.

Even until the first greying he lay as if dead, his arms bent strangely, his legs buckled under. In this posture the gatekeeper came upon him. He stood over the youth and his head shook fiercely with its affliction and at the sight: he noted how the youth had fallen, and searched the walls for some high window but could find none. He clicked and sighed at the impossibility of such flight, then crouched down and heard the youth's breathing.

S-s-so you ll-live, he said, straightening up. B-b-by the ch-chance of a-a haywain p-p-p-pulled here and n-no-nowhere else. As-as-as it is s-said, the-the w-wor-world is a hay-haystack and each m-m-man takes f-from it w-wh-what he c-can.

His head jerked with this wisdom softly spoken.

B-but you-you're not g-getting f-f-free-dom from it. N-no. You've l-landed r-right into the h-han-hands of ol-old Jack which i-is as g-goo-good as in-into the han-hands of de-des-destiny.

The gatekeeper prodded at the youth with a pitchfork.

C-c-come on, he spluttered. R-ri-rise your-yourself.

The youth groaned when the handle ground against his ribs, and opened his eyes. He saw the gatekeeper and how his head was shaken by spasms of agitation. He saw the man was fearful, that he held the fork now as a weapon with the tines ready to stab and pierce. And then the youth groaned at the ache in his body and the sear of each taken breath. Yet he sat up.

At this the gatekeeper stepped backwards, levelling the pitchfork, crouched and grimacing.

Y-y-you ca-ca-ca-can-cannot es-escape ol-old J-J-Jack, he said. Y-y-you i-is m-m-my-my cap-cap-captive.

The youth groaned again when he stood. Such was the aspect of his rising, the grime and grimness of it, that the gatekeeper gasped to see him. For he was thinned by deprivation, his face sunken to his skull like that of an old man, his hands like claws. He was clothed as a novice, but the habit was soiled with mud and straw and faeces, and he wore no shoes. He moaned, rubbed at his ribs to ease the pain while the fork tines wavered before him, matching the jiggle of the gatekeeper's head.

Th-they-they've d-done you a b-bad t-t-t-time, he said. Though n-none gets m-m-more than de-de-served.

In the youth the burning of his chest went dim: he hugged his ribs, began to comprehend the situation and the lessening of the dark.

They stood beneath the granite towering of the monastery, these two figures: one dishevelled and unsteady, the other jittering like a puppet, feinting with the pitchfork as at a wild beast. The ground about them was rutted and muddy from the carts come to collect hay, and everywhere was littered with this harvest. Black ice too had crusted where the rain lay pooled. On this they danced a nervous ritual: the desperate and the frightened. And from within the walls came the songs of mass; and from off in the woods a stag barked.

The youth's eyes never slipped from the gatekeeper, yet he measured the fields sloping down to the forest: the open distance where the dogs could take him or a man on horseback ride him down.

In-in-in-s-side, gestured the gatekeeper as the youth edged away from the wall, t-t-take your mis-mis-miserable life that's n-n-not wor-worth its liv-living, in-s-s-side.

He jabbed with the fork more from fear than menace, and the youth caught the prongs and swung with them, pulling the fork free even as a tine stabbed through his flesh. Yet in the mêlée the wound went unnoticed for they were both loose in the slush, flaying for purchase, but the youth was up first and running out into the open, away. Yet he stumbled twice and fell, glanced back to see what threatened, then was on again, crying with the pain of drawing breath.

And behind him in the mud yelled the gatekeeper but his words were broken, their syllables stuck and stammered even as he crawled towards the gateway where he hauled himself up shaking, arms akimbo, gagged. Some in the courtyard laughed to see his mad rantings, taunted him with imitations, mocked the silence of his stutter until one looked out and saw the youth fleeing towards the woods. Then the cry took voice.

And the chase began in a pandemonium, without consideration, in an uproar and in laughter with no earnest intent beyond the value of a hunt. Some ran out empty-handed, others took axes or the tools of agriculture; one who had a musket fired twice but his aim was amateur. The dogs too were unleashed and went baying across the fields towards where the youth looked briefly back, then disappeared among the trees.

As the branches closed behind him he felt the forest's safety: its gloom and its secrets, the mysterious way of its vegetation. He became of its shadows: a sprite, a dryad, of equal illusion and dexterity.

Yet the pain was still in his chest, rasping now, and he saw how he bled from the arm where the fork had scored him: a hole that gushed a free-running blood, a gore that coursed over his palm in a stream, dripping a trail brightly.

Behind him the monks shouted and again the musket fired, yet they were still upon the fields. Nor had the dogs come in.

He stopped to staunch the wound. Found moss to plug it, tore a bandage from his hem. Fumbled with the knot, and knew even as he tied it that the monks were on his blood.

He heard how they spread out along the forest's edge, their calls sharp above the snapping of the dogs they had now leashed, and he waited to know the extent of their reach.

He would have cried with the hurt of his body; he would have crawled like a fox into a dark place to die. Yet he was as rigid as a frightened deer, as alarmed as the hunted, tensed to every threat.

The monks beat into the forest. They came in a cacophony of howls and yells, tearing at the bracken and the bushes fit to flush all creatures from their hibernation. And the dogs took up the savage trail, frenzied by the scent of new bleeding.

Yet he stood.

Stood beyond his pain for there was now only the closing discord, the final strength of his desperation.

At first he could not see their approach, but waited to discern how they moved. He heard the enticements of the middle men, designed to lure him in. He heard the quicker progress of the outer men seeking to encircle him, to trap him as they would a pig. Then glimpsed in the farther gloom to left and right their hasty movement, and he fled.

Here the forest was open: the ground sponged with pine needles, the great solitary firs leaning together at their heights. No sky was visible and the shadow held everywhere thick and dark. Into this he dodged, yet was vulnerable and readily marked as he slipped from shade to light, from trunk to trunk across the gaps. Which was how some saw him and turned the chase, shouting for the dogs to be set free, cursing through the glade at his elusiveness. For he went lightly, could only be seen as a fleeting image that was more beast than human in its movement and its cunning.

Beyond the glade was wilder undergrowth, bracken and ivy and thickets of hawthorn, into which the youth plunged and was instantly gone, moving deeper and easily into the forest reaches. He heard the monks fall behind: their cries of exasperation, their sporadic calling and the frustration of the dogs at his escape. He stopped to make sure he was not followed and to ease the hurt about his ribs. He listened and knew the pursuit had ended. The youth went on. About him the forest resumed its stillness, and he moved as would an animal, with the surety of discretion.

### The dark rider

In the dusk the youth ventured upon the road. He had gone beyond the ambit of the monastery and its orders, and at this hour the few travellers abroad gave little heed to his limping presence. At the sight of him, people huddled into their cloaks, hurried fearfully on. He neither begged nor called for help yet he caught the glance of each one who passed. And each one turned away from his stare even as they saw his wretchedness: the filth of his habit, his arms clasped across his chest, the dark bandage, his naked, bruised and bleeding feet on which he seemed to stumble more than walk. All this they saw and averted their eyes.

At the last of the light the road was empty. The sky flared briefly orange where the clouds were broken, setting the trees in copper and likewise the way as it fetched south. None had passed him for some time.

In these moments the youth heard the slow approaching horse but did not look back. He went on with his limping hobble for he could conceive of no alternative. Behind him the horse and its rider kept their steady pace, gaining. At the smell of the youth the horse snorted and seemed to stamp its hooves harder with each step. They drew level. The horse measured the youth's pace. And the youth felt the tap of a crop against his shoulder, once, twice, and looked up at the giant form of the monk, hooded and faceless in his cowl, where perhaps his mouth was open and wet teeth quickly gleamed. For a few steps they walked transfixed until the youth staggered away from the looming presence. He would escape but his legs rooted him with their heaviness. He went down on his hands and knees in the dirt like one felled, his head hanging almost to the mud. The horse and rider stood colossal over him. And the youth knew utter impotence and terrible fear, yet the monk did not touch him. Nor was anything spoken.

Then the youth heard the horse step away and how it went off at a gallop, the thundering of its hooves trembling in the ground and in his ears. And he lay there until the road was silent. In his despair and in his desolation, he looked again about him. The last paleness had gone from the sky. The monk drew night like a curtain behind him.

### The succour of Tabitha

In the morning the youth still lay curled and delirious beside the road. Whoever chanced upon him crossed to the farther edge, considering him diseased and dying. Which is how he was discarded through the hours and how his life ebbed down. And such would have been his death.

But at this time there came a band of Romanies along the road who were bent into the weather squalls and would have passed by too had their dogs not set to barking at the body. Then they stopped: the men crowding round, the women coming down from the wagons and the children peering at the windows. And they pitied the youth, and took him up. He was laid upon a bed where the women could attend him, especially one called Tabitha who was creased in age, her eyes gone blue with cataract, her teeth stubbed. Yet her hands brought comfort at the touch, as did her words. In the secrets of her tradition she applied herbs and medicines and bound his ribs and put ointment in his wound. The band moved on and the youth with them.

Yet in the following days he was indifferent to her ministrations, like one who would rather die. Heedless, she brought him the bloodied rags of menstrual women, on which he was told to suck and he did so without compulsion, even at its reek and bitterness. His body healed but he lay listless without appetite or interest. Then the woman Tabitha saw the shadow upon his mind and conjured deeply into her craft for restitution. She sat with the youth and became part of his darkness. Together they moved in regions that were devoid of all matter except for a plain like glass beneath their feet. And there was no time here when it was light, nor any promise of it. She lived with him. Walked without exhaustion. Walked without bearings.

And she asked if he had a meaning and he would not answer.

And she asked if he had direction and he said he had.

And later they sat at the back of the wagon with the doors open and the road sliding beneath them. Sunlight came and went according to the clouds, dazzling in the puddles when it fell, bringing a sudden warmth to their skin. Somewhere in front the children shouted at their playing and the low cadence of the adults' voices rose and subsided like a drone of bees. A bird called in the forest, clear, close. Again it called. From a distance another gave response. The woman Tabitha sucked at her pipe and the youth watched the smoke go blue away from them.

On the road and when they were camped in the fields of towns or villages she slept at his side and would allow no other to prepare his meals. To dress him she went among the tribe collecting what garments could be spared, but, as none had extra boots, wrapped his feet in old rags and leather which was adequate for his purpose. The youth gave no thanks for this kindness. He was not of her, nor could ever be. She knew this but it did not trouble her. For she considered the youth's need as his love and his warmth as her comfort.

Then she took him upon her business in the towns when she foretold all futures from her cards. He saw how merchants sought her out and rich women sent for her services. He saw how each one took their cards with greatest trepidation, smiling to gain her favour, hands trembling as they laid down their strangely pictured fortunes. And she in a soft voice asked the youth for the depictions, which he gave: empress, juggler, lovers, fool, and where each one cast its influences. In sombre tones she foretold the fates, sparing no detail or bad tiding even if men cursed her or women fainted at her revelations. To the youth she explained the workings of these cards, gave meaning to each in the major arcana and their reverse. And he listened yet he could see no necessity for the knowledge she dispensed.

These are the markings of our souls, she said. See how the pope reversed brings false prophecy or those who draw the chariot ride to war.

She turned her sightless and marble eyes on him, shuffling and shuffling the cards through her hands.

Choose three, she said. It is an ancient method.

But he would not.

She sighed. You are right, it does no good. Yet we should have found the star among your spread. Also, I fear, the chariot.

And one other, he said.

The woman Tabitha rose from where they sat beside the town's river.

No one is without that card, she said.

She held out her hand to the youth: It gets late. We must go back.

They walked through the town that was still chaotic with marketeers and the last of their bargains into the quiet streets where windows were already shuttered against the night and no one was about to greet them. The youth led a step before the woman, her left hand resting on his shoulder, her skirts brushing his legs. She walked with the arthritis of her age and every while they stopped.

It does no good, she said when they were paused on a street that led directly to the fields, to live as we do.

The clutch of her hand on his shoulder tightened.

We wander from east to west, from town to village, one week here, next week ten miles away. All without purpose, all without direction. If it were not this town it would have been another.

She let her hand drop.

Tell me what is about us.

The youth described the houses on the street: how they were built of stone and wood and daub, their roofs of steep slate; all shuttered and closed for the night.

And that smell of smoke? she asked. They all have fires?

The youth confirmed it.

In their kitchens, she said, they are seated about their fires: man and wife and children. They do not crouch as we do, like savages in the night without shelter. They have their place. Among them may be liars and cheats, and those who have committed heinous crimes, yet they have their place. But we, we are called thieves and parasites, and chased off once the townsmen have had their fill.

She reached out again for the youth and he took her hand. They moved on.

Do not live by wandering, she said. It does no good.

They did not stop again until they were beyond the houses. The youth could see where the wagons were drawn together and the blaze of a fire. He could hear the notes of a sad fiddler, the crying of a child. Before they joined the band, the woman Tabitha drew him to her. He was taller than she, for age had shrunken her. She held him: her arms reached about his waist.

When you will leave, she said, then go. We take no partings.

The youth felt her like a bird against him such was the frailty of her frame and flesh. For a moment longer she clung: he stood mute, his arms hanging limply at his sides. Then she released him and he led her among the wagons.

That night the youth sat with the woman Tabitha as he usually did. The fire sprang up in their circle, the children ran wild in the darkness. Two men danced to the fiddler's play and others clapped the beat with rising crescendo: on and faster, on and on until the fury pitched climactic into a silence. The band was restless: women fretted, men argued, for in the morning they would move on; and their spirit itched in the youth. Yet he showed no agitation: none except the woman knew his mind.

## Return to the village

The youth went that night. He stole boots but they were all he took. On the road, he found she had put food in his coat pockets: nuts, fruit and bread which he ate while he walked. He gave no thought to the distance before him or the events that would unfold from his course. He was carried by the action and the purpose was in it.

He travelled now each night, sleeping in the day's warmth, or taking shelter in the woods from foul weather. Those he met gave him direction. Some shared of their food and of their stories, receiving nothing in return. Some fled from his eyes, drawing crosses in the air to protect their souls. In this manner he journeyed. And so he came upon the road he sought which ran narrow through the forest and brought him one early light to stand on the hill above his village.

He saw that the hour was quiet, and that the milking herd was not yet out to graze along the slope.

He went down.

At his coming geese broke squabbling from a ditch. He walked through them though they hissed and spat, malevolent in their unblinking. A dog growled, too, and snapped. Heedless he came into the village. No one was about.

The day would be low and hazed and hung now dismal around the cottages. He passed the beerhouse: a light glowed behind the misted windows, cats crouched against the door in sullen waiting. He saw how a drinker had shat immodestly beside the dwelling, and the piss stains along the wall. In the shadow of a hovel he paused to glance back at where the geese picked and scrabbled in the edge-grass and a black pig stood hesitant licking the defecation. To his right the road was empty of all life. In the hovel a person coughed long and hawked. There sounded the sting of sputum in a pot, and then a silence. The youth crossed from his obscurity towards the schoolteacher's house.

He circled through the weeds and rubbish until he was on the farther side, hidden from the village. Here he crept close to the window, and bent beneath the sill, alert for any noise, but there was none. Slowly he straightened. The panes were mired and showed only his image. Gently the youth wiped at a corner with his sleeve. Again he bent, hands cupped against the glass, framing too his eyes. He peered into the gloom. Yet nothing was discernible.

In the cold dawning the youth squatted down against the wall and looked out at a tree in first bud and beyond to the fields, unploughed. The ground about was littered with coal and feathers and the broken shells of hen eggs. Beneath the tree were stacked logs. The youth saw where they had been cut and how an axe was shafted into the chopping block. He stared at it: the arm-length of its handle and its dull head. It glistened with frost. Eventually he rose and went to it. His hand closed about the grip and he pulled the axe out, the wood squeaked as the blade came free. He stood feeling the weight of the axe at the end of his arm, then turned towards the house.

## A reckoning with the schoolteacher

He went in at the front door. The interior still contained the density of night. It smelt of smoke and a dampness and of rats, their droppings and their nests beneath the boards. He waited in this odour until his eyes had adjusted to the dimness. He heard the snork of difficult breathing from a farther room. He stepped inside and closed the door.

The youth remembered the design and went down the passage towards the inner room. He moved slowly, kept against the wall, felt his way cautiously through the clutter. Once the axehead chipped against a pot or basin and rang out. The youth stopped. He listened, but the saw of breath did not alter.

He reached the inner room. The walls he felt were still charred where in his capture they had been scorched by fire. He went in. It was lighter here: the morning a grey effulgence at the window.

The schoolteacher slept in a chair, head tilted back, mouth open, air rasping through this cavity. A blanket covered him and he clutched it at his neck. In the grate the fire was no more than coals, glowing without warmth. A bottle stood beside the chair, the liquor well down.

The room was heaped with maps and charts, papers and illustrations of strange people and strange beasts: men depicted in ferocity; horned animals that bellowed out their wrath. These were spread over the table and across the chairs, were pinned to walls, or stacked against the artefacts of his obsessions. On this piece the schoolteacher had drawn arrows and made notes; on another he had circled islands in the vastness of oceans, or marked places on unsurveyed continents. Here scuds of wax showed his concentrations, there a stain of wine washed red across the land. All this the youth noted, and how in a belljar swam a human foetus, arms raised in horror at this still and soundless captivity.

The youth eased farther into the room until he stood before the schoolteacher, the axe held carelessly beside the man's head. He reached down for the liquor bottle and smelt at the liquid and then drank. It took his breath, burning too at its passage into his gut. He let the flush die before he drank again, slowly, in two long swallows. He replaced the bottle. The schoolteacher grunted in his sleep.

In the kitchen the youth found a candle and lit it. This room was small and he could see that what he sought would not be concealed there. Yet he searched quickly in the cupboard that was greased with food and among the implements behind it. Then, cupping the candle flame in his hand, he went back through the inner room into the short and cluttered passageway. Neither was it there; nor with the man's own gun, a long-barrelled version, rusted and seldom used. The youth wasted no time on it, seeing in an instant where the weapon was faulty. Beyond was another door and he entered a barren room littered with papers and the refuse of rodents. He held the candle up to cast the light: a rat stirred in a corner, turned its violent eyes on him, but would not flee. The movement caught the youth's notice and was equally dismissed. He returned to the inner room.

He drank again from the bottle and waited while the liquor worked within him. Then he raised the axe and chopped lightly at the schoolteacher's chest. The man opened his eyes; the youth ceased his motion. In that time they appraised one another: the youth with his indifference; the schoolteacher waking into his alarm.

You! he exclaimed. You!

And pinned himself back against the chair.

The youth nodded.

How? blustered the schoolteacher. I mean . . . how? I was coming for you. In the spring I was coming for you.

You would not have, said the youth.

The schoolteacher did not hear him.

I was coming for you. I have worked something out. The monks are medieval. I could not have left you there. It was my obligation, do you understand? To you. To your father. All winter I have been at it. I have studied these maps to find a way for us. And now I have determined it. I have read of the places. I have charted them. It is all here. All of it.

And he gestured at the litter of his room.

I am here for the rifle, said the youth.

Yes. The rifle.

The schoolteacher glanced left and right in confusion.

Where we are going. In the south, you . . . we will need it.

Where is the rifle? demanded the youth.

Wait. Wait. I have it, said the man.

He made to rise. The youth pushed him back into the chair, half raised the axe.

I have it, said the schoolteacher. It is here.

The youth let him up.

It is here. Here.

And he thrashed among the charts. Then he straightened.

I have thought of this, he said. In the winter I thought of this. There, in the south, are streams that trickle with gold. Wastes where the very stones are diamonds.

He pulled a map free, stabbed a finger at the diagrams.

They are here. Here in this land.

He looked up at the youth.

Bring the light. You can see the streams. You can see where these places are.

The youth watched him, but did not offer the light.

Then the schoolteacher noticed the belljar, and snatched it from the table.

Ah, he sighed. See this, my friend. This is science.

He held the belljar up and towards the youth, turning it so that the brown and shrivelled foetus seemed to revolve in its own universe.

It is from the south, he said, staring with admiration at the object, and then back at the youth. I met here, here in our own beerhouse, a man returning home, who had fought in the south to tame the barbarous hordes. He told me of the riches. He showed me the stones, the clots of amalgam streaked with gold. Of how it lies littered about the land. And of the opportunities for science. An incomplete nomenclature. Or the study of these man-like primitives – and he pointed at the belljar. This very specimen he personally cut from the belly of a savage found wandering in the wilderness. He said it lived for an hour in this world, against all expectations. Then he carried it for days so determined was he to save such a fine example. And in time was fortunate to find a chemical man who could bottle it. I realised instantly its value. He let me buy it for a small amount.

The schoolteacher paused. I had thought we – you and I – should go there. To the south.

The youth ignored him. The schoolteacher scavenged again among his artefacts.

Look, see this, this tooth.

He held it out, dangling on a thin cord.

A leopard's, he said. Worn by warriors in battle. Take it. Take it.

I have come for the rifle, said the youth, yet he reached for the tooth and the schoolteacher gave it.

It's a charm, a protection.

The schoolteacher bent towards him.

If you agree, he said, we could . . .

He hugged at the belljar; let the sentence trail off. Then he smiled.

There is gin, he pointed, beside the chair.

The youth made no effort to acknowledge this.

The rifle, he said.

The schoolteacher shifted uneasily; papers, maps drifted to the floor, rustling. They settled. It was quiet again in the room. The candle flared suddenly: the flame reflected as if it burnt within the foetus. Outside, the milkherd passed lowing and moaning from the sheds. There came voices, and the village awoke to its necessities.

I was coming for you, the schoolteacher repeated. I would not have left you there.

He looked at the youth; the youth remained unmoved. The man went on.

There is nothing to keep me here. I owe no debt to this village, for these are simple people. I would have done better in the colleges, or . . . or out as a man of science in the wild reaches. I have some money. Enough for our passage. And afterwards, for a time. We can leave this place. Travel to another country.

He put the belljar down on the table, kept one hand resting on top; and it seemed the foetus recoiled at this darkness. Keeping his eyes averted from the youth, he asked: Will you come with me? Then quickly: You can have the rifle. It is here. You can have it.

No, said the youth. Just the gun.

No! said the schoolteacher to himself. He frowned. You will not go with me!

He bent his head and brought his hands up to cover his face. In this attitude he stood and was round-shouldered and seemed even to shake.

Gin, he said eventually, taking down his hands. The gin.

The youth kicked the bottle towards him across the floor, the liquor splashing on to the fallen charts. It fetched up against the schoolteacher's shoes, dribbling the last of its contents. For a moment the man stood indecisively, then bent down and grabbed the bottle

66

and raised it and sucked at the neck. When he was finished he f
the youth again.

I cannot give it to you, he said. It would not be what your father
wanted.

I will have it, said the youth.

The schoolteacher shook his head.

The youth raised the axe and swung it and the schoolteacher
watched the arc described and would have cried in protest but
there was no time because the belljar exploded into shards and
the reek of formaldehyde came at them powerfully. And suddenly
freed the foetus slipped across the charts of foreign continents and
seemed to crawl towards the table's edge until it plunged into the
underworld among the rats and ferals. The schoolteacher moved to
catch his precious object which he did but was repulsed by the feel of
this soft and slimy thing and let go and in a moment it was gone among
the accumulation in the room. He stood distraught at the weakness of
his hands and their ineptitude. He gasped, My God! My God! – and
went down on the floor, snuffling in his desperation, rooting like a
forest pig among the undergrowth.

Now began a turmoil in the room, for the youth was maniacal. He
obliterated from the walls the cases of butterflies and the mounts
of weasel heads, crushing each with a blow, hacking without
discrimination. He raised the axe again and smashed it down into
table and upholstery, and again into book and ink. He tore among the
vast maps and charts, single-minded in his destruction, moving in a
swathe through the furniture. At this outrage the schoolteacher leapt
upon him and they staggered about, the man on the youth: clawing,
biting, spitting. Which is how they went down on to the glass, into
the pools of chemical that stung their eyes. And with his face pushed
hard against the floor, the youth looked into the wise features of the
foetus: the hooded eyes, the lips parted as if they spoke. He saw how
the hands reached towards him, and that the legs were bent as they
had been inside the mother. He stared at this tiny form of silence
and would have screamed, except that he howled within himself a
noise that had no human attribute. Nor had his ferocity. He struggled
against the man's weight, coming free and striking upwards with the
axe haft in a vicious blow that caught the schoolteacher's chest and
drove out his wind. The man coughed and writhed, while the youth
stood above him surveying the debris and the hidden corners now
revealed. There leant his rifle, the pouch of bullets tied about its
stock. In two paces he had it and had hurled aside the axe. But the
schoolteacher was at him again, kneeling up, clawing at the youth's

waist, pleading. Twice the youth struck down with the butt into the man's face: once striking the cheek, the second time opening a long gash across the forehead. It was enough: the schoolteacher crawled away, blinded and gibbering. Where he stood the youth broke the breech and blew into the chamber and similarly down the rifling to rid it of dust. He cocked the hammer which had stiffened from disuse and worked it to ease the mechanism and did likewise with the trigger before he was satisfied. From the pouch he took a cartridge and laid it in the breech and brought up the barrel. It locked closed with a click which was the first sound he had heard in the tumult. Then he saw the schoolteacher bloodied and sitting on the floor, his face turned up to him, his mouth simpering the words he could not sound. The youth moved around him and out of the room and down the dim passageway. He heard the schoolteacher staggering behind but he did not look back even when he opened the door.

In the road were gathered some villagers, his aunts among them, drawn by the violence in the house yet too terrified to intervene lest it be devils. At his approach they huddled away. The youth walked past them neither daunted by their number nor acknowledging their presence. He carried the rifle in both hands, holding it at waist height: his right hand gripped behind the trigger, his left upon the barrel stock. None sought to interfere. Then came the schoolteacher into his doorway and leant there ravaged, visible to all. The women gasped at the sight and only now did the men shout after the youth, but no one made to chase him. The youth walked through the village and started up the hill towards the forest.

## A supper of quail and liquor

He took the road leading to an upland field. At the crest of the hill he glanced back at the village, its disorder and consternation, and the black figures of his aunts outside their house. But it was no more than a fleeting appraisal before he struck across the field and into the trees.

He found the invisible paths which not even his absence had erased, and where traps had been, and still were with their rotted catches. From the depths came the call of woodpeckers, their run of chiselling, and everywhere the scurry of furtive dealings. He circled through the cuts and glades, obscure in his purpose, attentive to each rustle or shadow, convinced that he was watched by cunning eyes. The youth came at last near Madach's burrow and here he paused, disappeared into his immobility, became of the wood. Yet in the hours he waited, nothing altered in the solitude.

Eventually he called out for he felt the other's presence.

Madach, he called. Madach.

And the name died quickly among the vegetation.

So you'n have come back, said Madach into the forest quiet. His voice came from the youth's right, but the youth knew Madach's trickery and searched elsewhere for its source, yet could not locate him.

Come out, he said.

In good time, replied Madach. You'n have betrayed me once, my peacock, you'n can do so again. First I'll know why you'n here.

The youth looked to where the voice had sounded. He spoke to it: I'm leaving, he said.

Ah, sighed Madach from another direction and the youth spun to that: You'n leaving are you'n!

Then from a way off he shouted: I thought you'n had already left.

Where are you? demanded the youth loudly, casting around. Come out.

I'm where I want to be, said Madach. All I need is to hear your words. As you'n need to hear mine.

He paused to change once more the location of his voice.

Now listen to this, my peacock. For a winter I've wallowed here, sick almost to death. Sick beyond all agony I thought possible. Like a cat I could've died within the burrow and gone to bone and been dispersed among the rocks and soil. Who'd've known that I'n had ever been? Me. Madach, who's lived through more winters than twice your age, who's shifted for himself without help from no one, who's sought no charity, stooped to no beggar's pleading, could have disappeared like smoke into the air. I was sick. Poisoned in tissue and organ. Too weak to set a trap. Too weak to leave the burrow.

He stopped. Then sounded again closer.

'Twas when I needed you'n.

The youth glanced down into the brush. Madach spoke next farther off.

But you'n would not have known that.

Come out, said the youth.

Come out. Come out, mimicked Madach. Why come out when you'n are leaving. Go on. Go!

The youth did not move.

I've learnt one thing, my peacock, said Madach. There is no trust to be placed anywhere but in oneself.

He said it softly, more to himself than to the youth. For a while neither spoke. The forest reasserted itself.

Then the youth slung the rifle on to his back and started between the trees. He was wary of movements among the shadows but there were none except those of birds or where the wind stirred. He noted them all; disregarded them simultaneously. His direction he took from instinct: his mouth set to his purpose, his eyes alert, their gaze black. In a moment he was gone and only another used to the forest could have followed his passage. Except he did not get far.

Wait! called Madach, and he dropped beside the youth, humped and smirking, dancing with the suddenness of his appearance. I've some food.

The youth stopped.

And spirits.

He grinned before the youth, and the youth looked at him without smiling.

Meat 'n fine potato liquor.

He took the youth's arm, lightly, hesitantly, but the youth did not resist.

Yes?

The youth shook his arm free, acquiesced.

In the burrow they ate and drank and neither spoke further. Afterwards the youth slept. Madach watched him: saw that the eyes had become deeply set and that the skin had thinned along his jaw. He smelt him too: the stench of travelling and also the sharp reek of wariness common to all hunted men. The youth lay on his rifle; once, briefly, he opened his eyes as resting animals do: they were fearless in their clarity.

When the youth awoke later he was alone. The fire still burnt; the bottle was placed before him. He took the gun and went out. Neither was Madach in the vicinity. He stood in the cold air above the burrow, for the day had never cleared and was now as damp and grey as it had begun, and listened but there was only the moan of trees and the cracking of inner wood. He returned into the burrow and set to the cleaning of the rifle. Which is how Madach found him.

The humped man dropped a brace of quail beside the fire yet the youth did not look up from his occupation, nor when Madach plucked them, filling the air with feathers and fine down, did the youth help him. Among the coals Madach scooped two hollows and in this heat he laid the naked, ungutted birds. The aroma of them rose into the burrow. The youth finished with the weapon, put it aside. Madach gestured at the bottle and the youth reached for it and drank. He drank twice more while Madach waited, his eyes averted, yet conscious of the level. Eventually the youth surrendered the bottle and Madach drank likewise without drawing breath until it was empty.

He laughed. D'you'n want more, my peacock? More of Madach's magic!

The youth looked at him, spread his hands towards the fire without answering.

From a corner, Madach brought two bottles: one he gave to the youth, the other he kept. Again he cackled. He poked at the birds to test their cooking and tore a strip of flesh and saw that it was done. Yet he left them until the skin browned crisp. Then he lifted a carcass from the coals and gave it to the youth who took it with the same equanimity, impervious to how it scalded. They ate; Madach crouching intent and serious beside the fire.

Afterwards they finished the liquor and slept the uncaring sleep of drunk men. And such was their inebriation that even the raucous birds at dawn did not stir them nor the sudden quiet that followed. Yet the forest knew that strangers trespassed: men who spoke in undertones, who carried weapons, and were pulled by dogs.

### The bailiff's men

The men were not of the village: they had been called from the town and the monastery and were the bailiff and his forces and two monks. In the predawn outside the beerhouse they worked by the light of lanterns to charge their guns, grumbled at the dogs they leashed, more irritable than cajoled bears. The monks looked on, being unarmed except for cudgels. And the villagers stood about them in curiosity.

All this for a youth, cursed the bailiff. When not a road is safe from dangerous men, we must go chasing a mere youth.

You saw the youth's doing, said a monk.

Bah! spat the bailiff. If others had any courage they would not have let the fellow walk free.

He is an animal, said the monk.

So are tigers, said the bailiff. Yet I have seen them dance to a man's whip.

He spat again and shouldered through the crowd.

His men followed him straining at the eager dogs and behind them came the monks and then the villagers, those who could labour the climb, except the schoolteacher who peered at the procession from his doorway but would not go farther.

Leave him, he tried to call. Leave him.

But he could make no utterance: his mouth was too swollen for articulation, the words were croaks, the sounds carried no meaning. Some villagers thought he praised them and waved what hoes and forks they carried as weapons.

No, said the schoolteacher shaking his head. No.

And so they left the village with his unheard protestation.

In the forest the dogs were true, went yelping at the chase and nothing could be done to hush them. The men followed quickly, half running, alert to any shape they should flush out. And they came to the oak in whose roots the burrow nestled where the dogs milled mad and pawing at the ground and about the tree-trunk. The bailiff had his men surround the site while he tapped with his rifle-butt to find the entrance. The villagers came up too, standing timidly among the trees. In the great bowl he found it, a rough-hewn plank that gave at his pounding, releasing from the cavity beneath a smell of cooked meat and fetidness. Alarmed he stepped back, rifle poised. But nothing challenged him. He shouted for whoever was there to come out, but no one yielded. Then he had the villagers collect brushwood and demanded men's shirts or the skirts women wore beneath their coats and three were donated. Into these he bundled the kindling, sprinkled gunpowder from broken cartridges, fashioned his bombs. The men watched, grinning with anticipation. The bailiff called for matches and had the bundles lit, which were dropped into the hole and there must have exploded into flames because they heard the dull burst of the powder and smoke poured from the opening. The men stood ready for the capture.

# CHAPTER FIVE

*The youth and Madach travel south to a port. In nightmares the youth's future is enacted. On the ship he displays his ability and for this is reviled and abused. Also he arouses in Lizzie an uncontrollable lust. A theme of slavery is introduced.*

## The way south

AS THEY HURRIED, THE YOUTH AND MADACH HEARD how the commotion stopped at the burrow, and eventually the hollow detonations. They did not pause although Madach swore.

This is your doing, my peacock, he cursed. No one has troubled me before.

The youth ignored his agitation.

There's no reason why I should go with you'n. It's not me they want. I'm innocent. Innocent, d'you'n hear – and he danced before the youth, gesticulating.

The youth kept on.

And later when they rested briefly, Madach proclaimed: I'll go with you'n some way, my peacock. I'll put you'n on the road. But no farther. D'you'n hear. This is my home.

The youth stared at him but said nothing. Later he arose, and in silence they proceeded.

They walked all day although they were not followed, and fared on for most of the night. Which was how they travelled in the coming days, keeping within the forest, passing through unknown and unsuspected: the man humped, beneath the sack strapped on his back: and the youth carrying nothing but the rifle which sometimes rested on his shoulder, sometimes lay in the crook of his arm. He wore still the Romanies' clothes, such as they were, bedraggled and stained from the journeying, and looked as wild in appearance as an outcast.

They went by mutual consent, although no route had been decided between them, yet Madach assumed a course and the youth accepted it. Nor did Madach complain further about his lot, but took it with fortitude until there came a day during the early warmth of spring when the forest thinned and the country fell broken beneath them on to a coastal plain.

On the escarpment Madach and the youth stopped among the shrill of insects and the baked vegetation, its smell tough with resin; surveying from high rocks the unwooded lowland where all that grew was scrub and olive groves. Never in their wending had they encountered such terrain: although they had crossed the sides of mountains, traversed steep valleys, yet always there had been forest and its prospect. They looked now on its end; the beginning of a new geography. In the distance the sky curved, a denser and a darker blue, towards the sea. And at this juncture lay the white gleam of a town, the houses like bones heaped and shimmering.

This is the direction south? asked the youth.

Madach nodded: And there's too the road.

He indicated a track which zigzagged down. The youth followed his pointing. He saw where it came out of the hill and its route across the plain. At this time none travelled there.

The youth shouldered his rifle and began the descent, threading a way carefully between the rocks because the going was treacherous, the ground unfirm.

I'm not coming, my peacock, shouted Madach after him.

The youth was out of sight.

I said I'm not coming, d'you'n hear, he called again.

The snap and slither of the youth's passage went on. The humped man squinted into the sun that rode like a white hole across its apex as if he could see there other possibilities. The glare was intense. He closed his eyes and sighed, steadying himself against a rock until the blinding image had gone. Then he, too, began the descent.

## An offer of employment

In the evening they were stopped beside the road, a meagre supper stewing between them. Neither spoke, which was out of habit but also from fatigue. Yet both were alert and could not be surprised. The light was failing.

Long before its appearance they heard a coach on the pass, a man's curses, whip-cracks, and how the wheels slid about the road. Even how turning down the final gradient that ran straight out, the man drove in a fury, lashing the horses which were done for by the day's travel yet could not deny the slope. They came on at a gallop until the momentum went out of them and they slowed to walking. When they reached where the youth and Madach sat they would go no farther. The man beat at them with the whip but the animals stood lathered and blown. In temper he hurled away the rope, and jumped down from the coach.

He glared at the youth and Madach.

Are you Christians? Or thieves? he bellowed.

Neither responded.

If you are thieves leave now or I shall kill you where you sit.

He took a revolver from his coat.

If Christian show your charity and help a distressed man!

Madach paid no attention, began eating from the stew. The youth watched the coachman.

You, said the coachman. You, lad. Come and help me.

The youth did not move.

He'd need a wage, said Madach. A wage would bring out his charity.

He handed the stew to the youth. The youth drank at it.

From inside the coach a woman yelled, high-pitched and angry: Let us out, Joe Silver. How d'you expect us to breathe in this dusty box when there's not a breeze to sustain us?

I'm about to. I'm about to, muttered the man called Joe Silver. Then turning to the youth: Come on, whelp, show some respect.

Again Madach answered: He's not one for charity or respect.

Is he dumb?

Joe Silver, let us out right now. Right now, damn you!

No, said Madach.

Then what's he got to say?

Nothing.

Nothing?

He's got words when he wants them.

Joe Silver!

I'm here, woman. I'm here, responded the coachman, unlocking the coach which was barred at every window. A woman, high dressed in embroidered satins, stepped down, and behind her came two girls, sorry-looking, unhappy. She eyed Madach and the youth like dog turds.

And these?

Travellers! shrugged Silver. Peasants?

Scum, said the woman.

Madach laughed. He took what was left of the stew from the youth.

We can't stop here, she said. Not with them.

Silver raised his face and hands to the heavens.

If you can get those beasts to go another mile, then do it, he said.

These are my charges, said the woman indicating the girls. The horses are yours. And now you keep those two where they are while we take relief.

Yes. Yes, Silver muttered.

I mean it, Joe Silver. And I mean it properly. Under the barrel of that gun.

The coachman raised the revolver tentatively and pointed it at the youth and Madach. The women disappeared among the scrub.

It's not good for you'n to point a weapon at friendly men, said Madach when the women were gone.

The man lowered his arm.

Bitch, he hissed, just audibly.

He approached the fire and saw for the first time the rifle lying in the shadow of the youth's legs. He stopped, hesitant.

You are armed, he said.

My friend has his weapon, replied Madach. I have this – from among his possessions he drew out the long bayonet.

You are not peasants!

76

We're what you'n see. Nothing more. Nothing less.

Does he shoot?

He does.

And true?

And true.

Silver considered this. Are you deserters? I have seen many on the roads. Some dressed as women.

Madach sucked at the last of the stew.

No, he said.

Mercenaries? Hired men?

Madach shrugged.

The coachman sniffed at the drifting aroma.

What did you eat? It smells of lamb.

Madach looked up at the man. He spat a small bone into the grass.

Squirrels, he said eventually. Shot even as they leapt between the branches. Is there more that you'n would know?

Silver crouched down on his haunches. He looked from the youth to Madach, and grinned. Then he spoke, glancing quickly at where the women had gone, but they were still about their business.

The young women are our wards, he said. Signed into our service by their father. But we would not call them maids. We would rather call them protégées. We would give them a better future.

He glimpsed the movement of the women approaching.

Perhaps you could help us?

Joe Silver, screamed the woman. We must go.

Those horses won't, Lizzie, he said, standing up. They've gone as far as they're going to on this day.

The woman called Lizzie spat.

In Mary's name, she cursed.

Neither the name of Mary nor anyone higher will prod them forward, said Silver. So you may as well abide.

The woman looked down at the youth and Madach. The two girls had gone into the coach.

They would slit our throats, she said.

Madach laughed.

Come here, said Joe Silver, and he drew the woman aside. They spoke in low tones. Sometimes the woman exclaimed, but the coachman talked harder to overcome her protests.

At last she broke away: You do as you want, but don't come whimpering at the consequences.

77

There'll be no consequences, he threw back at her, at least none that you're thinking of.

The woman Lizzie got into the coach; Joe Silver came grinning towards the fire. He went down on his hams and spoke without looking at either the youth or Madach but at the space between them.

He told how he and the woman had gone among the starving and destitute offering what solace they could in prayers or kind, until in a remote village they nursed an ailing man who begged them take his daughters to a new life.

We could not, said Joe Silver. They were his joy, his pride, all he had left. His wife was dead. Had died a wasting death of fever while he looked on in helplessness. Now it was in his lungs. He knew, as did we, how it would go. And how shortly. For mercy's sake, he would plead, tears at his eyes, take them now, give them hope, don't let them see my suffering. Yet we could not. But the greater our procrastination, the more earnestly he pressed us.

Joe Silver glanced quickly from the youth to Madach, then away into the thickening darkness.

You understand how we felt. We were torn. Our compassion was wracked. Each night we went on our knees to ask the Lord for guidance or sought advice in His Book. We heard His Word and let Him lead us. Consider, too, in good conscience, we could do nothing else but give this comfort to a dying man. At last, when it was clear he would not see another winter, we agreed.

The coachman paused.

We left enough money to cover his needs.

He crossed himself quickly: By now he is probably called.

Then he leant closer to the youth and Madach.

We need protection, he whispered. You have seen those girls, they are more precious than gold, and to many as desirable.

Still crouched, he waddled forward, his boots almost touching the coals.

Our meeting is indeed fortunate, heaven-sent, you are men of the world.

Again he shifted his eyes to Madach then to the youth, yet now it was too dark to discern their features. The youth seemed asleep. Madach gave no indication of his opinion. Silver spoke on hurriedly.

You see, we take passage in three days for a wild and distant place, a ridge of goldfields with its towns and industry. This is our mission. There is need of our work in these new lands, and to this we are committed. But the times are dangerous, the destination no less so, nor the voyaging. Dangerous enough for a man and his wife, let alone with two young daughters.

He stopped.

I can pay, he said. I'm not asking for your charity.

Nor would we give it, said Madach.

He dug at the coals with the bayonet.

You'n say the girls are sisters?

Yes, said Silver.

Suddenly Madach leered into the firelight, grinning. The man fell backwards in his fright.


### The port

The next day they travelled on together. Yet at their waking the woman Lizzie had changed her disposition: smiled at the youth and towards Madach also. The youth gave back nothing for this friendliness, but Madach bowed until his back curved higher than his head. Now the youth saw the girls clearly for the first time: their exhaustion and their grief and the fear of where their lives were leading. They went past him quickly to perform their toilet in the scrub with Lizzie laughing at the youth's stare, even lifting her skirts before she was properly hidden. Silver saw it but kept busy at his horses. Nor did the youth's curiosity cease. He watched them return: the woman brazen, the girls demure. Madach watched too, and sniggered at the youth's perplexity.

Before sunrise they began, and in this manner they travelled at a man's pace, for the horses would only walk: Silver preceding, the youth and Madach behind, the three women inside the coach. Often the woman gazed back at them, her face filling the aperture, rouged, quizzical, and caught the youth's eye and he squinted in return. Yet the scrutiny left him uneasy, so that he walked to the side where she could not see him.

In a late dark hour they reached the town: its streets deserted except for dogs and rodents, its houses barred. No one would give them lodging: either ignored their clamouring or met it with abuse. And they were forced on until the streets opened into the beach beside the harbour. Here they stopped, uncaring. The women slept where they had sat all day; the men lay between the wheels in the sand. Before them stretched the sea, great and black and loud: a booming presence in their sleep that would give no rest.

And at dawn they stood at the water's edge where it came hissing and sucking about their naked feet. Aside them ran the tideline like a necklace strung of polyps of weed, of feathers, of claws and carapace, each rearranged, each constantly renewed at the shallows' heave and collapse. Yet the sea's distance was as level as a board and as motionless. Low across it scudded cormorants. White gulls wheeled down to flock upon the sand.

And at midday they stood in a great spectacle of humanity that surged and cried about the docks: fishmen, whalers, parrot sellers and organ grinders as sharp-faced as their monkeys, jigging too with the tune's monotony. Sailors more alien than monsters. Gangs of chained men who stank from their captivity. And frightened emigrants, huddled together. Here they waited with uncommon patience shuffling towards the pursers' tables and were offered passage to wild continents, which others seemed to choose, although they had no real choice and would go where they were ferried. But which Joe Silver declined, naming another destination, and in accordance was given berths.

And at sunset they stood on the quays among the groaning ships: schooners, cutters, merchants, barques, those powered by steam and those square-sailed. Above them the forest of masts and spars swayed on the swell.

Then Silver took the youth and Madach and they sallied into the port that was even wilder by night than day. In the bazaars he bought them new apparel for which he got no thanks, it being no less than their expectations, and they shed their rags where they changed among the stalls. Thus newly clothed they moved on to the baths. In the steam sat naked men of every imperfection: those large-bellied, their genitals displayed like prunes; those hairy as bears; and some lean as skeletons where the penis dangled more ropey than a spastic limb. Some showed the wounds of petty fights and some those of historic battles, yet the scars could not be distinguished and each had healed in due ugliness. Silver bore no marks. Madach carried his deformity. The youth was scored only about his ankles like a common prisoner. Each was given a tub. Each soaked until the water lost its heat. The youth was first out, made uneasy by the place: the savagery of its nakedness and men's solicitation. Yet those who would approach him saw his eyes and hid their lust. He dressed and was followed by Madach who, like Silver, grumbled at the youth's haste. Yet they joined him quickly in the streets that still teemed with the day's transactions and were accosted by children offering up the flaccid shapes of octopus, or by men with contraband, or by whores who rubbed against their groins and poked in their ears with vapid tongues. And Silver fondled their breasts and buttocks in return as did Madach, preening at this attention, but the youth pushed grimly on, heedless. Through gin dens and the haunts of bootleggers Silver led them until they were well-liquored, crazed with this indulgence, arrogant and shouting.

Now he brought them to a house where in the downstairs rooms men ate and drank shrouded by a smoke so thick it was the equal of sea mist. Fiddlers played, and here too lounged whores of every caste and age. The men were captains and their proprietors, chandlers, merchants, bankers, and in the dim recesses some of lesser station yet who spent as lavishly their fortunes. Silver spread his arms, offering it all. He called for wine, for food; and they were brought fine mutton enough to feed them twice, and burgundy. They drank. Silver raised toasts to where they were headed, to the clipper that would take them, to the business they would do. They drank. At some time Silver was gone, and at some time he had returned, bringing with him women who let their garments fall free as they caressed the youth and Madach, kissed at their drunken lips. And she fondling the youth unbuttoned him which was when he hurled vomit on the floor that was laughed at, his back thumped by men he did not know who offered port in compensation. He took it, sliding down among the tables, ignored. There in the later hours at the carousing's end the woman Lizzie found him exposed as the whore had left him. She went down on her knees beside the youth, stroked at the hairs of his groin entwining her fingers there, cupped the sac of his testes, considered the unconscious sex; then fastened his garments. She cleaned too his face and sat him up in the debris of platters, bottles, the slops and shards of the night's hard living. He asked neither where he was nor how he had got there, but stood unsteadily even on Lizzie's arm. In the hall waited Silver with the two young women; Madach stood smiling upon the stairs.

They went out into the early town that was as empty as it had been on their arrival. Cats hissed and yowled among the garbage; and water rats of feline size stood up to mark their passing. Daylight was on the buildings. A stench more pungent than fish gone rotten being also of faeces and piss and sundry offal carried in the narrow streets yet they did not notice. They walked in couples: Silver with the girl called Florrie; Madach with her named Fanny; and Lizzie on the youth's arm although she gave support, not he. Which is how, like a band of penitents, the lanes brought them to the harbour stirred now by some activity: those preparing for the tide; fishermen hauling to the banks. Likewise they found the clipper readying and went below: neither concerned at the departure nor anxious at the fall-away of this land.

### The voyage: dreams, conversations, passions
The ship sailed out.
Beneath the loop and cry of gulls she went even before the port had

come awake, the sleekness and the slenderness of her going through the roadstead of awaiting vessels into the seapaths and the quickening winds. Her sheets came unfurled, cracked as she took the wind. There began a drumming in her timbers which the captain knew and loved for what it was, the measure of her speed and sailing. The jibs were out; the clipper was away.

And below in his drunkenness the youth dreamt that all the distance he had fled and the reaches he was still to cross would be rendered meaningless by the image, black and gross, that he could not shed but which was of him and in him and stood in cowled and unfaced silence, invincible in battles where demons leapt from the bodies of the slain, gored with their entrails and mutilations, bearing neither rifles nor pistols but spears and shields, their eyes ferocious white in the darkness of their deeds and bodies, their teeth snapping hungry for the flesh of other men . . . yet not even they could triumph over this man for he held grimly in their midst, unwounded, scything forth with his sword, a weapon as primitive as those of the men he fought, yet more deadly in its use until all were vanquished and the youth stood alone with this figure among the unmitigated horror.

From which he woke screaming to find he lay naked and solitary but with the scent of the woman Lizzie still powerful in the berth.

And in the coming days he dreamt this again and similar dreams of violence, inexplicable in their fury. Always he was in regions of devastation: ruined villages put to fire, the massacre of innocents. He wandered in this as blood-crazed as his partners without obvious purpose or intent except the cause of mayhem and revenge. For he was filled with profound savagery against his fellows. And he rode to endless upheaval, rode before a band of dread horsemen until the very ground trembled with their coming.

From these scenes and others of equal calamity he awoke in the narrow cabin, hot and listless. About him the ship vibrated at its passage, clipping swiftly before the wind. Then he sought solace on the upper deck.

Above the masts wheeled stars, high and multitudinous, appearing and disappearing as the sails flew like clouds across their universe. Below in the ink depths rose creatures of phosphorescence that danced in crazy motion.

Or he joined a company of strangers who sat out to talk. At their voices his other worlds grew distant. He listened to their disquisitions which carried no practical point yet none the less engaged their tempers.

A doctor among them said he had explored throughout the human body, both of those alive and of those dead, and could find no essence that he could label soul.

Nor was there any, mumbled a low voice.

You do not believe in salvation?

Or damnation?

No. Neither.

In what do you believe?

In regeneration. In death.

You are mad.

It is what I believe.

So you would excuse all bloodshed, all war, all revolution and the horrors that are perpetrated?

I would neither pardon nor blame.

You would condone suffering and misery just for the sake of seeing order collapse into anarchy?

I have said I would neither condone nor advocate. That is purely the way we are.

You would leave it at that? You would hold no one accountable! Surely there is right and wrong?

Once we chopped off a child's hands for stealing bread when he was hungry, now we call such punishments barbaric. Yet tomorrow we could have different views again.

You are a relativist, sir: the world is not like that.

At which the doctor grunted his disapproval and moved off as did others in the company until the youth stood alone. Below the dark water hissed and slapped against the hull.

The ship sailed on.

Across seas utterly empty, devoid of sail or bird or fish so that it would seem they were nowhere, that what they called movement was illusion, a gross deception in this boundless element. Or at other times they rode upon storms that pitched them, vulnerable and fraught, from crest to crest with the clipper in anguish at every moment. Then they feared the worst. Then those who still had the sense to fear cried in panic; while the rest lay wishing for that very death. Which was the youth's condition and likewise the rest of the group except Lizzie who tended them all, and the youth especially. Until the howling stopped and they entered the doldrums where on a glassy sea that slipped like oil beneath the bows they saw ships becalmed, limp-sailed in the windless latitudes, yet they passed on, graceful and silent, powered by the hidden airs none else could find. And whereas in the storms all had been damp, now the sun gave no relief. Above was shadeless, the berths below held their heat with the closeness of ovens. Even at night they would not cool, and the emigrants came up to sleep haphazardly upon the deck.

Against a bulkhead lay Silver and Lizzie with the young women between them and the youth and Madach as guards on either side. Here the youth did not dream. He lay in the blind darkness, his head filled with the creak and slap of the ship, breathing the scent of the woman beside him that was like nothing he could name. It belonged to these nights: became the perfume of the equator, all-pervading, ineffable, swirling out to trap men in a lassitude. And here Lizzie put forth a hand that settled on his stomach, lay there with its passion radiating deep into his organs, and he did not set it aside. Yet he was rigid, tensed beneath the palm and fingers that neither moved nor exerted any weight. He went erect; he ached in his testicles. Still the hand did not come alive, nor could he seek his own relief. So they lay: the youth beneath the woman's disembodied touch, her smell exquisite on the night. Both thus imprisoned. In time she bent over him, came to rest with her head upon his stomach and took his penis in her mouth, working at it with her tongue and teeth until he could contain himself no longer. Then she moved up and sought his lips and passed into his mouth that which she had taken into hers.

Swallow, she said.

The youth swallowed, though he felt it rise again, embittered with his gorge. Yet he stopped it; he kept it down. And he saw how she smiled, her chin spangled with his fluid. Then she turned from him, and the night that had been before came back.

It was this way throughout the tropics. Lizzie ate of him, and gave him too this substance. Yet she would not allow him on her, or even his hands. And in the days he watched her: the moving lips that spoke and smiled to reveal the exactness of her teeth, the warm lushness of her mouth, as she went grandly clothed and forbearing among their company, being nurse, mother, madam according to the circumstance: her own woman, not possessed, not possessing. And the youth saw himself in those times with Madach or Silver or on the edge of groups as if his other self did not exist, nor hers with it. Except each night they lay down to their ritual even while about them men and women whispered the prayers and awesome terrors of their lives.

For they were a company of refugees, aggregated from all corners of the old world and the new. There being numbered with them vintners whose crops had been withered by disease, and families thrown on destitution. Old diggers from faltering tin mines who stared crazed and bewildered at the changing times; also Jews put to flight by pogroms and similar persecutions across the provinces. These all, and gangster, mercenary, criminal: women who were prostitutes; men who were their pimps. Whom Silver knew. With whom he spent hours in reminiscence asking after one or another. And was told their individual fates. About Russian George who was run out of one city even by those who used his girls. Who went south.

To the goldfields?

The same.

Who was richer now than ever and trading in French and Belgiums, any ages, any size, because diggers weren't particular men. Because a hole was a hole to them.

At which they sniggered, and looked down the deck at where Lizzie walked and with her Fanny and Florrie and, a pace behind, the youth and humped Madach.

You've got it set up, Joe, one said.

Silver knocked clean his pipe.

Those are good women.

You might say that, said Silver. You might say that.

The ship sailed on.

In cooler climes they returned to their berths. The winds came up. The sea was white-capped and skimming. A pall of salt overhung them.

The woman still visited the youth who lay again with his dreams and went haunted at strange hours through the galleys and upon the decks. She saw how he was and mistook the cause for his lust and now had him look upon her nakedness, yet he was given no right to touch her, neither her breasts nor her genitals which reeked of her secretions. In this state she leant back against the door, her legs splayed, and had him kneel before her. He stared at the dark mat of her pubescence; the flesh beneath turning copper and rich into her sex. And she said she would have him lick her and pushed his face against her hair. The youth stuck out his tongue to its extremity, lapping among the soft enfolded flesh. She stayed emotionless, except that her fingers clawed about his head.

Then she would leave him. Push him away with her knee thrust hard against his chest. Dress while he lay sprawled upon the floor, face down, cowering as a dog cursed. She never spoke then either, but would bend at the last to stroke her nails along his thigh, his stomach, dallying. Still he would not raise his eyes. And she would lift her hand and straighten up, glance once more at the prostrate form before she left. Later the youth would go up to see the morning star diminished by the dawn.

At this time he first dreamt of a sand reach, his coming to it with others who were equally besotted, frenzied in their outlook and behaviour, who had the skulls of humans at their waists and pouches filled with fingers. They were in flight. Being hounded without leadership or direction from the land. Some bore gaping wounds and were attended by flies in swarming myriads. Some cried in the manner of abandoned children. He was whole, nor did he cry. The beach curved from them like a crescent moon, as white, as empty. They went down it to the water and in the shallows they fought against no visible enemy but were still grotesquely slain. He had a rifle and it was properly charged. Yet he did not use the weapon, but stood with the sea about his ankles gazing upon its enormity. When he turned from this prospect neither the dead existed, nor their attackers: the beach was vacant except at its extremity where a figure came on. He dreamt how he began to run. Towards, not away.

And Silver was shaking him awake and Florrie screamed and Madach stood with his unsheathed bayonet in the passage. At Fanny's door Lizzie pounded with her fists, screaming too. Beyond them quaked emigrants in terror and curiosity. Silver's face came close against the youth's: his breath held liquor, he brandished a revolver, shouted at the youth in panic. The youth swung off the bunk: he was trousered in large pants, the cuffs rolled, the excess belted at his waist, his chest bare. Lizzie yelled for him and he heard her voice, yet it was not one he knew. He saw where Madach crouched in malevolence, grinning at the play. And Silver's fear. Then he took the rifle: broke the breech, laid in a cartridge, snapped it shut. Doing it by rote, as men do who fight in wars. He went from his berth towards the woman. She spoke through the door and Fanny answered and then a man answered with threats of violence. Again Fanny spoke, begging them off. The man said he had a knife and would not fear to use it. They went quiet; only Fanny sobbed that could be heard.

Bastard, spat Lizzie, turning on Silver, you weak bastard for allowing this. And these? – meaning Madach and the youth. Where were these to give protection?

You know where he was, sneered Silver towards the youth.

Bastard, said Lizzie, again. Just get him out of there.

Silver called to the man.

You've had your time, he said.

The man responded with a laugh.

When she gives what I've paid for, then I've had my time, he said. But she's not done that yet or shown any inclination to.

Just do it straight, and get out, shouted Silver.

There sounded a tussle in the berth.

I'll do what you took money for, said the man. He was panting from the struggle.

Do it straight and you can have it back, Silver offered. Every bit.

You lying shithole, came the response. You dogfart with your fancy talk and boasting.

Only Lizzie saw that the youth reached for the doorknob . . . Which turned in his hand. Which had never been locked. Which in their fright no one had tried. They all saw the door swing open to show Fanny stark on the bed, bound face-down, and the man filling the narrow space with his size, his knife hand extended towards them and the thinness of the blade. In this no one noticed the youth. Their focus was on the man: who took a short step forward, his free hand coming up to push shut the door. It moved through half its arc before the youth fired and the man was thrown back and fell propped against the wall. He stared at them and would speak but there was no room in his mouth for both blood and words.

Then they looked for the first time at the youth who was now absorbed in his weapon, the cleaning of it and the reloading. Only with its completion did he glance towards the man he had killed, yet it was no more than that, a glance, before he went back into his berth.

The next day the captain came with two sailors who took his gun and manacled him. He did not protest or offer resistance at this arrest.

'Twas you who killed the man? asked the captain.

The youth gave no answer but stood before him chained, of a similar height, their eyes level. And in them the captain saw what he had seen in no man and could not describe except that he felt disgust and soiled and over that a fear.

My daughter could have died, said Silver in mitigation, speaking from out the group gathered in the open door.

The captain spoke to Silver yet kept his eyes on the youth.

So you have said, Mr Silver. Repeatedly.

He should be commended not treated like some common criminal.

That is not for the likes of either you or me to venture, sir, said the captain. Now stand aside. Let us pass.

Surely there is no need to have him chained, pleaded Lizzie.

Madam, replied the captain, there is a man who has been killed. By all witness, yours included, I have him who did the deed. For the rest there are laws and justice to decide the consequence. But until then, this youth is in my custody and I will have him locked and chained.

And he commanded that the youth be led away.

We will free you, shouted Silver after them. Be sure of that. We will free you.

And they took him into the forward bowels, to a hold that had been designated as jail and had held some savage men but until then none accused of murder. In these places it was dark despite their lanterns, the air reeking of tar, and the noise of the sea here loud and close. They set with him a candle which offered little light and less comfort in that blackness, and withdrew, riding home the bolts. Yet such was the captain's curiosity he could not leave but watched at a peephole even until the wick burnt out. In which time the youth had not moved.

Thereafter the captain came often and would renew the candle and keep scrutiny but the youth was insentient. Except sometimes he chose the dark and would snuff the new candle as it was placed, raising the captain's ire. Which led him to rail at the youth that he was either mad or animal, a beast in human form not fit for society and men's commerce who was best forgotten in some bedlam among nature's other freaks and that he would see him there without bother of a trial and argument. At other times he would hiss questions of the youth, asking of his background and his family, but he got no response nor even the youth's attention.

Similarly came Lizzie to breathe at the peephole, naming her bodily parts that she now exposed, now covered, now caressed, now fondled, pretending her hands were the youth's and for the first time could roam her flesh. As if he was with her and they lay together. She described what she would have him do and how she imagined he did it and the pleasure she took, until her words lost their syllables to the sounds of her masturbation. She moaned, shuddered, seemed to collapse against the door. Once in her ecstasy called out a name which was not the youth's nor Joe Silver's either but ended in her sobbing. The youth heard it out unaroused. And afterwards she cursed him. Described a rape she would inflict and his emasculation. Beat on the bars, vowing revenge.

Then it was Madach, fraught by what had befallen them and the fate in store.

My peacock, he whispered, there's only death for this. And what of me then? What of me, my peacock, in this hostility without forest or friend? Silver would leave me without a backward glance. I know it. That's his way. He's no loyalty to those he would call friends let alone such as I. Even now he scorns me. I can see it in his manner and his attitude when we're with the women or he talks with the others of his kind. They laugh at me, shift away considering me dung. And Lizzie has no liking for me, nor the young women, who cringe at my appearance. We are lost now, my peacock. We are lost, you'n and I.

The youth heard and did not hear them. Their rantings distinguished one period of silence from another yet he could not say if they came once each or often. And because there was no telling day from night he had no awareness of when to sleep or when to wake and may have been in either state throughout. Nor did he know if he imagined this imprisonment or if his condition was the scenes of war he dreamt. Each imposed its severity. And in each he lived without words; the terror dark inside him.

Until a day she entered; the door closed quietly behind her and was bolted. Upon the floor she placed a lamp; turned towards him smiling what was no smile but the mask of Nyx. He watched her coming on; how she reached out and undid the buttons of his clothing, her nails red clicking swarming and furious insects, until the trousers fell and the shirt was loose which she pushed back on his shoulders so that he stood revealed before her. She who wore transparent fabric, the loom of her nipples stained in it, even the shadow of her crotch. He made no action against her: his arms hung limp in tightened fists. She leant towards him: their bodies did not touch, nor the fabric brush him. Yet she smeared her mouth on his, chewing at his lips, sliding in her tongue, leaving him wet with her saliva. She licked her lips: tracing their outline, that of the top and that of the bottom, a pink slug deliberate in its motion. Then did the same on the youth. He reached for her but she knocked away his arm. He retreated, step by step to the wall. Now she rubbed against him without pleasure, grinding her bone upon his stiffness. He grimaced at the pain. Which she saw and ground harder considering him all men: those that had been and those that were unborn. She said this was what she had promised in revenge for the power in him and the weakness in her, for all that she hated and that bound her, the form that imprisoned her and its injustice. Words he could not understand. She made him lie upon the floor. And straddled him standing. She looked down at his body that was tough and ribbed, the bones dominant in him, yet it was invisible to her, except where lay the puce sac of his testes and the veined erection. Then she came down on him: hitched her skirts, exposing bloodied thighs, and the place where once he had licked now in gore. And he was taken up into the darkness and the blood. And the ring of muscles tightened about him, and he believed they were about his neck and he could not breathe. Thus was he strangled. And when she was closed, gripped about him, she rose and he was pulled from her like a root, torn out, screaming at the rasp of his skin. Then the woman Lizzie glanced at him where he lay curled about his hurt and she said it was as it should be, and there was nothing in him worth redemption or in any of his kind. She called him motherless base-born fool, railed at the life coursing wasted through him, the inconsequence of it and the audacity that he should live it. Yet she cried, and turned away and was gone. The youth lay still. A man laughed in the passage. The door slammed shut. Nor did she come again.

## An arrangement

Now the ship no longer sailed but rode at anchor, rolling on the slow back of the swells. He could hear waves, too, their distant booming. And the clatter of seabirds such as there had not been on the voyage. He knew then with a surety that they would come for him and waited in readiness before the door.

Which is how they found him, the captain and Silver and a guard, who came to fetch him up. He stood out of the darkness into their lantern-light with the suddenness of a spectre, gaunt as the incarceration had made him. The captain stepped back, holding up his lamp as a shield.

You are evil, he said. You have no place on my ship. Not even here.

Silver laughed. He gripped the youth's arm.

I have convinced him, he said. He will let you free. He has agreed.

The youth nodded.

Where is my rifle? he said.

The rifle? Are you crazy! shouted the captain. No. Never. No. God forbid it, no. You are a murderer and a savage. You should be hanged. You should not be let among the living.

Nor should you, captain, said Silver, grinning without humour. From the tales I have heard my girls tell, you are a strange man with stranger lusts.

The captain turned fiercely away.

Let us finish this, he said. I have my schedule.

Of course, smiled Silver. Of course.

They left the dark hold: the captain leading. The youth was chained still and walked between Silver and the guard, who drove him on with a rifle barrel in needless prodding. They mounted through the galleys and the gangways into the light of the barely dawned sun. The youth saw there were none about except the men of the watch idling upon the starboard rails and with them, yet not of them, Madach in clear anxiety. Across a placid span of water rose a dun coast and a headland that loomed like a death's head over it.

There, said the captain, pointing at a column of smoke in the stillness, is a settlement.

The youth and Madach followed where he showed.

It is better than the gallows, added Silver.

We'll be drowned in getting there, said Madach. We're not boat men.

Bah! exclaimed the captain. It takes no skill to row nor keep a straight line. I have given you easy passage here. In all justice I should have set you down among the surf.

Then do it, said the youth, if that is your will.

Then he turned on Silver.

What of our wage?

Silver shrugged, holding out his hands in empty gesture.

This is it.

This what?

This . . . he nodded towards the hidden settlement.

Madach's face contorted into violence and he lunged at him, conjuring his bayonet like a wand into his hand, and would have had the pimp stabbed and bleeding on the deck had he not held back at the last. He released the frightened man who scrabbled backwards, shouting, pulling out his gun.

Get them over, ordered the captain.

And the youth was unshackled and he with Madach forced over the side. They went down on knotted ropes to a dinghy that bumped and flailed below, and were cast off.

# CHAPTER SIX

*The youth and Madach wade ashore at a desolate whaling station through shallows of blood and see a beach strewn with the bones and gore of these leviathans. They encounter the whaler Hansen; and later a strange colonial named Schmidt.*

## The settlement

THE CLIPPER WAS QUICKLY GONE AND THE YOUTH and Madach left on the quiet sweep of the sea. They took each an oar, bent to it and struck at the surface in clumsy fashion.

Yet they gained motion. And so they progressed, inexactly, with painstaking, glancing back at the rise of the skull-like cliffs to keep their direction. It brought them beside a rock where seals swayed in awesome performance, baring canines, barking at their intrusion until the rowers pulled away, yet they saw the dark shapes of these creatures roll beneath them in the green clarity, streaming bubbles at their mouths, as though anticipating the flesh of drowned men.

When the cliff loomed over them they found the coast was a deception and that a channel broke through it upon an unseen lagoon. Some people now watched their approach, gathered not waving or excited, but intent as people are who live in such isolation, complete and enduring. Beneath their gaze, Madach and the youth rowed into water that was no longer sea but blood, a vast stain of it that leaked from four half-flensed carcasses drawn huge upon the shore. They saw now too that the smoke issued from a cauldron and smelt how the air stank with its fumes. Here they beached. Here they waited in the wash of blood to be greeted.

The people came up and bunched on the shore which was strewn with the bones of whales, their entrails and the mess of this enterprise. Nor were they bothered by the stench of cooking blubber or the incessant flies drifting in black clouds across the vicinity, but stood in this foulness dumbstruck. They stared at the two in silence, even the children. Then he who stood slightly forward of the rest and carried on his belt a broad-bladed knife spoke.

We are righteous people, he said using the German language, we would not have wrongdoers among us.

Nor're we such, replied Madach, squinting up.

You were put off ship.

Yes, admitted Madach, through no fault of ours.

That is your story.

It's the truth.

The man considered them in close scrutiny. Madach returned it, but the youth looked off along the water where the great whalers swung at their moorings and over at the poor houses as if this matter did not concern him.

I have no way of knowing it, said the man at last. It is just your word.

'N it's good enough, said Madach.

The man nodded and lapsed once more into contemplation, his face scowl-masked and furrowed.

You have no choice, Knut Hansen, said a woman at last.

She bore a baby on her hip and pushed through those gathered until she was beside him.

The man she had called Knut Hansen looked at her without seeing either his wife or his child.

You can take them south when you go next, she said.

He did not alter his posture; did not seem to hear her.

There is no harm they can do here, she said.

Knut Hansen broke his stare. He glanced again at Madach and the youth in the way he would glance at sharks circling a harpooned whale, then strode off towards the cauldrons and the flensing. The woman, too, turned away, as did the others.

## Whaling

This was a desolate place, this settlement: greased on every surface with the residue of blubber they boiled down; permeated in such a stench. A place of outcasts and those shipwrecked who lived in desperate fashion between sea and desert and of consequence had more demented in their number than otherwise. Not simpletons by birth, although them, too, but those deranged by how they lived, by a diet of fish and poor crops and the dagga they smoked. Here the youth and Madach worked with the flensing crews, wading about that flesh and sickening gore. Day on day they fed the pots, amassing a great quantity of oil, yet Knut Hansen was not satisfied. He walked among the carcasses to see nothing was wasted, grumbling at their efforts when the bones were clean. Or he stood upon the headland scanning the sea for a whale's blow. Behind him, pale and bonneted, went his wife, dressed for winter in coats worn threadbare, and carried everywhere her child.

Soon the fires died: the smoke no longer hung above the settlement, and the pots were empty. The men sat about the days in idleness, the youth and Madach among them, and waited to sail south; but Hansen would not until his casks were full.

It's what she promised, harried Madach at the captain.

In due course, scowled Hansen.

And the men laughed that no one ever left the settlement; that all were cursed to die there.

Except us, said the youth.

Except no one, they joked, for there's a worse death waiting those who do.

And in these days the youth learnt, too, the weight and balance of the harpooner's lance; was taught the distance of the throw and a [whale's regions of mortality] Some mocked him that such business

94

was inborn and could not be acquired which he did not dispute but stared upon those taunting until they drew back, their words failing. Nor did they deride him again, but went warily of him.

Then came the call of whales seen drifting down the inshore currents. And those men drunk were quickly sobered; and those in dagga were carried aboard. Soon Hansen had the whaler under sail on a fair breeze that brought them to the creatures which lay unconcerned at their approach: now placid; now crashing down their flukes; now sinking, for a moment their great tails resting black enormous moths upon the surface, then, too, sliding down without a ripple.

Two boats were lowered: the youth and Madach taking oars in the first where Hansen and his chief harpooner already waited. Hansen sat back at the tiller; the lancer stood ready in the bows, leaning on his dart.

Pull, whispered Hansen.

And so they stroked slowly towards the nearest hulk of a black size that made them puny against it. They drew in closely not more than a dozen feet off and the whale let them come. In the swell an eye rose clear and fixed on them.

At this Hansen yelled: Give it to her, give it to her – and screamed a mad high yowl as the harpooner pitched the iron straight and deep into the body.

The whale started, a massive shudder, churning the water. Out went the second iron and that stuck too.

Stand the oars, shouted Hansen, and they backed water as the line smoked after the running whale. Yet their efforts were nothing against that terrible power and they were dragged behind with the bows lugged down and shipping water. They rushed through a heady foam clinging to the oars and gunwales for fear of being tossed into the sea. Hansen screamed throughout: some orders, some songs. In the bows the harpooner balanced ready with other darts to stay his foe.

Then their hurtling stopped; the whale sounded.

Play it out. Play it out, cried Hansen when it seemed they would be dragged down too. Which eased it; the boat rocked freely yet they sat to their calves in slops.

The line went slack; they waited.

Hansen looked about.

Can you see her? he called out. Where will she rise, harpooner? Where is she now? Where? Where?

Then the whale rose beside them and stood for an instant its full length above the surface showering a rain of salt water and blood. It fell like a detonation and wallowed.

Now haul in, Hansen bellowed to the bowman. Quick man, haul in while she's blown.

And at his crew he shouted, Row. Row before we lose her.

Which is how they came upon that dying creature. It rolled in a slick of blood, even spouting a fine red mist from its blowhole. Yet none could be sure its fight was gone.

Row in, called the harpooner and they did. Now the youth stood in the bows and he drew out a lance from the creature and leant over pushing it again into the body almost to its length. A gout of blood broke over the whale like a fountain, drenching the hunters too.

It's dead, said Hansen.

⌊All sat in wonder at the vast corpse they had made. ⌉

In like fashion they killed another before dark, nor did those remaining take fright but seemed even to gather nearer, watching with their great heads riding upon the surface. The sight of them so steadily within reach caused a rage in Hansen. He railed at the oarsmen to row faster when they had scarcely strength left to hold an oar. He shifted about the boat in such excitement at the chase that all might have been tipped into the sea. He would have thrown a dart had there been space for another man in the bow. Such was his fury he had them work until the last rays; and if there had been lanterns strong enough would have hunted through the night.

Now it was at the end of twilight; the dark coming over the sky. They had drifted well out in the hunting and could see neither land nor the settlement's fires. The wind was down, the canvas slack against the masts. The carcasses lay strapped to port and starboard of the whaler which drifted in a bloody sea. And were being rendered by sharks: their heads rising white and pointed from the depths, their jaws distended in a crown of ragged teeth. They rose all about those hulks and in the silence of their frenzy took away the flesh.

None slept that night. Hansen was continually about the deck: now calling for the watch, now straining into the blackness for the shapes he sought. Such strange hours filled with the groan of the ship's planking, a rasp of carcasses against the hull or the thrash of some vicious strength eating. And in the silence between, the whales breathed ghostly across the sea.

By first light Hansen was once more in pursuit for the whales lay off at no great distance. In this the harpooner gave the youth the lead and he stood forward at the approach and sent out the lance and watched it strike and the line tauten at the sounding. He neither smiled at this success nor hesitated in the actions but threw again; and the harpoon went true. Behind, Hansen screamed his bloodlust throughout the turmoil, wild at the danger and laughing, singing the process of slaughter. Only when one was lost did Hansen curse the youth and the harpooner. Demented in his attitude, swore at each who had laboured for him through raw and blistered hands. At which the youth drew a knife.

So, yelled Hansen, you vile body.

Don't, my peacock, cautioned Madach.

The youth came on; the oarsmen parting at his advance.

No, screamed Madach.

And the youth reached back to strike, the blade seen short and silver in this, but he did not. He lowered his arm and Hansen would rise to take away the knife yet wavered at the impulse and desisted. None moved for none would have stopped the youth. Then he turned back to the bows; the oarsmen hauled on towards the boat.

In the next days more whales were taken, the hunts being long and the men's hearts not in it, except at Hansen's exhortation. Then the whales disappeared. The sea lay unbroken. Hansen had no other course but to put back.

### Experiences of bondage and freedom

At the end of the flensing they sailed south. Went out beneath the gathered stares of the settlement people, and the muttered prophesies of bad deaths. Some saluted their passage and Madach acknowledged it but the youth did not.

At the first port of call they drank among those who dealt in ivory and slaves and held little candle for their fellow men. Here a man appeared who would cleave Madach's skull with a blade as broad as a cutlass but the youth beat him away. Then others rose to the fight and the youth was laid down and rose with a mess of blood about the temples and swung berserk about him a harpoon that had once served to ornament the wall. Now occurred the plunge of glass into a man's bare face; the ripping of an ear between clamped teeth; here blood spurted from an eye at each heart-pump; there another spat teeth out of a wound that was once his mouth. Then at the door there burst in men wielding half-oars who came as a phalanx until they filled the room and had beaten every fighter into submission.

These men hauled them to the pits: caverns in the bedrock outside the town, and entered through a hole over which an iron grille was bolted into the stone. The youth and Madach stood among some twenty men crammed with little space to sit nor enough height for a man to stand upright. In the morning Hansen appeared, and singled from the knot of men his crew. The youth and Madach stepped forward expecting to be called but he ignored them as strangers.

What of these two? asked the jailer.

Hansen looked down at them and shook his head and turned away.

Captain, shouted Madach, we've an arrangement, you'n and us!

But the jailer pushed him back and the grille closed on them.

They were a clutch of foreigners in those stinking pits, none of whom had seen that town before, all of whom were passing through on missions of their own devising, yet had somehow fallen foul. They lived among offal and their defecations worse than swine. By day they sweated, for the pits turned furnace; by night they froze in an iciness of stone. And always they had no notion of their fate.

Until the youth and Madach were taken with six others and made to walk for numerous days into the wastes. In this journeying they saw no other humanity except its traces where bones lay brilliant in the ruins of mud villages or heaped bodies leathered beneath the sun. At night they were stalked by savage beasts and in daylight overflown by carrion birds. Yet still one of their number ran off and was later found dead of adder bite, his eyes crow-picked, the sockets clean.

He to whom they were bound was called Schmidt, who lived without women or children in a house gothic and immense, the rooms vacant, the windows shuttered. There came a time in his fields when Schmidt went wild at the way they worked: shouted, unwound the whip to lash their backs. It cracked about them until one, a freeman, could abide it no longer and bellowed out in rage and rushed upon Schmidt. Yet was whipped down instantly and rolled howling upon the ground. Some among them made to attack and would have but Schmidt beat them back with threats as much as lashes. And they submitted.

Then he had them tie the freeman to the cartwheel and he was kept there through the afternoon and night into the following day. The man called out and moaned but none could take him food or drink, under pain of a similar punishment. Already the freeman hung from the wheel without the strength to move. He drooled. His eyeballs rolled loosely in their whites. His skin blistered.

It was then they conferred to intervene and Schmidt heard their deputation and at the end said if it was water that was needed the freeman could have it by the kettleful. Which he set on to boil. And when it was done he took the kettle from the stove and went out to the freeman. He pulled the man's head back and put the spout between the man's lips and poured out the kettle's contents. The man writhed but made no sound except some choking noises and was then still.

That night Schmidt fetched the youth up from the labour pound and showed him to the only room he used. Here he cooked and slept in spartan circumstances, the place furnished with no more than bed, table, chair, stove. He had him sit on the chair and poured brandy into two jars. He sat upon the bed. They drank in silence three or four jars and the brandy worked heavily in them. Yet the youth was cunning and did not match him. Nor said a word; nor did they look one at the other. At some time Schmidt stood upon the chair and the youth was made to stand before him. Then he sang lieder. Now he marched and sang and had the youth join him. They circled the room until he called a halt. He drew two rifles from beneath the bed which both shouldered and proceeded again, him in full song. With all the youth complied neither wholly drunken nor terrified. Throughout they drank, until the empty bottles Schmidt smashed against the walls. Then he lifted a trapdoor and they descended to a cellar which held a great quantity of liquor from floor to ceiling. Schmidt held a lamp towards the casks and drew a bottle and tapped the spirit out.

This, he said, bringing it towards the light, was the brandy of Napoleon.

And he swayed even as he drank the spirit and fell down inebriate. Nevertheless the youth clubbed him where he lay.

# CHAPTER SEVEN

*Madach is wounded and slowly dies. And in his anguish and his grief, the youth goes out to become what had been decided. There is more on the theme of slavery.*

### Enlistment

IN THE FOLLOWING MONTHS THEY TOOK UP WITH those who prospected and those who hunted and those who hired their labour for no return but food; and at times were sufficient and at others went hungry and desperate. Which is how it happened that they stood in a military camp to enlist with men of every description and creed, drawn from the bars and the jails and the mining encampments, who were united in nothing but their indifference to this calling; and were told they stank and were asked where they had fought before and if they had weapons and horses. In answer they stared blankly at those who recruited them.

The youth and Madach came to ride behind a captain as slovenly as his crew: ill-attired in worn jacket and trousers, his hat shapeless and stained with sweat, its colour run to dust. He carried neither a rifle nor was slung with a bandoleer as were most following him, nor seemed to be armed with anything beyond a sabre. At his neck he wore a silk scarf and across his waistcoat looped the chain of his fob, yet otherwise, from the dilapidation of his boots to the strength of his odour, he was of one with his men. They followed him at a short distance, riding singly or in pairs on horses which had been better left to perish such was their condition and wretchedness. The men's weaponry was assorted: each bore a Mauser or Martini and carried too an English Adams in his belt.

On the road they hanged five men for no greater reason than vagrancy, leaving each strung to his tree at the height of a horse's back. A homestead, too, they destroyed: setting fire to the timbers, slaughtering the sheep, when it was learnt the family had sheltered rebels. But their lives were spared as evidence of mercy. Such was how they rode to war. And in this manner garnered trophies from those they slew and soon wore necklaces of assorted items and some were decked, too, with skulls.

Until a day when the men followed doggedly a trail that seemed hopeless for they had come too late to the pursuit. They were in a desolate region passing along a red and sandy drift that gave succour to no other vegetation but knobbed-thorn trees. The sun was huge with its heat; about them all shimmered as if it would dissolve. Here they dismounted to rest wherever shade lay. And here they were attacked by a horde of warriors that stood suddenly among the trees and rushed upon them.

In this tumult of screams and smoke and the discharge of rifles, the youth sat fumbling to take bullets from his pouch and heard the explosion of Madach's gun and glanced to see Madach turn towards him holding out his blasted hands. And the hunched man screamed, looking at the tatters of his fingers. His face was blackened by powder and ran in rivulets where blood oozed and in this glared the whiteness of his eyes.

See this, my peacock, he shrieked, waving the loose digits as if to shake them free. See this for a thing.

And the youth looked from the wounds to Madach's face then bent again to his business. He filled the cylinder; clipped it home. He clasped the butt of the Adams with both hands and raised it, but he did not shoot. Nor, he realised, did others, and assumed them all dead. Beside him Madach still whined, shook his arms, amazed at the sight of them. Again he waved these wounds before the youth and laughed hysterically. The youth struck him once with the revolver and he sighed down unmoving. Using the waste of Madach's blood with dirt, the youth daubed himself and lay in feigned death, the Adams gripped ready beneath his jacket. And kept this way. The warriors went about looting the dead of their weapons. So did a figure rear up over them although the youth did not flinch at this or give any notice of his living even at the removal of his rifle. Nor when they were pissed upon did he stir although he was sprayed about his face and tasted the man's filth. Afterwards he heard their going but for hours lay stiff and may even have slept.

### The youth tends Madach

In the afternoon the youth helped Madach down to a river which flowed shallowly between the sandbars and the fording was easy. On the farther side they stopped in the ironwood shade and did not go on again that day. For hours the youth watched the way they had come, drifting in this landscape and his fatigue: but saw nothing of men nor heard their activity. In the last light he left their hide and scouted along the bank. Where the path they had followed took to the south he noted hoofprints and from their spacing knew the horse was not a stray but ridden, although with no urgency, and imagined, too, the rider. In him rose a horror that was from fear and from what had been described and was now possible. Over a short distance he followed the tracks but they did not alter their measure or direction. He reckoned the passage as earlier in the day. With dusk he gave up on them, returning to where Madach waited, yet he did not speak of his dread.

In the following days they progressed badly for the terrain was broken rock and gorged and the heat endured. And always the hoofprints were before them. And Madach bled from his wounds and cursed their luck and the pain that he bore.

You'n do not have to do this, my peacock, he told the youth.

No, said the youth, yet he persisted.

Another day they maintained their course. Now was Madach partly conscious and their going even slower. At stops he ranted delirious about his life or in moments of clarity he wept.

They went higher along a rising path and sat out the afternoon on a krantz from where the country behind them lay rugged and that before them endless and dense. At night they saw fires flickered in the reaches they had left.

D'you'n see that? said Madach.

The youth nodded.

They know we're ahead. They'll find us.

The youth looked out at the points of weak light and considered them and said, It may be any tribesmen.

You'n know it's not.

It could be.

He pared thin strips of dry meat from the last supply they had and fed Madach as he now had to.

The next day they did not travel: they could not for Madach was defeated by his wounds, writhed at their excruciation and howled out for the suffering to stop. The youth tended him and saw the lesions festered but had no antidote for this or the pain.

At night the fires showed closer.

The next day they walked off the krantz into the flat thorn country beyond. Here the path became a wagon track but was weathered clear of any human use showing only the spoor of animals and the hoofprints of a single horse set at an unhurried gait. Their going was slow, Madach persevered, his arms strapped upon his chest to ease their throbbing. In the afternoon a jackal took up like a dog behind them and would not leave even when the youth hurled stones at it. They went on, considering this ill-luck. But later Madach glanced back and the creature had gone which seemed now favourable. Towards dark the track led beside an expanse of water that could have been lake or river but was of such an extent no opposite shore was visible. It stretched placid and black and unbroken. Here they stopped; here they waited out the night, sheltering among the driftwood trunks debris'd along the floodline by some storm.

During these hours the pain came up in Madach and he cried, maudlin about the state of his life and coming death and the horror of their condition: 'Twas as nothing, my peacock, he sobbed, as nothing. All these years, as nothing. And in their repetition his words became no recognisable sound except that of fear and hurt. These faded too, went beneath the night that was loud with its own language spoken now as it had always been without emotion, without meaning. The youth heard it all but could offer no words of comfort or gesture. He lay prone where they had settled and gazed into the night at the stars d the depths between them until these pulsed and he shut them from his sight.

In the morning they followed the shore of this water through a mist that muted all sound; went warily, the youth with drawn revolver, for about them shrieked the terrors of a bestiary. At their approach hadeda ibis put up on slow wings, hooting into the whiteness; buffalo lumbered among the reeds. At each fright they stopped, going on only when a stillness resettled. For some hours they walked in the opacity until with a higher sun the vapours burnt off, revealing the ease of their route which lay flat beside the water. The youth sighted at where they were headed and from where they had come but both distances were devoid of men. He searched the track for hoofprints but there were none: neither did they lead in the grass nor along the shoreline, and he knew the rider was now behind him.

They went on: the youth more vigilant than before, watching their backs. And in the early noon rested among mangroves with the curve of the shore giving on a region of bright dunes where there would be no shelter. In the northern vista herds shimmered upon the floodplains. These the youth heeded: and in time saw some bolt and then others, dust rising at the disturbance. A shape appeared and floated ragged in the mirage but in time disappeared.

In this landscape and in those subsequent of forest, high-canopied and vined, Madach would renounce his life, would go down where monkeys screeched in the foliage and the green snake uncoiled. For his being knew only pain which was his new country. But at every refusal he was helped up and taken on by the youth; the passage; the direction. And he, the youth, was compelled because his footsteps existed in the track before him, and could have existed in none other, and had been formed there at his nativity. Was compelled to match each print to its boot, and did so with neither reluctance nor hesitancy, did so with grim unthinking. Such was the manner of their journeying.

And in its time this track had delivered those in chains and those brought seemingly of their own accord to the end of this land and to this sea; and now it opened from the forest wall on to cleared patches haphazardly planted, the crops standing brown and foraged by cows. Across this came the youth and Madach leaning on sticks and they progressed haltingly in no rhythm. Now they stopped; now they moved on again. Towards. Towards.

### The slave station

This was a place called o Inferno by those who traded there and by those who inhabited it and was a place known by other derogatives as well. It existed in the minds of hunters and slavers and was embedded in the knowledge of those sold and bought there. It showed on ships' charts designated by a Christian cross although it had no church or priest, nor had one prayed there ever. Those who knew it spat at its recollection, and those who lived at it could live nowhere else. These numbered some two hundred souls. Among them came the youth and Madach in the humid, breathless hours of the day when none stirred from the shade, not even livestock or fowls, and the dogs were laid down panting. They entered first at the fort which was a wooden stockade partly destroyed by fire, the ruins of this still standing like five black ribs. A structure of brick and corrugated iron leant against a farther wall, being offices or jail or both. One room was empty; in the next slept a man in a hammock and beneath him on the mud floor lay a woman and child. The child whined low and incessant. The woman was awake. She stared at the interlopers without surprise or fear. The youth prodded at the sleeping form. The man grunted and turned over and looked at them from bulging eyes. Eventually he spoke.

Que queres?

Madach held out his hands, wrapped in their stained and bloodied rags. The man shifted his eyes to the raised limbs and considered them and yawned, the spittle webbing between his teeth.

There is no doctor here.

He turned back to face the wall. The youth prodded him again.

There is no doctor here. Compreendes!

Água, said the youth.

The man spoke quickly and incomprehensibly to the woman and she got up and showed them to a barrel in the yard. She did not wait while they drank but went back to the room. The youth tipped the barrel and what dregs there were slurred towards the lip. The water was stagnant and coloured with sediment. Small beetles swam in it. He drank and then Madach. They left the barrel on its side, dripping.

Outside the fort clustered a slum of dwellings that were of mud and unbaked brick and drift-timber and corrugated iron and canvas and skins through which chased narrow paths, pooled from rain and slops. Shells of mussel and limpet littered these alleys as did the claws of crabs and other crustacea. Where the way led hung a sculpture that was of shark jaws, white and ragged, and of brass buttons, and of some shrivelled objects and small bells all strung by gut from an arm of wood, and balanced. Against this Madach brushed causing its sudden dance: the artefacts knocked, jangled. Which brought from a shack a man who leered toothless at them, then was as abruptly gone. The youth drew the Adams and held it at his side. They entered this maze, passing through it: in dim interiors saw prostrate bodies, or heard the hawk and cough of them and smelt everywhere the fetid stench of excrement and rotten vegetation. Children watched them. Where a woman squatted above her water and strained to shift out a turd was chalked a sign: CANTINA. The youth lifted aside the skin that hung for a door and they went into the darkness. Both waited close by the opening until their eyes were accustomed. They knew others watched them and could see the lighted tips of where men smoked and in the gloom picked out their shapes. None talked. Before them at the counter the barman drummed his fingers and it was the only sound in the room. The youth pushed the gun into his belt; they crossed the floor.

He said, Boa tarde.

The man did not cease from his drumming.

Gin, said the youth.

The man raised his eyebrows: You have money.

The youth undid his belt and threaded loose a skull that was strung there through the sockets of its eyes. He put it on the counter. The barman snorted.

This is not money.

He addressed those in the dimness and spoke his language and someone answered in the same dialect and a few laughed.

What does he say, said the youth.

He says that if I give you drinks for this then tonight he will chop off his woman's head.

The youth pointed at the skull: This is not a woman.

The barman shrugged: That is what you say.

The youth ignored it: This is a feroz.

But it is not money.

At the door the hide was pushed in and the woman who had shat beside it stood in the light, the rags that were her skirts still hitched about her waist. A man called her and she went, letting the darkness resume. The youth gestured again at the skull.

Do you not listen, snarled the barkeep. He pulled some coins from his pocket and spread them on the counter. This is what I want. Not bones.

A man stepped towards them: I will buy it. How much?

One shilling, said the youth.

Nay, said the man and put three coins on the table. He picked up the skull.

One shilling.

The man put down another coin: Genoeg! he said.

The youth pushed a coin at the barman and he was poured two beakers of a fluid that was not gin or wine or any recognisable liquor but stank powerfully and burnt to the swallow and where it settled. He drank without pause until it was finished. Then he held the other beaker to Madach's mouth and he drank similarly. Afterwards their containers were refilled.

How many? asked the youth.

The barman held up a hand of six fingers.

The youth nodded.

He who had bought the skull asked for a candle and was given one and it was lit. The man peered at his purchase, held the flame so close it licked darkly upon the bone. He scraped at where tiny traces of skin still clung about the fissures and mouldings; these flaked away in his fingernails. He examined the teeth, counted them, felt their firmness in the jaw, then held the skull at arm's length and seemed to weigh it. The youth watched this. At last he set it on the table but kept his hand on the cranium, caressing the smoothness.

It is good, he said. Very good.

He indicated for the barman to give them more liquor.

Will you tell me where you got it?

The youth shifted and drank, then he helped Madach to do the same.

It makes no difference, he said.

To me it is most important. Was it close?

The youth shook his head.

Good. The man looked down at the skull, his hand still stroked over the bone. Did you kill him? You, yourself?

The youth did not respond. After a length of silence he pressed again: I must know. These are important details.

You have bought it, said the youth.

Ja, the man nodded. Ja. But this is not enough. I must know the full details. Perhaps some other time you can tell me this. My name is de Graaff. Often you can find me here, or on my ship.

He picked up the skull and started towards the door.

They sat through the afternoon, the youth and Madach, and drank what they had paid for and what extra de Graaff had accorded. The liquor worked in them: twice the youth staggered into the outside blindness and retched forth a bitter spume. When he straightened he saw children had gathered about him who were naked and scabbed and stared as the spasms racked him. He waved them away, but they would not go. Again he lunged at them and they withdrew into the alleys but stood waiting like scavengers at a death. He felt for the gun in his belt and pulled it out, grinning at how they vanished now. Thus sniggering he went back through the dimness to where Madach leant upon a table among the waste of their drinking. He smashed down the Adams; Madach raised his head as the youth swayed before him.

They drank until the liquor was finished and sat stupefied, unconscious of their whereabouts, and uncaring. In the cantina some entered and some left and voices rose or murmured about the darkness. In due course they went out and passed heedless along the alleys, both reeling inebriate and cursing at their excess. None interrupted their passage; nor offered shelter. Upon the beach they lurched among the hulls of skiffs and boats, dragged above the tideline. Here they fell drunken, and seemed corpses fetched by dogs from the shallows. Neither moved, nor moaned, nor knew of the world about. The light went down. Beyond lay the ocean, and bright in the indigo a risen star.

### The branding of the slaves

At the coming of the slavers the youth and Madach stood with the gathering crowd drawn by this event. Children ran among them chased by dogs; and women shouted and men laughed and the spirit was festive. De Graaff waited with some others outside the stockade of the fort, sighting through a glass at those approaching across the cleared lands.

This was a column of chained tribespeople and of others who carried tusks and the traders who drove them on. They came slowly issuing from the forest. In greeting a call sounded and was answered by those welcoming and went back and forth in chant stirring the crowd. Some raised their rifles and fired; and the whips cracked as echoes of these shots.

Then the first of the traders rode up, with the crowd surging about to offer liquor and food which was rudely taken. These were a mixture of men being blacks and whites who spoke in a pidgin of constant invention and were led by one scarred according to custom and wounds. Although he gave no orders his gestures were obeyed.

They swaggered among the people and were followed by women bargaining the price of sex. The men laughed, and grabbed the women at the crotch saying they would pay no money to paddle in those sewers. Still the women persisted, convinced of the desirability of their commerce and the knowledge that these would be paid men soon.

Before the stockade the ivory was stacked and within its derelict enclosure the slaves bolted to stanchions embedded for that purpose.

The bondaged numbered over two hundred men and women; and their cacophony was ceaseless. Now the ship's doctor began his examination of the slaves for which all were rendered naked, although that was the condition of most. He went along the rows with his instruments of detail and was followed by de Graaff and the trader, the latter vexed at his fastidiousness. For he peered into the eyes and seemed to search in the pupils for hidden disease and tapped at the teeth of each and at their joints with a small hammer. He felt the firmness of their flesh in leg and arm and measured with calipers the fall of each testicle sac and the length of each vaginal slit. He looked too at the anus for signs of nematodes or the inflammation of dysentery; then chalked on those considered fit a white cross.

The others, which were few either aged or dying, were unchained. These did not flee but crawled away and begged of those about for sustenance. Or wandered confused throughout the slums and in the surroundings and some would even go with their fellow captives when later these were taken to board the ships, but were beaten off.

And those crossed were then sold in a quiet negotiation between the trader and de Graaff and one other the youth did not know. Likewise the ivory was purchased and carried away to the ships.

At this conclusion two sailors went among the slaves: they dragged between them a brazier and hot irons which bore the insignia of distant owners. The crowd packed closer and climbed upon the stockade and the roof of the jail and into trees to watch this spectacle. They jeered at the fear of the slaves and were greatly entertained by their panic. The sailors completed the task as if they worked at wood or some metal and were not part of this diversion: branded each slave upon the chest according to consignment. With every imprinting the crowd rose in cachinnation.

And after the branding they went with the crowd into the alleys where revelled the traders and those women now whores. Here men played on xylophones and the beat was frenzied and those who tired were replaced and there was no end to this sound. Here old women roasted giant prawns brought clapping from the shallows, and sold too crabs and other sealife and a distil of their own concoction. Here children offered pipes of dagga. All rollicked, all were boisterous as this occasioned celebration. And through the confusion threaded the youth, who had bought cheap liquor where he could, and with him the weakened Madach. They drank this and ate meat scraps that may have been rat or snake or monkey; and both were soon sodden.

Later the youth raised Madach and supported him, and they limped down the alleys into the night.

## Madach's operation

On the next morning the youth found de Graaff in the cantina and took him to where Madach lay groaning among the boats. The bandages were off his hands and of the fingers displayed some were blackened and oozed a yellow fluid and some were stuck through with bone. Sand-flies bothered at them.

De Graaff looked at the hunched man and at the hands held out and shook his head.

There is nothing I can do, he said.

The youth shifted his sight to the long boats drawn up the beach where men loaded water. In the bay rode two ships, placid on the pewter sea. De Graaff followed his gaze.

You have a doctor out there, said the youth.

Yes, agreed de Graaff. But what can he do? It is too late. Long ago you should have cut off those fingers.

It is not too late.

The youth eyed de Graaff; the man avoided him, turning away.

How much? said the youth.

De Graaff glanced round: You have more skulls?

No.

What then?

The youth drew out the Adams and offered it on the palm of his hand. De Graaf took the gun.

Ah, an English. He appraised it, wiped sand from the metal, spun the cylinder.

It shoots, said the youth.

De Graaff unloaded the cartridges: I would not doubt it. He examined the chambers then reloaded each and clipped the cylinder shut. Again he weighed the gun, nodding. Ja, he said. Good – and returned the gun. He gestured at Madach: Get him more drink – and for this flipped a coin that sank in the sand at the youth's feet.

The youth bent for the coin and sifted through the sand until he found it: You will bring the doctor?

But de Graaff did not answer except in gesture to affirm their contract. He started towards the long boats, and the youth watched him go.

'Tis no use, my peacock, groaned Madach, 'tis no use – and he cried from the pain.

They sat out the hours in the shade of a skiff until the heat and the agony of their condition grew intolerable. Then went back into the alleys and wandered lost in that maze, confounded at each turning. A boy saw them pass once and again, and on the second time the

110

youth bent to him saying, Cantina! Cantina! – and the boy pointed and led them on through a passage formed of sharkskins and those of crocodiles.

In the afternoon de Graaff took them to a room where two others waited. They had Madach sit at a table and place his hands on the surface. The older one peered at the wounds, moved some fingers that caused no pain and others that made Madach shriek. He prodded at the swellings and bent closer to smell the wound's rankness and did so in various places as if he tested a fragrance. Then he stepped back, stroked at his beard in contemplation. At last he spoke to de Graaff in the Dutch language and indicated two fingers on the left hand. De Graaff spoke back and the man nodded.

To the youth de Graaff said, He must cut off the right hand and those two fingers on the left.

Madach was too drunk to comprehend. Neither did the youth respond. De Graaff shook him.

Do you understand?

He mumbled that he did.

De Graaff spoke again at the old man who agreed wordlessly while he fetched from a case two knives and a saw. These he placed upon the table. Then the other, who had not moved throughout, produced a bottle and drew its cork with his teeth and soaked its fluid into a cloth. This he held over Madach's face and Madach pulled back at the cold of it then slumped as the ether overcame him.

De Graaff said to the youth: Come, we will wait in the cantina.

The youth said he would stay.

It would be better . . .

No.

De Graaff shrugged.

Krijg hom uijt, said the old man.

Hy wil niet gaan.

Krijg hom uijt.

But the youth had sat down against a farther wall.

Tell him to do it, he said.

He wants you out.

It doesn't matter. Tell him to do it – and he handed de Graaff the Adams.

The youth stared up at the men and saw them through a drunkenness of diffused light that was yellow and allowed only vague features of the shapes swimming in it. These and others came to him as a tableau that contained also his aunts and the blind woman Tabitha and her named Lizzie, naked at her loins from which hung a

etus head, unhaired and the eyes lashless; and he numbered next
the monk invisible in the blackness of his habit that showed neither
his face nor his hands nor his feet. And the youth shrank back against
walls patterned from bones and skulls in ancient design. Hear me,
said the monk, leaning close, and hear me this last time truly. In this
world each is left to his own devices. What you have seen and done
and what has been done to you are the actual condition of this earthly
occasion. Nothing more and nothing less. Yet it befalls only some to
wend through this way and know it. Whether you speak of it or not
the fact of its existence is not denied, nor is its continuation. Yet on
this horror a similar horror must be exacted.

At this the youth cried out and those operating looked over at him
and the one picked up the ether and held the cloth to the youth's
face until his thrashing stopped. Now was Madach grinning at him,
holding before him a brace of pheasants: We can eat, my peacock,
he said, this night we can eat, you'n me – and they did in a place that
seemed a burrow, natural and partly built, the walls of sand and stone
and roots. Here Madach said, Hear me, my peacock, 'cause there's
neither vengeance nor retribution there's only how it will be and for
that we are to blame. Each for his choices; each for his actions. You'n
for yours; me for mine. With which Madach raised his face but his
eyes were closed.

### Anguish and grief

In the dark the youth woke and lay disorientated. There came to him
the howl of cats and the scatter of them across the tin roof and then
a silence which welled deeply and contained no familiar sound. He
sought to stand but collapsed in dizziness. Nor could he crawl. He
panted like a dog on his knees and hands, straining into the blackness
where nothing was discernible. Words formed yet he could not say
them and lay down again insensate.

In the light he stirred. A greyness edged about a shutter at the
window and this pervaded thinly through the room. His vision, too,
was grey: some objects standing darker in it, still unfocused. He rose
up against the wall and leant there. With extended hand, he felt the
wall's corrugations and its skin of rust as he slid towards the shutter.
This had no catch but opened to his push. Beyond lay hovels; fowls
pecked in the dirt. At this different air he was seized by racks of
coughing and bent out to hawk away the loosened phlegm. Then
slowly he turned already knowing what he would see and that it
could have been no other way. Still he was not prepared. And the
sight raised a cry in him that seemed endless and constant yet was

inaudible. He stood while the anguish lasted and was renewed and faded down into sobs and into a quietness after the final echo.

Upon the table lay Madach slumped with his arms outstretched to their bandaged ends and his head between them face-down. The youth saw this and the blood that was soaked in the floor and still wet upon the table. Again the anguish sounded in him: came to him as from a distance and passed into a fastness beyond. Then was all still.

### Destiny manifest

The youth went on to the beach which stretched deserted before him except that herons waded in the shallows. No person was about at this hour. Likewise the bay was void, the ships with their human cargo put to sea. He went; and the birds lifted at his approach going heavily away; and at his coming the bush quietened its chattering so that he passed in silence. He was ragged; without possessions. He was demented by the liquor. He was grieving. Neither the thickening heat nor the grit of his thirst could stop him. He went against this. He went. And behind him a thin smoke rose from the slums where those who had danced and those who briefly had coupled and those who had pulled knives and those who had cried their unhappy hearts were drawing into another day. He did not look back. He walked on this white strip between the sea and the forest and crushed underfoot the delicate bones of dead birds.

# CHAPTER EIGHT

*Across an inhospitable land comes a horseman, alone, whose passing is watched by the wild creatures and whose manner is depicted in the cave paintings of ancient tribes. His name is Daupus. He meets with a disparate company of men.*

### A vacant land

HE RODE SOUTH THROUGH DESERTS WITHOUT TRACE of human venture or of animals. The distance was sand, level and endless on every horizon and neither vegetation nor rocks interrupted this monotony. By day there was no direction: everywhere was the same and he could not tell where he was headed or from where he had come such was the immensity of the plain stretching about him in its whiteness and in the whiteness of the sky. Then he rested. Rolled in his blankets, no skin exposed to the sun, he suffered the hot hours: partly sleeping, partly tormented by images of water or the appearance of complete cities that existed so finely he became convinced of this new reality, yet it would shimmer and disappear even as he watched. Then, too, he doubted his course and would move on haphazardly until the stars could correct his wandering. Or it seemed he made no progress, that in this world all movement was illusion and he was going nowhere, his senses stopped: confounded by space, deafened by silence that held no natural sound except his own. Yet in this solitude he heard ancient voices and other noises without apparent source, and sometimes believed himself a ghost passing through villages of activity, invisible, alien. And his appearance was ghost-like, powdered as he was by the desert, both his horse and himself, into pale apparitions which floated more than trod upon the ground.

On the eleventh night he rode out of the desert into a country of low scrub and thorn. With the risen sun he did not stop but continued in this new geography which gave him outcrops and the distant view of hills to set his way. This land was as vacant of men as the other. If any had crossed it they had done so lightly or their passage been quickly erased. For it was an inhospitable territory. From their burrows suricates came up and stood at full reach to note the passing of the man, slumped in his saddle like one dead. Above him a kite wheeled on the upward air, its cry diminished by the height and of no consequence to any below.

Such was the country he traversed and such was how he rode: his clothes had become rags and he wore a blanket like a hooded monk against the sun. The man swayed in the saddle and his thighs were rubbed raw with the motion yet he no longer felt the pain. He carried a rifle on his back and about his waist dangled assorted containers for food and water and ammunition. All were sparsely supplied. Nor was the horse better than its rider, being emaciated and frothing, its head swung low, its eyes feeble. Which is how he continued.

In the hours of furious heat he came upon scattered heaps of granite and dolomite that seemed arbitrary to the landscape. Under the shadow of a red rock he went in and sat on his beast until his eyes were adjusted to the gloom. He saw nothing lurked in the recesses, yet an uneasiness prevailed; the crickets gave no relief. The man dismounted. His horse expected water but the man offered none nor took any himself. The horse stood bent in acceptance. In the farther reaches he picked from the dirt splintered bones and shards of pottery and the stone heads of arrows. On the walls of the rock loomed depictions of buck in large numbers that moved from a fissure to issue forth as ghosts. And of giant men who hunted with bows and arrows, and of others who were tattooed with stripes and dots. Here ostrich, there eland: a multitude of detail beyond reality. He found, too, the illustration of a battle where men on horses fired guns at those who fled clasping their meagre weapons against this onslaught. And everywhere milled cattle and antelope in a scene of great confusion. Among them stood a warlock, fighting this malevolence with his power. The man stared at these broken images without comment, then retreated to the mouth of the overhang. Before him the plain swept baked and vast beneath the sky and nothing moved on it.

He could not sleep in this shade despite his exhaustion. Yet in the height of the sun he could not leave. Nor was he equal to his fatigue. The man sat against the rock fighting his condition which was filled with the painted figures whenever he succumbed. Men who became the shape of animals, their feet gone to hooves, their heads bearing horns, and from their noses streamed blood. They danced, their arms thrown back, their bodies bent as they writhed in spasms, round and round, mixed with eland and snakes and elephants, dancing through the geometry of hallucination, their spirits drawn from their heads, their forms attenuated. And among them were fish and birds, for they were underwater and flew simultaneously. Then the women clapped with a slow monotony and the figures loomed and swayed. But to one side always stood a man wrapped in skins whose head was of a rhebok turned away, yet he walked on human feet.

When he awoke from these figments the crickets were still; only the flies gave disturbance. The place had lost all animation. In this hiatus he took up his weapons, having been told the people of the plains killed with poisoned arrows and knew no mercy. He edged into the light and mounted and rode again upon the flats.

Through the afternoon he led the horse, passing over a terrain of iron rocks, split and blackened by some primordial conflagration. And in the final light came upon a pool in surroundings as bleak as any he had crossed. Yet here a source bubbled up and simultaneously seeped away within a small circumference, surrounded by stones. It offered a brack water, hard and saline, which he drank without concern. His bottles filled, his horse watered, he rode on.

In the next days he rode into a canyon and followed a river's course until it turned west. Then he left this way which had been easy, well supplied with water, wild fruit and meat, and went up on to the grasslands. Here he found men had been. He rode through the ruins of clay villages long abandoned, overrun by grass. On the perimeters grew wild spinach and edible roots that became for a time his staples. He rode through herds of antelope he could not name and watched a spectacle of buck passing in their millions through a valley for three days and nights. On an open stretch he came upon a prospector's wagon down on its axles and the wheels smashed. From the boards still stuck a spear, and there were empty cartridges sprinkled about. He found bones, too, which had been chewed by animals and were unidentifiable. It was a desolate place, filled with wind and the rustle of grass. He rode on towards the south.

### The outcasts tell a story of betrayal

On a night he came across the fires of men. From a great distance the glow was visible and the man headed towards it, stark and unhurried. A way off he dismounted and approached, standing his horse in the darkness until he had counted the group's strength and observed their behaviour. These were six men who kept no watch but had their horses tied within the circle of the fire. None talked, each kept to his own contemplation as if they considered themselves cast to such outer reaches as to be beyond interference. Two were well-weaponed with bands of cartridges across their chest and their rifles beside them. In the belt of one other was stuck a revolver, but the three remaining were unarmed. The man noticed this and the poverty of their spirits. He unslung his rifle, and walked the horse towards the camp.

The men heard him coming. They all stood; those with firearms pulled their weapons; the others drew out of the blaze. The man stopped while he was still invisible.

Who are you? called one who carried a rifle.

A traveller, said the man.

The men considered this before the one spoke again.

There's no one travels here, he said.

That is God's truth, came the response.

Let us see you.

Neither the horse nor the man shifted in the darkness and seemed invisible.

Let us see you.

Have you no word of greeting?

Words mean nothing.

Yet we use them.

The men at the fire laughed. The one who had spoken put down his rifle.

Come, he said. We are not wild men.

The man walked into the light and the men gathered there saw he was as rough as themselves and as put upon, yet his face was still hidden in the cloak of the blanket. He looked at each from his hoodedness and they stood uneasy in his black gaze which was not relinquished even after each man had looked away. Then he lifted off the blanket and they saw the skin peeling from him, his lips puckered into open sores, his face drawn close upon his skull.

The men took their places about the fire yet none would sit near the man. No one had spoken, nor was it yet time to speak. The man saw they were a disparate company of all nations, motherless men. And one among them nursed a stinking arm. The stench of his gangrene drifted about the night.

The men had little food except what dried meat they carried and some fruit, wild and sour. This they offered to the man who accepted it as it was given. Now he drew a bottle from his pack which he uncorked. The men eyed him, sullen, expectant. He drank, swallowing the liquor like water, and the men watched every mouthful he took. His chin shone in the light where the liquor had dribbled. Then he passed on the bottle and each took his share until it reached the man with one arm who finished what was left and gave the bottle back, knowing the preciousness of glass. The man took it and drove in the cork and returned it among his possessions.

That is good liquor, said the man who spoke for the group.

It is, the man nodded.

He looked at the speaker across the flames and again the other was the first to drop his eyes.

There's not one of us been in liquor all these days since our catastrophe, he said. But that taste brings back a remembrance.

He kicked at the coals.

You have any more of that distil?

The man said, You had the last of it.

I thank you.

He spat into the fire and his phlegm sizzled briefly.

We were men content with cheap jack that could give a three-day drunk on a mugful, and that's how we should have stayed. But in recent times we've had fine whisky which alters a man's taste.

Liquor is liquor, said the man.

The one who spoke for the group shook his head.

No, he said. You had some of the best of it. As did we.

118

They were quiet around the fire. From the night's depths came the deep coughing of lions that stirred the horses uneasily. And it was answered by an ungodly sound that whooped and broke into laughter more terrifying than the initial roars. The man looked away into the dark as if he could see where the beasts prowled. Again they coughed, but they were moving off and the men relaxed with this knowledge. Nor did the hyenas call again.

After a time the man asked for their names and they introduced themselves as: Podumo, Clarence, December, Ruyter, Dubois, and Harsent, their spokesman who claimed the rank of sergeant. Each raised a hand in greeting with his name, except Dubois for the pain of his savaged arm consumed him.

Are you running men? they were asked.

Not as you imply, said Harsent.

Which is?

Common arrants.

The man smiled.

Then as what?

As honest men played foul.

I've heard that said by some who were taken by the magistrate's men just five minutes later.

It won't happen here, said Harsent, even if you're the magistrate's man. We've no crimes, no matter what others think.

Are you Royal Levies?

Neither them. Though once we were of a kind. A better kind than usual, that ended mayhem in adjacent regions. Deputed horsemen you could call us. And Harsent named some troubles, unknown and unrecorded, that they had quelled. Such is the profession of justice, he said. Some call us heroes. Some thieves tremble at our names.

He glanced at his companions for confirmation and they acknowledged it.

Let me tell you, friend, of one brigand and his types who rode on long-horned cattle and came drumming a thunder into the earth that was terrifying. These were bloodlust men, governed by no other compulsion than killing. It was told in the settlements of how they came at night wearing fire in their hair, brandishing spears and bows and rifles, and trailed pillage in their wake. Of how they slaughtered children for their pots, and danced when the smoke was in them. Their stronghold was on a mountain, encircled by thorns and patrolled by lions, and no one had broken its defences.

There we went. Truly this mountain stood alone and conical upon a plain but this caused no deterrent: our approach was brazen and undaunted. Similarly the ascent, encountering neither lions nor thorn barricades, nor even watchmen. We ambled into the fastness unchallenged. And between the huts killed men where we found them drunk or asleep. Most died that way; a small number cowered in surrender.

Then we brought out the leader, naked because he had been surprised with women: a fierce man who cursed when we forced him to kneel. I circled this captive in wonder at the evil of humanity. We tried him and judged him as such men should be, and passed sentence. Later his head was cut off; it rolled in the dust and came to rest with the visage upwards: the mouth open, the eyes unblinking at the sun. It was a just retribution. Believe me, friend, when we left that place of man's wrath the vultures drifted down like a dark cloud on to the mountain.

Harsent looked quickly at the man, who had stared at him throughout the telling. The man nodded, his head spectral, and none could tell in that hesitant light if he was young or old.

He said, And you come from?

Harsent gestured into the darkness: Various parts. The mining towns. He pointed at the turbanned Podumo: He was an honest laundryman. Of the others, we met as men do in such circumstances.

That being.

Chance.

Harsent swallowed but his mouth was dry.

Yea, brother, we are truly righteous men. Upright and moralistic, commissioned to our actions by signed government decree, who have been sadly betrayed.

His companions grumbled their agreement.

Betrayed for no just cause in a most devious method.

How was that? asked the man.

Ambushed, replied Harsent, if you can use the word for types who appear as friends yet who slit men's throats while they sleep.

He spat.

The other said nothing but seemed to wait.

We were headed, said Harsent, for a distant place that was neither town nor settlement but a mission of Rhenish priests that once we'd saved from certain decimation by banditmen. It had no store or any liquor, no loose women or card-sharp men, offering only prayers and solid food. A dusty place of mud huts. Yet a place of refuge we sorely needed for we had been warned that others sought our deaths. We rode without much spirit, more as men abandoned. I remember that night we lay, as now, about the fire talking, restless through to the dawn. Then we saddled and rode on.

Here he broke his telling and focused across the flames at the man. With his silence the other looked up. Of the rest, two seemed asleep as they sat; Podumo listened; Clarence kept the fire; Dubois moaned softly at his pain.

Harsent said, Your liquor would be welcome now.

The man shifted his legs to gain a greater comfort.

It would, he said. But as I told, you saw the last of it.

Harsent nodded, scratching at the ground with a twig.

Maybe you have forgotten some?

No, said the man. None is forgotten.

It would be a pity to find it later, Harsent persisted.

There'll be neither pity nor later, said the man.

Clarence offered a bladder of water and Harsent took it and drank three slugs loudly.

It is a poor story that must be told without liquor, he complained.

No one responded. Podumo passed the bladder back to Clarence. Eventually Harsent continued.

The parts we travelled towards the mission were barren. Lonely spaces of rock and shale. We expected no sight of men, neither trekkers nor San. Yet in the early afternoon some days later two trackers came up, and I believe now they searched those reaches for us. It is joked that the army does not venture often into wild regions. But at the time it seemed no more than welcome coincidence. A divergence. Something to distract us from our black humour. For they were from a platoon camped not far off under the command of one Major Jackman, a thin-lipped man, speckled and ginger. Even his moustache was clipped into a sneer.

Harsent hawked, and shot forth his sputum.

Major Jackman! It is a name I shall carry until our confrontation. Because meet we must. This world could not be so unjust as to ignore my plea.

The man laughed.

You disagree, friend?

No, he replied.

Then Harsent told how he and his men were welcomed among the soldiers.

They were a platoon of some thirty, said Harsent, hard-bitten types, who could have been among our number just as we could have ridden with them. But they were hospitable and for the most part liquored, and we, facing a dry future, were eager to toast their health. We settled among them and the jugs came round.

Myself, Podumo, Clarence here and December, being given to cards, set up a game and were joined by five soldiers and played long into the evening. Around us the men bedded down, those who could. The others lay where the drink collapsed them. I recall Jackman lurked about, sometimes a spectator to our hands, sometimes wandering off into the dark. We played on, losing the troopers gradually until just the four of us remained. Then we, too, gave it up and found a place to rest slightly beyond the others, out of the light of the fire, there being no beasts in those parts to need guard against.

I sleep like the dead when liquored and if Jackman had had his way would have gone from sleep to death without knowing the transition. But because we were to the side, and the drink had addled Jackman's men as much as it had addled ours, we were forgotten.

At some time Jackman woke his men and they went among our company slitting throats without even a moment's retaliation. But they killed one of their own in the process and missed Ruyter and Dubois even though they lay obviously exposed, just as they missed us. Believing their work done they took our guns then loosened our horses, and themselves stole away.

Next morning Podumo was the first awake. He saw the horses had wandered free, and then the signs of our betrayal. I woke to his alarm. On the veld I saw how the horses strayed: two remained where we had hobbled them; three stood forlorn. The rest had vanished. Then my eyes came down to the slaughtered, still wrapped in their blankets, seemingly a band of men sprawled around the fire, asleep. Nothing. Nothing said they were killed. Except as Podumo rushed from one to the other in search of life, flinging back the blankets, I could see their fatal wounds. At the commotion Ruyter and Dubois staggered up and they seemed like the dead rising.

Here Harsent stopped. He asked for the water bladder. Clarence reached it across, and Harsent took it and drank. The man watched him and saw how his hands shook while they held up the skin. When Harsent lowered it, his face gleamed with an ugliness, contorted as pain pulled at his bowels. The spasm passed, but Harsent remained silent.

Soon the man said, You have six horses now.

What? said Harsent looking up, his eyes blank. He stared at the man. What of our horses?

You have six.

Yes, said Harsent. The mare is a mission horse.

122

You rode there!

The man shook his head in disbelief.

Where else? said Harsent.

It was where your Jackman could have gone on his patrols.

But he hadn't.

The man kept his counsel although he still shook his head in wonder at Harsent's reasoning.

There was nowhere else, said Harsent. We had nothing. Neither water nor food, nor much in ammunition, nor proper guns. Three days in those wastes would have had us dying. There was nowhere else.

He glanced at the man.

You do not know this country, he said. It has no concern for men.

Unexpectedly Ruyter laughed. A derisive, forced laugh.

Ask Dubois, he said. Ask Dubois how savage it is.

And they were left with the man's moaning in confirmation.

Then Harsent told of how they had travelled through the invincible heat for two days and a night without water until they came upon the mission. There they were provisioned by the priests and took the best of their horses and fled into the wild terrain where they had been drifting since.

Now you see why our estate is so sorry, said Harsent.

The man smiled: No worse than mine.

Harsent nodded.

A coal cracked in the fire and the men flinched as at a rifle shot. Only the man sat unmoved as the shower of sparks spluttered about them, then rose on the updraught and quickly were extinguished. Harsent shifted and glanced at the man and away.

And you are? he asked.

What you see, said the man.

I mean by name, said Harsent.

The man gave no response, waiting, but none looked at him.

I am named Daupus, he said.

Harsent nodded and Clarence, the rest kept their attitudes.

I am recruiting.

Now Daupus was the subject of all eyes, and in each there was a pleading and a scepticism.

On what wage?

A wage of takings.

And what would they be: scrawny cattle and shell beads?

Daupus ignored him.

Or weapons! Herds! Land! Gold! We've heard it before.

123

No, said Daupus. Revenge.

Harsent laughed: We all want revenge. We are all played foul. I shall have it.

And none doubted him.

Then Harsent asked for whom Daupus was recruiting.

And was told for himself.

And the night with its multitude of sounds, harsh and threatening, circled the men again. On the veld lions were about once more, grown savage with their hunger. They growled and it was as if they hunted these men. One, Clarence, drew brushwood off a small pile and some bigger logs they had collected, and threw them on the fire. The tinder caught; the flames came up. The men shifted closer. Dubois moaned as the effort disturbed his arm and the movement brought the stench of the wound on to the air. Daupus fanned at the pervading odour.

He named Ruyter grinned across the blaze.

It is the smell of death, he said.

Dubois heard him and bent his head. He cried out with the pain but the men ignored this.

The cats did it, said Harsent. They dragged him from the fire while we slept. So dangerous have they become.

They dragged; we pulled, said Ruyter. In between his arm was torn.

Some of the men laughed.

If you know any medicine . . . began Harsent.

It is a saw that's needed, said Daupus, not medicine.

It's true, said Harsent, and the men acknowledged it with silence.

Eventually Harsent asked for what specific purpose Daupus recruited, and he replied that such as them were always needed.

You have no contract?

Not signed.

What then?

Have you not read: I will destroy man whom I have created . . .

No.

It is scripture.

That gives you licence?

Yes. And you.

We have no mission.

Daupus lifted his blankets against the night. He leant forward until the coals seemed to glow in the hollows of his face.

Hear me, he said, In the beginning was the Word, and the Word was Kill.

You misquote, whispered Clarence.

Daupus laughed softly.

Maybe. But think on it.

Now they shrugged into their blankets for the night had become damp with dew, and they turned into themselves, into a darkness and a loneliness all-embracing that offered little of promise and little of hope, but what did exist was sufficient: a thin comfort that they still lived. Clarence put the last wood on the fire; it flared, reaching arms up and up towards the sky, then dropping back into its own combustion. The men lay down to sleep, even Dubois, and eventually even Harsent.

### The recruitment

In the last transience of the morning star came the suzerain howls of jackals across the veld, most bitter and forlorn. Then too did the night's species cease from their shrieking. In these moments Daupus woke. None else in the camp stirred. The fire had gone down to white coals in which red eyes opened indiscriminately at a stir of air. He lay as dead, straining for any sound of the living world, but there was none. Neither did Dubois moan, nor did any other mutter at the torment of their dreams. It was as if he had passed into a place without noise or movement that held its light constant, grey and dim. Into this entered the dawn revealing shapes seen only by firelight as body parts: heads, faces, an extended arm, a single booted leg, that became now the whole forms of sleeping men. So, too, returned faint noises: the clink and shuffle of the horses and the start of the day's insects working towards their stridency.

Daupus rose still wrapped in his blanket for the desert cold was not yet abated. He stood tall as some unhatted misbegotten, his hair long and lank about his shoulders, his pinched features skeletal in that half-light. Only his eyes, flickering from holes puckered and creased, denoted his living as he gazed upon the landscape forming relentlessly in the rising sun. It offered a monotony of stone and sparse grassveld. Stunted thornscrub grew here and there no taller than a man's waist. It was as unyielding as any he had ridden through. He took his rifle; walked off across the black scree.

Daupus headed for some low rocks which were the only variance in those surroundings, a petty distribution of eozoic matter, scattered and sudden. Among them he shat and saw that the place was a general latrine for it was polluted with the stools of the other men and informed of their time in that camp. Beneath him his faeces steamed, and were bejewelled with emerald flies gathered from the surrounding filth.

Others were awake at his return. Clarence tended the fire, coaxing small flames into the tinder. Podumo sat turbanned and cross-legged, seemingly at prayer, although he was not. December and Ruyter rolled dagga into cigarettes, their hands trembling after the fashion of wasted men. Harsent still lay in his blankets. Dubois seemed to sleep. He came up, stared down at Harsent, prodded with his boot until the other responded.

Ya fuckard! Harsent swore, hurling aside his coverings in a sudden rising. What's your calling, friend?

The two stood close until Harsent backed slightly away.

What's it, brother?

I'm no brother or friend to you, said Daupus. I gave my name. You heard it.

Yes, said Harsent. I heard it.

Daupus jerked his head towards the southern distance.

Harsent shut his eyes. With forefinger and thumb he pinched at the bridge of his nose. In this attitude he asked with weariness: Are you suggesting something?

Daupus kept eyeing him.

Harsent dropped his hand and stared back.

What? he said.

You know what, said Daupus. These others are recruited: we wait on you.

I didn't hear one join up.

Maybe not in so many words.

Did you? shouted Harsent, pointing towards each.

And they all answered it was so, except Dubois.

Harsent looked down at how Clarence tended the fire, then up again, his face contorted in its anger.

Who're you? he screamed at Daupus. Who're you to do this?

Daupus did not answer but turned away and took from his possessions a bottle of liquor. The sight of it drew a bellow from Harsent that was part agony, part fury. He spluttered with temper, flecking spit on all about him. Daupus drank and passed the bottle to Clarence who took his share and returned it.

You . . . You . . . stammered Harsent, lunging forward.

Daupus levelled his rifle.

Harsent stopped.

You lied, he shouted.

Daupus nodded.

You lied!

I lied, he said, bringing the bottle to his lips. He swallowed three

times and in good will was to have passed the liquor to Harsent v
Dubois rose screaming from his litter.

He held out his ravaged arm, bloated and gored beyond all
recognition of such a limb: the skin peeling back in large translucent
flakes, the stench all-pervasive in their nostrils. But it was not this
that caused his panic. For they all saw how there dangled from his
wound the tail of a worm which lay burrowed in his flesh. Then, too,
they saw the swarm of other creatures be they maggots or lice where
they spawned in the festering.

Dubois howled further at the sight, and the men stood around him
sickened. He beat at his arm, striking the dead flesh of it which was
beyond pain. Some creatures were shaken off. When he was still they
saw the worm had disappeared. Yet it was not on the ground. Dubois
collapsed, exhausted by this flailing.

They looked at him while he whimpered in the dust until December
bent to aid him and hold him up sitting. Daupus gave him liquor and
he drank and quietened. Ruyter held a cigarette for him and he smoked
it down. Then he lay among the squalor of his stinking skins. Soon
he was laughing. Shuddering with it, crying even, his mouth open in
laughter, his whole person ashake. The others laughed too. Sniggering
at first, then chuckling at how the drug worked wonders in him.

Daupus took more of the spirit before he offered it to Harsent.
Harsent accepted it. He drank slowly. And when he was finished
Daupus nodded that he should hand it on. Harsent wiped his mouth
against the back of his wrist.

It is for him we cannot move, he said.

Which Daupus acknowledged.


## The death of Dubois

They languished there for three days further and on the third night
Dubois rose up while they slept and went crazed with dagga and
the pain he bore into the darkness, disturbing no one. Daupus
watched him go and saw that Harsent marked it too yet neither
prevented him. They smelt the scent of his decay stir over them
and heard him stumble once and then how he walked on until the
incantation of his foreign tongue grew faint and could no longer be
discerned; he passed into silence. The night was dense about them:
shrill with insects, intermittently called by bird and animal. Of this
Dubois became part, indistinguishable from that around.

Daupus raised himself to squat before the fire, stoking new flames
into the coals. In the rags and haggardness of him he looked not
human. He rocked upon his hams, then poised like a heron, pensive,

listening. But nothing carried from the night that was evidence of Dubois. Nor did he rouse further.

Harsent hoisted himself on to an elbow.

Where is Dubois? he whispered.

Daupus glanced across at the man who would not meet his eyes.

You saw him go, he said.

Harsent lay down again.

He will come back.

No, said Daupus, he is gone.

He fed more brush to the fire: the flames licked up, spat and hissed.

Then Harsent said, He has no mind to reality. The man is dying.

Daupus said nothing.

Why did you not stop him? asked Harsent.

Why did not you?

Don't question me, said Harsent, rising again. I have said I didn't hear him go.

Daupus stared off into the dark.

It is what you say, Harsent. But I know otherwise.

There came a cackle and the following whoop as they had grown accustomed to hear.

Leave it, said Daupus.

He settled among his paraphernalia; and now Harsent hunched beside the fire.

The bones of their meal lay blackened in the ashes as did some gristle, charred and glutinous. He poked at this, shifting it without purpose but to melt it viscid about the stick he used. Daupus listened to his scratching, then spoke.

There is none will keep you, he said.

Harsent paid no heed.

You can go tomorrow. You alone or with whomever. It means nothing particular to me. Nor perhaps any of us.

He turned to face Harsent, propping his head upon the stanchion of his arm. He stared across the fire but Harsent ignored him.

I said you should go.

The words were softly spoken, such a whisper Harsent was not sure he had even heard them. He kept at his scrapings.

You, Harsent! Do you hear me? There's no place for you here.

These words too fell like the flecks of spit into the fire and were consumed. He stared more intently at Harsent: saw how his features were distorted into hardness and the distraction in him. Yet there worked in his face a distinct alarm.

What's in you, brother? said Harsent after a time. We're all men here, but there's in you something besides. Something I've not sensed before yet I suspect there's priests would call you evil, truly evil beyond the doings of men. Which perhaps it is in you.

Daupus smiled, yet in that light Harsent could not see it.

You have good eyes that can see so much.

I've been reading men a long time. I know what keeps them.

Yes, said Daupus without belief.

Yes, said Harsent.

On the veld the hyenas laughed again. They loped across the night, hideous, of sloping gait and dog-like, spotted, heavy-headed and jaws agape, giggling at the scent of putrefaction. And skirted about the men's camp, yet close enough to run anguish through the horses which reared and whinnied. Likewise the men felt their passing. From the distance came the dread whoop again and was answered and it seemed the beasts summoned their kind out of every direction.

Podumo woke and Clarence. But not Ruyter or December who lay in drugged sleep.

Podumo glanced at the scattered skins where Dubois had lain.

Where is he?

Daupus waved a hand into the night.

Out there. We saw him go.

Both looked from Daupus to Harsent.

You did not stop him?

No, said Daupus.

Harsent studied the ground.

Jesus, said Clarence. Holy Jesus.

It was Dubois's scream that woke Ruyter and December. Clearly it sounded: Mère – yet was only briefly heard among the giggles and shrieks of those that brought him down. But was enough to thrill their blood.

At it December echoed the cry, leaping in bewilderment, shaken with the horror of it.

And Ruyter rose to half crouch, the fright rigid in his attitude, shrieking unformed words.

Podumo swung into the night, his rifle clutched ready, and would have run towards the madness but Daupus gripped him.

No! God damn you, no!

Podumo wrenched free.

You cannot let a man die like that.

Like that! yelled Daupus. Or die slowly from the rottenness of his flesh.

It would have been better to have shot him.

You could have done that while he slept. Any night you could have done that.

Podumo let the rifle sag, and stood himself dejected.

He was dead from the first, said Daupus, you couldn't have spared him anything.

This is bad, cried Podumo. This is bad, you should not have let him go.

Now the night became filled with the death of Dubois: it snapped, snarled, came yelping at them and they heard too the sharp break and crunch of bones. Podumo blocked his ears as did Clarence. But the others listened through it to the conclusion.

# CHAPTER NINE

*In their progress across stark and wondrous vistas the men encounter both hospitality and fear from those they meet. They see some who are diseased and shunned, and the graves of others who died in search of their dreams. They enact, too, a gratuitous killing. Finally they arrive at a town on the goldfields.*

**Daupus among his men**

WITH THE DAWN THE MEN RODE OUT.

They came upon the spot where Dubois had died: it was with no sign that a man had been eaten there except for some disgorged rags, darkly stained. Not a bone remained or even the skull. They saw the scuff-marks of the hyenas' frenzy, yet none imagined how the man was torn apart with the muzzles bitten into the soft parts of him, or how the beasts ran off with what they had shred from him to chew and swallow it uncontested. But they traversed the ground with due reverence and December drew a cross ephemeral; the others muttered what prayers they could.

Here Harsent rode against Daupus.

Are you happy now? he taunted. Now you have your way.

Daupus neither acknowledged him nor swerved his horse from its course. Harsent spat and moved ahead. In the afternoon Daupus circulated among them all.

He spoke first with Podumo getting no reply but a rolled cigarette of dagga which he smoked and greatly relished, moving on to Ruyter and December. They shied nervously from him even when he called them back in all friendliness. Yet they could not slight his advances but allowed him between them. He came up, frowned at both which glance sank fear into their hearts as palpable as any stabbing blade. Then reached towards Ruyter who leant away, suspecting a blow. This incurred Daupus's irritation; he snapped his fingers. Ruyter slowly straightened, still wary of the hand that stretched ever closer until he could feel the fingers fondle at the fleshiness of his ear. They stroked gently yet caused a sharp pain as the skin ruptured beneath them. Ruyter grabbed at his ear and there came away in his hand a bullet, flattened and bloody. Alarmed he dashed it to the ground. Then Daupus turned towards December offering him a severed finger which wore a cheap ring of agate stone, such as December had. And the latter held out his left hand which was missing the ring finger. Then his eyes turned up and he swayed in the saddle and would have fallen had Daupus not held him. When December was recomposed he saw his fingers splayed intact. With relief he snorted. And Ruyter forced a laugh. Then Daupus nudged his mare towards Clarence who declaimed from a stained and ragged book the measured alexandrines of Chapman's Homer.

He came up and rode beside the other while he read. Clarence continued some further stanzas then closed the book. Yet they heard still the lamentations of Troy's women and held the image of Hector's mutilation, vividly. Daupus looked up to see that Clarence watched him. He raised a hand in greeting, and asked what it was Clarence read and was told.

You know the poets? asked Clarence.

No, said Daupus.

There are not many who read the poets any more.

Daupus nodded: Why do you?

Because this landscape has not heard it, said Clarence.

Again Daupus nodded but made no comment.

In the late afternoon Daupus took up with Harsent; and they proceeded thus not talking.

At last Daupus spoke.

There is something I have for you, he said.

Harsent did not reply. And Daupus allowed a silence to lengthen between them until Harsent said there was nothing he wanted. Perhaps not, agreed Daupus, yet dug in his pocket and drew out a cord on which hung a tooth that was of some beast, polished and honed and bored through the neck. It was a canine, its yellow scored with black veins. Daupus held it out and it swung between the riders like a metronome.

Take it, said Daupus.

Harsent looked at the object then spat out the gristle of the dried meat he ate and dug with a fingernail at that lodged between his teeth.

You will need it.

It is not powder or lead.

No, agreed Daupus, it is a talisman. Some would believe it greater than ammunition. I am told the man who last kept it vowed as much before he died.

Yet he died.

So must we all. Some before their time. Take it.

Still Harsent would not. Daupus let it swing awhile, then withdrew his hand, gathering it into his fist.

It is old, he mused, a true relic of this place that has hung about men's necks for generations and was once a leopard's fang. There is no telling what veins it severed or what flanks it tore, or how it came to be carved thus, or who has worn it on grand occasions, or carried it when they committed war, or stood aside as witness of such. Yet it is history. Will you have it?

No, said Harsent.

In a glob of spit, he hawked out the particles he had loosened.

It was a gift, said Daupus, meant in no other way.

Then he took off his hat and slipped the necklace over his head. The tooth came to rest against the bare thread of his coat. It seemed most primitive, as though it glowed. Daupus reset his hat.

It is yours at any time, he said. Such is the spirit of my giving.

Then he drew his horse to the left and took up behind the riders. Harsent did not change his pace, nor was there outward manifestation of his unease yet he knew a fear that he had known before in the face of death and could well remember. Later, at their night-stopping, Harsent told Clarence he had a great mistrust of Daupus, that he found him strange. They stood apart from the others, pissing.

Clarence shrugged that he was no stranger than others of their outfit.

He was, said Harsent, in the things he said and the way he smelt. For he smelt of earth.

Others stank worse, Clarence allowed.

Not of mould and rot, said Harsent.

Clarence agreed not of that.

Their water fell heavily, susurrating into the dust. Before them the aspect was black with only the evening star punctured in it. Otherwise what was land and what was sky were undifferentiated, the planes enfolded one into the other; themselves and their kindled fire the star's juxtaposing light.

### Ruyter's lust; peacocks; trekkers

In the days to come they passed through a multitude of places.

In the kraal of a chief they were welcomed with beer and meat and feed for their horses and offered huts in which to sleep. In exchange they gave ten rounds of ammunition and a knife that had been Dubois's. Which was not equal to the hospitality but seemed sufficient for their host. From the shade of these mud abodes they watched the village about its life: those who went to the fields or those who drove the herds; those who cooked and brewed or brought them beer in gourds.

With the drink in them they contemplated the young women. Ruyter said he would fill his mouth with the teats which some carried so firmly and big-nippled. And described how he would suck one and trace its contours under his tongue until it stood solid and raisin-hard, while with his fingers he squeezed at the other until it too was aroused.

And they laughed at his lustfulness.

And Clarence said he would trade his pistol just to cup a pair of young bubs in his hands and feel the softness and the weight of them.

And Ruyter pointed out for him a woman with fallen dugs which hung pendulous where she bent stirring a pot. The men hooted and slapped themselves with the thought of those piled in Clarence's hands.

Then Ruyter said what he truly wanted was to thrust into a girl's cleft, one that was unhaired and tighter than a fist.

At which Daupus warned him off, saying he would not allow such carnality.

No? challenged Ruyter.

No, repeated Daupus. For these were not whores.

All women were, said Ruyter, there was no other use for them.

Again Daupus warned him, now with threats of emasculation, and they sat sullenly afterwards.

Yet in the dark when the men ate with the chief and his tribe, Ruyter took a young girl and did what he had fantasised and left her seemingly dead in the hut. Then he went out to eat and talk with the rest of them. Later they found the child still lived. Daupus was called and he looked at the girl by the light of a brand which showed her thighs blood-streaked and blue welts about her neck. He turned, and smashed Ruyter's face with the butt of a gun and had drawn a knife to carry out his threat but the others resisted him.

When the kraal was asleep they rode out.

On the afternoon of the following day they passed through a region of red dunes bald of any vegetation and found before them a river coloured as violently as the parts they had left. Here they watered, contemplating the river's vastness. Yet it did not seem to flow swiftly. On the banks opposite palm trees stood at a height above the greenery. They walked farther choosing their crossing. At their coming a creature rose from the sand and plodded towards the water, its great tail dragging, and disappeared into the murk.

Son of God, breathed December.

Crocodile, came the answer to what had not been asked.

Then Clarence pointed at the washed-out stumps of trees drifting across the surface and they saw they had been deceived by this ancient reptile. And they realised, too, that what had seemed a cluster of rocks in mid-water were the shifting backs of hippopotami which turned to face them and displayed huge ivory in menace.

I have known them tear a man in two, said Clarence.

None doubted him.

They walked on until the beasts were behind them. At a bend, a spit of sand pushed into the flow and along this they filed, with Daupus in the lead, his rifle held ready, which action Podumo and Harsent imitated. They splashed into shallows, the level rising quickly up the horses' flanks to set them swimming. The current was weak. Once Harsent fired and caused a threshing in the water but no other trace of what he hit. They went on; crossing without further incident. And came out on an island when they thought to have forded the width. Here they unsaddled for the night.

But at sunset the quiet was rent with such terrifying screams that were merely peacocks going in to roost, yet it disturbed them deeply. And simultaneously there rose from the bushes hosts of dragonflies until the air vibrated with their sound. The men beat at the insects, except there was no defeating them. They became a cloud shifting above the island.

We must go, said Podumo. He stared wildly about.

They will cease with the dark, said Harsent.

But the peacocks did not, nor did the dragonflies go down.

Podumo saddled his horse. As did December and Ruyter.

You will die in the crossing, warned Harsent.

It is a chance, said Podumo, but no more a risk than staying here.

Again the peacocks cried. Now Daupus too saddled as did Clarence and finally Harsent: they all went into the dark.

This stretch they forded demented with fear, lying hugged against their horses' necks, awaiting moment by moment the truth of which Harsent had spoken. The river was black to either side and the horses picked their way over its treachery snorting at the danger of it with the water washed up to their bellies. Yet they came out unscathed, and each rode hard and shouting through the reeds until on the flats beyond the riverine bush they stopped again to muster. Exhilarated still, they sat their horses, grinning; then turned into the night and rode for its duration.

On the fifth day they saw wagons that looked like sailboats adrift on the plains. The distance was hazed to water, liquid and insubstantial. Across it floated the wagons, their covers filled with wind: billowing white and distorted beyond proportion.

Trekkers, said Harsent.

Scumboers, said Podumo. With his forefinger he pushed the flange of his left nostril closed and blew from the right a clot of mucus; then closed that hole and shot from the other a clear emulsion.

Daupus shrugged: They will have food.

They feed none but their own, said Podumo.

Even so Daupus set his horse towards them, and the others followed, compelled by hunger. They ambled, of no concern to travel faster but gaining steadily against the trekkers' oxen. In an hour they had traversed half the distance first separating them and could see now the spanned teams being driven on. Also how three horsemen broke towards them at a gallop. Daupus stopped, the others grouping beside him: a ragged line of ragged men.

They are armed, said Daupus.

Harsent unslung his rifle, as did Podumo his. Clarence pulled his pistol from a bag.

There will be no trouble, said Daupus.

Yet even as he spoke, the trekkers raised their rifles. The men saw them smoke and heard the lead zing between them. The trekkers curved aside to reload.

Wait, said Daupus as Podumo brought up his weapon. They'll talk, if we hold off.

He told December to call them in their language which he did but in response they fired again, their aim closer, enough to knock down Harsent's hat; then backed off, preparing their rifles meanwhile.

Podumo laughed.

Harsent scooped up his hat, cursing.

The trekkers were grouped out of rifleshot, hesitant.

We don't need their fight, said Harsent wheeling his horse.

The rest would do likewise, when Daupus headed towards the trekkers and they let him approach. He stopped before them and smiled, nodding from one to the other. They spoke at him, gesticulating, too, at the men grouped beyond but Daupus sat silent and hooded in his blanket until they ceased. Nor did he look round to see what the others did; nor did he call them. But they drew near and the trekkers edged about on their horses in due nervousness.

Daupus spoke to December: Tell them we are peaceful men, he said. That all we seek is food and water.

Which December did. But the trekkers were still unbelieving.

Wij hep genoeg gesien zoo gij, en het geweld van uw doen en laten gesien. Weg is uw, omdat den volgende tijd wij zal niet genadig wees nie.

They say we are bandits, said December. That we should go before they kill us.

Tell them we mean no harm.

Wij is vreedsaam.

Ha! Gij is dieven. Bandiete. Dit is beter om jakhals te vertrou as den zoort mans gij is.

Al wij vragen is 'n stukje kos.

Uw kan skiet vir kos overal.

'n Stukje brood?

What is it? asked Daupus.

I have asked for food, for bread, said December, but they do not trust us.

Tell them if they will show hospitality we will unload our rifles and guns.

No, warned Harsent. They are scumboers. They are treacherous. Tell them.

And December did. The trekkers considered this: Wij zal veruilen kos vir patrone, one said. The others nodded in agreement.

They want bullets in payment, said December.

Pah! Harsent spluttered.

It is a fair price, said Daupus, we will pay it. Ask them how many.

Hoe voel?

Twintig.

Twenty, said December.

Daupus shrugged in agreement. He drew five cartridges from a pouch and took four from Harsent and the same number from Podumo, and Clarence offered three which were all he had. Ruyter said he had none and December drew one from his bandoleer which was the only one in it. These seventeen Daupus showed to the trekkers and the one held out his hat to receive them but Daupus wagged his finger and retained the payment.

The trekkers shouted at him demanding half in advance but Daupus paid no heed and nudged his horse towards the wagons. Still they grumbled yet did not prevent the men's passage.

The two wagons were now stopped upon the plain with the oxen in span and the drivers beside them trailing whips. Daupus led the horsemen to the lead wagon so that they passed before the sullen stares of those behind who did not seem afraid. This was a rude collection of families, pocked by disease and their poor living, grimed, and abject in rags and skins. Some carried old muskets: all watched the men intensely with no slackening of this attitude even when one gave orders to the women and they turned grimly to their preparations. Then the men dismounted and Daupus had them sit to await the hospitality. Yet the trekkers would not talk with them; except the children came to stare closely until they were ordered back. And about the men circled two curs that never ceased their growling. Of the group only Daupus seemed unconcerned by the silence of the gathered trekkers; the others shifted uneasily, muttering at the danger of their predicament.

But Daupus said it was not such; that their own panic caused the fear.

We are unarmed, hissed Harsent. They can kill us.

They will not, said Daupus, these are God-fearers.

In time they were served a meat and stiff porridge, tasteless and unflavoured, which Daupus blessed before any were allowed to eat. Then they ate without pause, ravenously, even snapping the bones to suck the marrow. But each watched about him suspiciously. The scraps they threw to the dogs, leaving no remains. Except Daupus, who held out a knuckle of meat towards some children and drew three from the group who came timidly at his offer and were not stopped by those watching. He enticed them on with smiles and words they could not understand yet they seemed unsure, as if the meat would vanish from his hand. Until a girl rushed forward to grab it as a jackal runs in at the carcass and he caught her and stood with her neck locked in his arm and had brought out a revolver which was held rigid beside her head.

Two among the trekkers shouted and raised their rifles but Daupus eased back the hammer and they heard its click as the chamber came into place.

Tell them we hope she will come to no harm, Daupus said; and December complied.

Now fetch their weapons.

December and Clarence walked towards the men: Geven ons de fuseliers.

Wij zal skiet.

Dan zal zij sterven.

Stop! Wij zal skiet.

Geven op die fuseliers.

Tell them her blood will be on their hands, said Daupus.

I have, said December.

And Daupus squeezed on the child's neck so that she gasped at the pain, and somewhere this cry was echoed. Then Clarence reached out and took the rifles without effort. The men stood stricken.

Nor did anyone move while the horsemen mounted; nor when they rode off. In the veld Daupus set the girl free.

### A storm; a leper colony; the graves of prospectors

The band rode that afternoon across grasslands where grazed herds of sundry antelope and those of zebra and quagga. Sometimes the shadows of vultures, or of marabou, or eagles wheeling against the sun, passed over them and they gazed up, but the sky seemed void. In later hours it filled with high-stacked cumulus which darkened and thundered and swept towards them. Lightning struck at the edges. On a wind came the roar of hail whitening the plains and they cursed at the first pelting of stones. Yet they rode through it, bent into the storm and the sting of the small ice, shivering and sodden, their horses less sure-footed on the sudden pebbles.

By evening they had entered a range of hills and here they camped, fireless. The next day and those following they continued through this broken country, and none questioned Daupus where he headed. Not when they rode in the higher reaches of mountains or came down again on to the flats. Nor when they rested.

On an afternoon they entered a pan and crossed its mosaic leaving dusty scuff marks on the tiles of dry mud. On the farther side was a colony of lepers who were some without feet or hands and some without parts of the face and some whose stumps decayed in a bluish powder. And at their coming these outcasts crawled among the horses' very feet and begged abjectly for tobacco, but were given none. Daupus and the men stared at this congregation arranged about them, and at the huts patched of reed and buckskin seemingly on fire with smoke issuing from the low doors and through the holes, and shuddered at the sight. They rode on. Behind, the lepers pleaded in sibilant chorus.

In later days they came upon diggings, deep holes laying bare the igneous bedrock of shale and schist and lime. And themselves sifted through the sortings with long-abandoned sieves that yielded a refuse of quartz crystals, garnet and mica, and stranger artefacts: stone chippings, arrowheads, shell fragments, bits of bone. There were, too, the graves of prospectors, marked only by heaped rocks, the headstones unnamed, undated. At night they saw fires in the distance and dampered their own to avoid detection. And travelled away secretly before dawn. Which was how they proceeded, passing over the landscape without presence, seen neither by herdsmen nor by settlers.

### Devils

Except upon the flats where a lone man with his dog watched them go shimmering into the distance, and then watched them return. And when they were still a way off he started to run, the dog slinking beside him, its ears pinned back, its teeth grinning. He ran strongly in the full knowledge of his territory and where it offered refuge. And did not ask why he fled or if he was chased, or why. But ran because a man alone had to at the sight of horsemen, who did not want to be enslaved. He ran towards a river course that cut deeply across the flats, knowing that in the banks were antbear holes and further tunnellings. Behind him the horses galloped thunderously upon the hardened dome of the veld, the riders yelling at this sport. On the ridge of the bank he paused, scanning the slopes opposite, and saw what he sought and slid down the erosion into the dry riverbed, heedless of where his legs were skinned or the cut of stones against his toughened soles. The dog went after him, silently. And he clambered up the shaded side towards the hole which he reached before the horsemen appeared, and went into it, but the dog would not. No matter how he called, the dog would not. It stood whimpering at the entrance. From the hole the man hurled stones and clods of earth to chase it away, but it would not go. It was perched there when the horsemen rode up on the farther bank, one abreast of the other.

They were laughing, so badly laughing that December fell from his horse and sat laughing harder, and the others at his clowning. Daupus sat his horse to one side. In this state the men tried to shoot the dog. Harsent first, then Podumo, and Clarence: the dog turned and slunk and scampered as the bullets struck around it, but returned always to the hole.

It's luckier than a drunk barman, said Harsent.

It won't be this time, vowed Clarence, who shot and missed and they laughed wildly at his attempt.

Then Harsent's shot broke the dog's pelvis and it howled and spun and rolled down the bank. Yet tried to go back up, its hind legs useless, dragging.

Dogs are stupid, said Harsent. Even worse than men.

He sighted on the frantic animal and fired but it was wide.

Hawu, sighed Podumo, you all watch a marksman.

He dismounted and lay with the rifle steadied in his arms. They waited. Podumo shifted his position, pushed the turban off his brow.

When're you going to shoot it? chided Harsent. Today or tomorrow!

Which set them all to laughing. In that laughter Podumo fired: the dog was knocked down and did not rise.

The men cheered.

Podumo rose, waving his rifle.

Heja, amawasha, he called in triumph.

Then Clarence fired and December: both hit the carcass which shuddered at the impacts.

Ruyter swore bitterly.

You all forgot the kaffir? he sneered.

No, said Daupus. None here's forgotten him.

Give me a gun, said Ruyter.

Daupus looked at the man.

All right, he said.

He called Clarence, and Ruyter took the offered pistol.

They turned back to examine the opposite riverbank where nothing moved.

Daupus ordered Clarence to the farther bank; and December and Podumo into the riverbed. He and Harsent remained watching the hole, but the man stayed hidden. Then he told Ruyter to fire the grass which at this time stood tall and yellow and grew in clumps along the riverbanks. Ruyter did so; and the fire flared and crawled up the gully, fanned by a following breeze. The men were dismounted now, their faces masked in cloth against the smoke, their rifles ready. They trod on the fire's path, ash and smoke billowing about them as in a tableau of hellish apparitions.

He's going to die down there unless we see him soon, said Harsent.

Daupus did not reply.

The fire leapt about the hole which was suddenly obscured.

They heard Podumo yell, and December, and one fired.

There he goes, cried Harsent, as the smoke drew back.

The man came out of the hole and could not breathe and could not see but could hear the flames and sensed the men would be behind it. He turned away, coughing and stumbling, screwing his fists into his eyes which gave him a watery vision. He blundered along the sand, fell, crawled, stood, and ran on. He could hear the men shouting and the shot fired, yet did not think that he was going to die but did not think he was going to escape either. He ran as an animal runs before poachers, in hopeless terror.

When he was first hit, he did not feel it, nor did he alter his pace. He could see where he headed and that it held no shelter, except in the bends of the course. He ran slightly stooped, wheezing still, yet he ran strongly, even believed he was outrunning the others. The bullet took his ear: it bled but he did not notice the blood or the pain. He heard more shots. He was knocked down and stumbled on to his knees but forced himself up and ran with his hand covering the wound in his side. The riverbed turned from its straights. Out of sight he slowed to a walk. He looked at the blood that seeped through his fingers. He looked at how the gully narrowed and the steep sides. The men were gaining. He limped on, then suddenly stopped. His action was not reasoned but he felt no value in running farther.

Ruyter was the first around the bend. He had not fired yet. The man stood within pistol range, leaning into his wound. Ruyter walked forward. The man watched him, watched him raise the pistol, watched him fire. The gun did not work. Ruyter swore, hurled the weapon the ground. The others approached and gathered before the wounded man in a half-circle. Two reloaded their rifles; Daupus stood away. He, the hunted, sat on the sand, his legs straight out, fresh blood staining his trousers at the thigh. He would have spoken to them but he could not move his tongue. He did not want to ask them why or who they were, but for water. He knew that in the sand below him it flowed and that if they dug a hole he could lie with his face in the coolness, sipping at the seepage. This is what he would have said. Instead he stared up at them, his face impassive for all the pain he took.

One came forward and spat at him. The mucus hit his chest and gleamed there. The others stood round, squinting. Finally he spoke.

Hobaneng oetsa tjena? he asked.

Daupus squatted before him.

Re banna kaofila. Hobaneng oetsa tjena?

What does he say? said Daupus to Podumo.

That we are men like him.

At which Daupus laughed and likewise the others of the company convulsed by the dagga still strong in them.

Le banna ba babe. Ke bone seo le se entseng.

He is no one, called Podumo.

No, said Daupus. Wait, wait. Let him speak.

Ke monna oyang lapeng le ntja ya hae. Ke tsamaile masiu a mahlano ho tloha molona banna ba basweu leneng lebatla ditaemane nkeke ka boela morao koo, kapa bana baka.

Daupus glanced over at Podumo: What does he say?

He says he was a diamond miner but he won't go back there, or let his children work there.

Has he run away?

Hobaneng otlohetse dimane?

Eo ha se tulo ya monna. Rene re kwaletswe mo, mo dikampeng, re hloletla le hoya hae.

He wants to go home. He doesn't like being kept in a cage.

No, admitted Daupus, nor would any of us.

Then Ruyter hit the fallen man and he dribbled blood from this blow. He turned towards Podumo: Lebo satane, ke monna o yang hae le ntja ya hae. Hobaneng le etsa tjena?

Podumo forced a laugh.

What is it? Daupus said.

He wants to know why we have killed his dog.

Tell him we are going to kill him, interjected Harsent.

He knows that, said Podumo.

Tell him, said Daupus.

Monna omosweu ore oile ho shwa tje kantja ya hae.

Lebo satane! said the wounded man.

What? queried Daupus.

He says we are devils.

Daupus laughed and the others with him.

Tell him the devils will not kill him like a dog, said Harsent. Tell him that a man such as he deserves an honourable execution. Tell him the devils will shoot him by firing squad.

No, said Daupus, and he walked up to the wounded man, and no one stopped him. He raised his rifle in one hand until it was an extension of his arm and was inches from the man's head, and no one stopped him. He looked at Harsent who returned his stare. Daupus fired.

Harsent turned away. Began walking back along the river course towards their horses.

The others moved off too, glancing at Daupus who stood over the body.

They went back with his horse and found him sitting in the shade somewhat from the corpse. Although each watched him none would meet his eyes. He mounted and led them back on to the flats.

### A town on the goldfields

All day they rode across the grasslands. They passed beside kraals where naked children stared at their passage. Men hailed them but were not greeted in return. Women fled away like guineafowl. At a village they bartered Ruyter's pistol for beer and were given four calabashes-full. Towards evening a rise of mountains stood out starkly on their left, but Daupus veered from it, keeping to the escarpment with the great panorama arrayed below them. On this ridge they camped.

And after they had drunk the beer and each man had prepared to rest, Daupus said that beyond the night lay their destination.

What of it? said Harsent for one place was as good as another.

Daupus did not answer.

I've heard it claimed, said Ruyter, the goldfields have no women but whores.

Just so, said December.

More than you'll need, said Harsent.

Ruyter grinned in the dark.

They say fornication brings a kind of death, said Clarence.

Who does?

The poets.

There's types who write with their cocks.

As you would know!

I'm told, said Ruyter.

Clarence took from his possessions a book and paged through it, bent forward to catch the firelight. Then he read of a man who pleaded with his woman to no other end than copulation. And the men whooped and hooted at the poet's deviousness and the arguments he used.

Tomorrow, drooled Ruyter, tomorrow, I'll tear a whore's pleasures with rough strife, as the poetman says – and thrust with his hips against the ground.

The next day they rode along a ridge named for its white waters although at this time it was dry. Here they joined a track which linked settlements of tents and rudimentary houses fashioned from sheets of corrugated iron, their roofs weighted down by rocks. About them swirled a red dust scraped up on the sudden winds. And through this wandered livestock and fowls and small children clothed only in vests. On the veld they saw naked men who laboured in pits and trenches. Others, formally attired, stood by in supervision. And they passed men who were raw tribesmen who sought work to meet their taxes and had walked from unknown regions with this hope. Each called up at the horsemen a singular chant, each went unacknowledged. In time they came among mining concerns where chimneys gave off a foul pollution. Between the buildings, towering headgear fed cables into the earth and Harsent said he had worked their infernal reaches and vowed he would rather die than work it again. Here touts approached who would indenture them but Daupus shook his head and these agents hurried off after a closer inspection of the band. Likewise a vendor would sell them grilled corn and another a meat proclaimed as rabbit which was the size of rats but both were spurned and neither was vexed that the men did not stop.

They entered an outlying area of bricked houses where the road was trafficked by all manner of transports: coaches and carts and rickshaw men who ran between their shafts with the strength of horses. In this hustle Daupus led them through the town that was a cacophony of cries doing trade in every possible produce. For here vied the hawkers of sundry nations: the Asiatic, the northern Jew, the oriental and the Christian orthodox, their wares spread upon the pavements and in the market square offering clothing and the trinkets of remote countries. And cunning pedlars would sell them hairbrushes and gilded mirrors. And others would wrangle from them the price of tonics and lotions. And beside them ran fruit sellers holding up baskets of bananas which Daupus's men desired but could not afford. On these streets too was done the commerce of script and men stood for this purpose in a section chained from the thoroughfare and here bought and sold their shares. The horsemen passed by, and were caught again in a flurry of people which took them to quieter quarters of the town. From the balconies women stared at them and they raised their hats, even blowing kisses with great exaggeration. Some returned this gesture; some turned away in disdain. A woman leant over and spat; the men laughed and felt light and truly happy. They called up at the women all manner of lasciviousness.

Then they were beyond the town in a place that stank. Water lay stagnant between the shanties and in the roads that were not roads but tracks flattened through the marsh. Baked bricks smoked in the vicinity. Daupus said here they would find rooms. And he led them among the tin huts and narrow courtyards that were slop-sodden, rank with the dung of humans and animals. The men looked on this filth in displeasure. And Ruyter complained he would sleep on the veld in preference, even in a jackal midden than in this slough. But Daupus ignored him, inquired about for lodging. They were offered it in a house that flew a yellow flag. And were told that a lodger had smallpox but took the rooms none the less.

# CHAPTER TEN

*Scenes of drunkenness, gambling and whoring, and the machinations of a banker and a government agent. To Harsent, Daupus explains the ambiguities of vengeance. The missionary Thorne enlists Daupus's men as his private army.*

### On the ridge above the town

THEY RAN DOWN STREETS OF BOARDED BUILDINGS where none were about and were convulsed with laughter and drunk and December still unbelted and erect having had no time to shoot his seed. There came shouting behind them but it soon died away. They slowed, began to walk. It was always best what was not paid for, said Clarence, grinning in the dark. And Ruyter joked about the woman, the dryness of her yet how he had forced in. December spat, knotting the rope that was his belt. And they laughed at the image of him standing into the woman and her screams at his thrusts, mocking him that the size of his penis was too small and her screams were for a manly tool. December cursed them, yet laughed himself at their humour. They crossed on to the ridge above the town. Below, the lights spread like a galaxy into the farther darkness. They were Harsent and Podumo and Clarence and December and Ruyter.

### In a canteen

They stood in a canteen that was low and dim, lit only from a door open starkly on to the white day beyond. And remained there until Ruyter alone was standing and he with no conception of his whereabouts. Again they were without Daupus as they had been every day. The place was tin, the floors of dung, the air unmoved and heavy in the rising heat. Men entered who were diggers or cabbies or house servants or rag men or nightwatchguards who bought them wild liquor labelled differently as brandy, whisky, rum, yet indistinguishable in taste. They drank as it was offered. Here Clarence won at cards and with his luck hosted gin for all in the house.

### Dutch gin

They sat in the yard as they did each morning having grown accustomed to the latrine's reek. A woman hung washing. The sun beat fiercely in the small enclosure. They were Harsent and Podumo and Clarence and December and Ruyter. Each was jaded with the night's surfeit. Each ached as if nails were driven through his skull. They sat maudlin and degenerate. A bottle of liquor marked DUTCH GIN FOR KAFFIRS which was a recipe of proof spirit and tincture of orange peel, and turpentine, syrup and juniper oil, stood frothing before them. Ruyter drank from it mostly, and December. The others could taste it when it rose and subsided in their gullets. The woman went inside and the men were left alone in their stupor.

### Dust

They watched the dust come up from the town in a billow that covered the afternoon, the sun gone blind and white behind it. And the air was red, and the sky filled with it. In this miasma sounded the curses of those demented by it, both men and women, and throughout children sobbing. They witnessed, too, peculiar caravans: hunters clothed in skins, and coming after them naked bearers hefting ivory tusks; and chain-gangs that rattled past, singing. The dust revealed them, and the dust consumed them as if these men held no other reality than in imagination. Nor were the men convinced by what they saw, only by the dust that covered them.

### A boxing contest

They went on a sabbath, electric with storms but yielding no rain, to view a travelling exhibition of dwarves and freaks and every conceivable monster that could be fashioned from the human shape, set up on the veld beside the town. Here the malformed drooled and squirmed and shuddered before them. And in the boxing ring a man who seemed a giant, stripped to his waist despite the blaze of the sun, proclaiming himself a champion in twenty cities who would take on all comers at a fixed price and pay back double to any who knocked him down for the count of ten, and triple that to whomsoever put him out for longer. But he warned that none anywhere had yet achieved the second and very few the first. Then he taunted the spectators that he had heard of men there who could drop a donkey with a single blow and of others who fought hyenas with their bare hands, and consequently he expected good sport for the afternoon. At which some laughed but none went forward and he had to chide them further saying that he had heard tell of how mining men were men as men were known without fear or trappings of finery, with the courage of heroes and the tenacity of animals; that mining men were spoken of with trepidation in the drawing-rooms of the gentility but that it would seem he should revise this view and advance opinions that mining men were cowards, bad sportsmen, afraid, that their reputation was as soft as ripened bananas. Which stirred some into angry threats that he would regret his life had ever led him to this place and that he would wish his mother had been barren and his father seedless. At which he merely laughed and called all the men there cocksuckers. Such disparagements could not be made with impunity. Men yelled and raged and would attack him as a mob which drew more of his vitriol: funks, yellows, dastards, poltroons, he hurled at them. Until Harsent entered the ropes; and even while the exhibitionist was prancing round the ring closed on him. The other had not prepared his defence before Harsent crumpled him to the dirt, then kicked him twice before Clarence and Podumo pulled him off. Men whistled and hooted their laughter and considered this was fair sport beyond expectations. And Harsent held up his arms in triumph, acknowledging the crowd. Again they squared up, gave blow

149

for blow, and clinched, pounding each other's backs, until Harsent drove in short stomach knocks that left the champion doubled and gasping for air. Then was he most vulnerable, bent over with his face stuck out for the right hook Harsent would unleash. And it came. And it missed. Unbalanced by the swing Harsent stood for one clear moment amazed, then he was felled by two punches that came faster than a cobra's strike.

### An earnest conversation

They saw Daupus in the street: on his right walked one they recognised as a banker and on his left a government man they had not seen before. And Harsent would accost him for deserting them but Clarence argued against it. Instead they watched these three walk for an hour in earnest conversation, sometimes stopping to make a point, then walking on again in thought. At nightfall, when the street was left only to urchins and outcasts, the three went in to dine at the Hotel Royal, and Harsent and Podumo and Clarence and December and Ruyter off to find cheap liquor in the yards.

### The contract

The room was dark, the drapes drawn. Two lamps were lit, but gave little illumination, their light being lost in the velvet furnishings. And the air was weighted with cigarette smoke, and a low table before the three lay strewn with empty cups. The banker seemed to sleep; Daupus eyed him, his face skull-like and deep-socketed in that dimness; the government man wrote, the scratch of his pen loud in the room until his notes were finished and he looked up.

He will be sent for, he said.

Daupus smiled and placed his hands upon the armrests and they lay there long and tinged with a green hue.

### Clarence's advantage

They were drawn to the whippet track by Clarence who was compelled to gamble what the cards had won him. Of an early morning they went. He and Harsent and Podumo and Ruyter and December, each in the spirit of it and excited, vowing all winnings on the best whores in town. On the veld beyond the shacks a track was beaten on to the hard, red earth and being swept now in preparation. Men gathered: serious, frowning, sucking on unlit pipes. Such is how they considered the merits of the dogs which stood ashiver and seemingly afraid, their eyes terrified, their demeanour cowering. Clarence marvelled at them and went about learning their achievements. He was advised. And sometimes placed his bets accordingly, and sometimes by intuition. Then the dogs were set and raced in pairs to the howls of the men and their delight or defeat, but always to Clarence's advantage.

## At the Villa Sylvio

In the evening they went, as had been agreed, to a bagnio chosen for its renown on the goldfields, and spoken of in northern cities. They were bathed and pomaded and shaven and were liquored but not drunk, singing with the exuberance of their day, uncaring of the past or future. Even as they turned into the street of bordellos, women called them from balconies and windows, and the men waved and bowed in appreciation of the attributes displayed. For the ladies stripped off their lingerie and showed their breasts and rubbed themselves, all in enticement and invitation. The men stopped and joked with one another about their stirred machines, using the metaphor of engines to describe their lust. Then they passed on towards the Villa Sylvio, which stood brightly painted, its door hooked ajar, yet no girls but a dim light at the windows.

'Ello, boys, a voice called out. Come in, come in.

And they entered a lounge that was rich in its ornamentation and furnishings, lighted by lamps which left shadowed alcoves and niches where could be faintly discerned the entanglements of ladies and their clients. And all was hushed after the clamour of the street. The men stood dumbstruck in the garishness, tinged by a red glowering.

Towards them swept a woman with outstretched arms who seemed like porcelain and as delicate, whose hand Clarence caught and brought to his lips, kissing the fingers in all gentleness.

Lovely boys, the woman said, smiling at them, stroking her hand along their arms and faces, admiring the clean smell of them and the scent of money. They stood about her sheepishly like pets weakened by this adoration.

Ah boys, she sighed. This is the place for you.

And she smiled at each one in turn and none would look her in the eyes, not even Harsent. They shuffled, and Clarence drew out his money roll.

No. No. The woman held up her hand. There is time for that later. After the pleasure.

At which Ruyter giggled, and she took his arm.

So that is foremost on your mind, she whispered, her eyes crinkled with delight.

It is always on his mind, said Clarence.

Then he is a wicked man, she said mock-sternly, slapping at his

151

hand in admonition. Surely we shall have to find someone to rid his thoughts of this naughtiness.

Surely, said Ruyter, twice thrusting rudely forth his pelvis.

The woman let go Ruyter's arm and although she smiled still there was in her eyes a grim distaste. Which was fleeting and quickly gone. She turned, beckoning them after her.

Come with me, my lovely boys, she said gliding before them into an ante-room as plush as the room they left, redolent with perfume and the faint acridity of cigars. Here on the deep leather they were installed. Young girls brought brandy of a type not found in the canteens which was smooth and rounded in its aroma and spread warmth across their bellies.

It is good? inquired the woman.

The best, said Harsent.

Ruyter held out his empty glass and it was refilled. The woman waited while he drank off half the measure received.

So boys, she said, I am Madame Blanche Bocage of Paris . . .

Clarence rose to shake her hand, and they each did similarly, introducing themselves by name and country.

Madame Blanche stood amused at this mannerly display.

We are all foreigners then!

Except Podumo. Except December.

No, no, she insisted. In this town we are all foreigners. This is a place no one can call home. But here we all are. And we must enjoy ourselves, and bring a little happiness and love into each other's lives. Do you not think so?

The men grinned.

Now, in a moment the girls will be here, but you have the brandy and there are cigars in the mean time, yes?

The men raised their glasses to toast her.

Is there perhaps anything else?

Nothing, they beamed, at ease in the house's comfort. Except Ruyter.

Ja, he said, there is. One thing.

And that is?

Ruyter indicated the child waitresses. Madame Blanche stared down at the man, her face severe, her hands become fists, but she did not refuse him.

Chantal, she called out, in hardened tones.

And a child appeared from the dark like an angel, rouged and pink-lipped. Madame Blanche pointed at Ruyter. The girl came shyly forward. Ruyter patted his lap. He held his arms wide for her to nestle against him. She did so, even slipping her hand into his shirt. And on his cheek reached up little kisses that left a shine of dew.

Madame Blanche swirled out.

They sat ensconced within a haze of smoke and listened to the house about them: its creak of floorboards; the ascent of boots upon the stairs; or the undertone of voices and the giggled response. In slight bewilderment they awaited what would happen, too nonchalant for regulars: Harsent stretched out and languid; Clarence also, a glass caught in the bowl of his fingers. Beside him perched Podumo and then December, whose heels drummed a constant tattoo. They said not a word, nor disturbed their reveries when Ruyter had the child take him to the rooms. Quietly they sat until the girls came in.

Who were like swans descending. Who wore white gowns and had their hair fallen loose, and chattered, circling, stirring in the air a breath of lavender and were among the men with kisses and caresses. Who seemed brilliant in the gloom, more bird than woman, before they settled on the knees or at the feet of he whom she had chosen. And the air stilled.

And the men were enraptured. Entranced by these appearances. Would offer them brandy or a draw on a cigar, which the girls took laughing, blowing smoke into the men's adoring eyes. And the men ran their hands through the girls' hair, so soft and floating, and touched their cheeks that were more of silk than skin. And sighed with this pleasure and could have cried as Clarence did, remembering the words of the poet, Celia, Celia, Celia drink to me, which he mumbled while the woman licked his tears. At this time their worlds became their own, and none existed beyond them. They were complete. Each was led away.

It happened later that Clarence sat self-satisfied alone where he could watch the night's patronage. From his leather comfort, he studied them; imagined how some would go where he had been and how they would slide in the milk of his spasms. And he nodded at these thoughts. At the levelling of all men. For here was some justice and some vengeance made manifest.

When at the door there appeared one who paused in the attitude of a suricate, wrinkle-nosed to sniff the air before he entered. Then came in like a shadow, his eyes seeing all. The man nodded with winsome smile at some who called out in greeting, but did not approach them. He put down his hat. Pulled free his cuffs. Signalled a child to bring his drink. And was brought whisky. Which he sipped, taking barely enough to swallow. Then from the ante-room streamed Madame Blanche to kiss the man's cheeks and take him on her arm across the room until Clarence rose towards them. And he inquired if the man was a gambling man and was told he was.

Now Clarence showed his money and the man drew from his pocket a small bag and untied the strings. He emptied three gold nuggets on to a table.

Clarence looked upon the gold and reached out to touch it but the man caught his sleeve.

It is gold, sir. From right beneath our feet. You can believe me.

Clarence nodded.

My name is Joe Silver, said the man. Should we play?

Again Clarence nodded.

Ah messieurs, you are sporting men, smiled Madame Blanche. Come, I shall prepare the table.

Which was done in a velvet room lit by a low chandelier. Brandy and cigars were brought; new cards laid out. Silver took his seat and Clarence his and those who were bystanders grouped around, among them Ruyter and Podumo. Harsent sat beside. The hands were dealt. Silver held an ace.

In a room above, December lay at rest between a girl's thighs. Tears coursed her face but he neither wondered at them nor at why she sobbed. He rose yet she clung to him, crying the story of her despair, until he broke free, pushed her down, but could not stop what she told.

Which was of a damp morning, the windows iced and the fire gone to ashes and the clawing of her hunger that could not be assuaged. Of herself curled beneath the covers shutting her ears from the whine of the little boys, her brothers. Of her father angry at their destitution. Her mother offering a cold broth that was not broth but last night's boiled snow and the bones of a raven, found dead when they scavenged in the plots for unfound beets. How the father hit the mother and her too, pulling her from the rugs to stand wasted before him, crying himself with the fury of his helplessness. In this famine without remorse. Then he left them, running into the frozen landscape: the white fields; the black woods. And her mother wept at the table and she huddled with her brothers throughout the day. None expected to see him again.

He returned before nightfall with another, bringing bread and eggs and potatoes in a sack. He was livid with liquor, who seldom was, except at May and the harvest. The stranger looked about him in distaste, and at the girl. A stare that was undisguised appraisal. He nodded with self-congratulation, uncorked a bottle, passed it to the woman. At first she refused but he cajoled her to accept. She blushed and would not. But he persisted and there was in him something that could not be gainsaid. The woman acquiesced, bringing cups. She gave the children bread.

And the girl told how the foreigner, for he spoke in a strange way and was dressed as a townsman, whispered ardently at the woman, her mother, and how her father nodded in agreement even when the woman shook her head, crying against their proposal, gone frantic at the suggestion of it. The stranger poured more spirits which she took, quickly, in a single swallow. And another. Reluctant to give in. Whereupon he entreated her with all kinds of promises. And the man, the girl's father, repeated endlessly that it was for the good, that it was for their sons who would be surety in their later years. What of her? sobbed the mother. But the man spoke in placation. How it was for her benefit, that she would want for nothing in the service of the rich. The father echoing these words. And that she could return after a year. The mother sank her face into her hands, unable to resist them further. She, the girl, hid within the quilts and coverings while the money was counted, hearing each coin slid across the table, disbelieving.

She fastened to December, naked, her head pressed against his groin that was rank from their sex. She still knelt upon the bed; he stood by it rigid, deaf to all he had heard. Half-dressed. But seemingly trapped by what she now did. For he did not move to go. The girl held him.

Later he dressed and went on to the landing. No one was about. Except Daupus mounted the stairs in slow deliberation who raised his head at the sound above him. December started down. They passed, but December kept his eyes downcast and was unaware of the other. Daupus watched the latter's descent, watched even when Madame Blanche came from the shadows and took December to where Silver and Clarence sat at cards. Then he continued upwards.

In the card-room Clarence spread his hand and called Silver to show his who did so card by card that could not be beaten. Ace. King. Queen. Jack. Ten. All diamonds. He stretched back, taking his brandy.

I win.

And Clarence nodded, confounded that the cards should turn so sharply against him. He sat dejected.

It was a fair game, sir?

Silver rolled the nuggets into the pouch, drew the strings.

Clarence pushed the money towards him.

It was fair, he said. Though I've never played one like it.

Silver laughed.

155

Tonight I was favoured.

It comes down to that, said Clarence.

Then smile, my friend, you have lost nothing but money. And the brandy is free. I am a man of my word. Similarly if you will choose another woman. Is that not so, Madame Blanche?

Who smiled, her arm linked in December's, tenderly.

Of course.

But each declined.

Then one last toast, gentlemen, declared Silver. To fortune. To the fates that hold our destiny.

They drank.

The gods must always be appeased, he said. Sometimes we forget that.

Silver bowed slightly to the gang of ill-starred men.

Now please excuse me. I have other business.

And in the hushed aftermath Clarence sat fingering the cards, playing it over in his mind round for round, each card stacked against him. The others drank until there was no more. Then they went out into the streets.

So long, boys. So long, my lovely boys, Madame Blanche called after them.


### Smallpox

Podumo fell ill. In the hot days he shivered; in the cold nights lay fevered. Again the yellow flag hung before the house, and all expected he would die. He was brought nourishment but none would sit with him, even Clarence, for fear of contagion. Sometimes he heard them shuffle at the door, their whispers, or the enamel ring of food being left which he would not eat. Mostly he lay in peculiar worlds, delirious with the room warped about him.

He staggered into the yard and no one stopped him. From the house the landlord watched, as he had watched so many stricken, but offered no help. Podumo urinated in wide arcs, his water splashing up dust. Once he fell and lay squirming in the dirt that was of offal and faeces and men's vomit. Then he crawled about and finally stood, a sight from nightmare: fouled, his garments torn open. The landlord stared at the man's nakedness, the genitals hung without proportion. Podumo came past him yet was not aware of him.

Later he stretched sweating upon the floor, seeking its cold. The room ticked from the heat of the sun. He stared at the tin roof filmed with the disease of others, seemingly dripping. Pigeons skidded and scratched upon its surface.

At first the house was silent, and he did not know if he woke or dreamt. Then came street sounds: a bone man calling, a rattle of wheels of the brick carts, children, dogs, a hammering of construction. These he recognised.

Beyond midnight December found him naked in the latrine, slumped beside the pit. Clarence brought a lamp and in it showed Podumo's skin puckered and poxed, his face massed with pustules.

Jesus, said December stepping back.

Clarence drew water from the hole adjacent to this sink. He doused the man.

Get up, said December, prodding at him with a stick.

Podumo eyed them but did not move.

Then each tied a cloth about his lower face and wrapped their hands in rags before they pulled Podumo out. They dropped him in the yard.

He's mad, said December.

Clarence shook his head: It's fever.

They stood back from Podumo and watched him in the dirt. He was quiet now, yet he glistened from the sweat and water. December moved off.

We cannot leave him here, said Clarence.

Then take him in, said December, himself going in.

And Clarence did, dragging him. In the room he hoisted Podumo upon the bed and pulled a blanket over his body.

On the fourth day the fever subsided and Podumo lay in his disease, exhausted. Except he was tormented by the itch of his sores which he scratched until they bled and matted in scabs. Yet he was still shunned and now kept under lock. None visited him. Only a wizened black man came who brought food and cleared his pot. He grinned at Podumo from a face so pocked it seemed a mask, and then exposed his chest that was similarly pitted. He did not speak but gestured at his ravaged face and the scars that already marked Podumo, and cackled. Podumo blinked and was alone, except he could smell fresh porridge and boiled meat from where a plate steamed beside the door. He ate. And afterwards sat through the afternoon in solitude. From without came the laughter of Ruyter and December and Clarence where they drank in the sun.

### A disquisition on revenge

During this time Harsent sought the man called Daupus who had recruited them and owed them this allegiance.

Was at first denied that such a man was known or heard about,

157

even by those he knew must lie: the government agent, the banker. In the offices of each he charged duplicity, conniving, that he and others were contracted and would not easily be renounced. Both tilted in their chairs and smoked cigars and smiled at his exasperation. No, they said. Such a man was never met. He stood dumbfounded: I saw you with him. They shook their heads. Get out, they said. But he would not. At which the government agent pulled a derringer, forcing Harsent out, yet he went vowing this was not the end. And in his turn the banker by a secret alarm summoned henchmen who pinned Harsent against the panelling. You have your life, he was told. Be content. Be discreet. Live on. Then was he taken still urging his suit and hurled on to the streets.

Nor did he hear of Daupus in the canteens where every rumour of strange men flourished, even those of chiefs recruiting warriors and of planned rebellion and like apocrypha which Harsent dismissed. Until on an afternoon he sat in a canteen thoroughly maudlin and considered the passage of events believing all conspired against him. He cursed at Daupus and the banker and the government agent, and at his own gullibility too, vowing to search no further but to turn to other ways. He poured the last of his Dutch spirits. Then rose unsteadily to call for another bottle. And was brought it and paid with the few coins he could muster. His glass refilled, he said aloud in mock salute, The man is dead. Some looked at him.

But he ignored them and they saw the colour of his mood and kept away. Then Harsent rose to throw his stomach, staggering among the drinkers, holding his vomit until he could disgorge it outside along the drains. He bent afterwards spitting out the residue, until finally he straightened, groaned.

And went back in and ordered more and drank it. Later he stood declaring: On this earth justice will not be found – and pitched forward, going down. Some laughed; most gave no attention to his collapse. Or thought again of him, until his name was called, by a weasel man all knew as the American.

Then the diggers parted to reveal Harsent where he lay propped upon the floor, drunk beyond sense, beyond even the capacity to walk, gibbering in no spoken language. Which was how Joe Silver saw him.

This is Harsent? he asked, contemptuous.

And was told it was.

He's pig-soaked.

Those near by looked at Harsent and confirmed it.

Get him up, said Silver.

But each time they stood him, Harsent reeled and buckled again. He vomited over those who handled him, even grinning when they dropped him for his inconsideration.

Do you still want him? they asked.

Silver nodded, drawing out money.

Here, barman, he said, my pleasure – indicating all who drank there.

Men cheered. Then some gagged Harsent and hauled him up and rushed him out to where a cab waited in the dark.

In the late hours of the next morning Harsent woke, his head riven, pain beating at his temples that was inexorable, vindictive. His eyes opened sightless to a sheer void where no shapes formed. His tongue stirred bloated and foul. He craved water. Slowly he sat in a spinning world, hands gripped hard upon the bed-edge, eyes screwed shut against a violent pressure that would drive them out. He coughed, and each disturbance quaked across his skull. Yet as he sat the room stilled. Now gathered ghostly objects about him in this brilliance: a chair, a door, a basin and jug. He stood, but the pain pressed down, forced him to sit. He whimpered from it, from the throb of it, even as he slid to the floor. Then Harsent crawled towards the jug and filled the basin and drank from it like a dog. And the water could have been spirit, for he became intoxicated again: the room slipped from him.

It was night. A candle lit the room where Harsent lay open-eyed upon the floor. The hurt still surged in his head, but duller. He sat and was amazed that nothing moved and grunted approval of this constancy. He finished the water, wiping some behind his neck. He rose swaying to his feet and went quickly into a passage. At its end an open door cast out light. From there a voice called him: the voice of Daupus. Harsent stopped, listened, a hand braced against the wall for steadiness. The floor creaked beneath him. Elsewhere someone played a piano.

Harsent.

The voice was without query.

Come in, Harsent.

Still he hesitated, seemed to blunder in some fog of his own devising. Then went on. Until he stood at the doorway, yet unsure. The woman now sang in accompaniment, her tone lusty and foreign.

Every evening she sings, said Daupus from inside, obscured from Harsent by the angle of the door. I would not say hers is a beautiful voice, though you might disagree. Certainly it is not an angelic voice, but you cannot dispute that it has power. How would you describe it, Harsent? Perhaps you would say that it was raw, or that it had passion?

You would be right on both counts. At least I would agree with you. And to think it comes from such a delicate woman, from one so fragile that you would not think she had so much energy in her. It is almost a contradiction that this bird-like, this tiny woman, should have such magnificence in her voice. But that is Madame Blanche, a remarkable woman, as I am sure you would admit. And now, Harsent . . . Come in, man. Come in. I cannot talk to you hidden behind the door.

Harsent stepped into the room which was clouded with a smoke seemingly solid in the air. Daupus lay dressed and coated upon the bed.

Ah, Harsent, he said, letting smoke curl from his nostrils and the corner of his mouth. The world has strange ways, do you not think! Strange ways of doing things. Sit down, my friend. Would you have whisky! Or gin!

But Harsent declined.

Water, perhaps?

No, said Harsent though his voice croaked no comprehensible sound.

He perched upon the cushions of a chair, taut, unrelaxed, bent forward in some misery, his face turned down. Which Daupus noted and smiled to see. Then Madame Blanche's singing came strongly to them, demanding attention, keeping the smile on Daupus's lips that twitched like lizards. For a moment he seemed oblivious of all else: lost within himself Harsent waited, wretched in his sour stench. The song ended but the piano ran on.

She tells me, said Daupus, that they are ballads of nostalgia and romance, our dreams of idyllic pastures. Have you ever thought of such things, Harsent, or are they not part of your world?

I have thought of them, said Harsent. But never seen them.

Ha, laughed Daupus, that is because you are a cynic. If you had more faith in human nature you would not doubt their existence. You should fall in love, Harsent, that is the only way you will be convinced. Perhaps you should speak to Madame Blanche, she understands these things.

Perhaps, said Harsent.

Daupus swung from the bed and stood.

You are a good man, Harsent, he said. A good man. I have been told you were searching for me. Did you think I would not honour our contract?

Harsent looked up. Saw the form of Daupus towering yet could not clarify the features. Could not see how Daupus stared at him, crossed the room, poured whisky.

Do you remember your story of Jackman?

Harsent grunted.

He is dead.

Dead!

Disembowelled. I saw his corpse.

Harsent nodded slowly. His eyes again tracing the carpet's faint pattern, his shoulders hunched.

A long death . . .

Harsent kept silent.

. . . Which should please you.

Daupus stood before him, but his boots were all that Harsent focused on: the shine of them and the patterned tooling of the leather.

Is it not what you wanted, Harsent? The sort of revenge you would have desired just to watch him in that final agony and to recount his sins? Come, it is a fitting end to his mean life. It speaks of a balance in the universe. Yet I could also tell you that he died in his bed from no obvious cause. I saw his corpse. It is a fortunate man who dies like that. Some would say only the good die so peacefully. You were cheated, Harsent. It is of no consequence how he died, except that you did not kill him. You have been allowed no retribution.

Harsent kept bent and crouched upon the chair.

We were betrayed. Someone gave him orders.

Of course someone gave him orders. Of course you were betrayed. You were wild men out of control: those who had set you loose needed to kill the beast they had created. To them you were nothing, Harsent. You are a dog.

The boots moved from Harsent's vision; the carpet stretched as a desert before him. He was aware Daupus stood to one side.

So how should you revenge yourself!

Harsent knotted his fingers, shook his head.

Well?

I have no answers.

There are no answers. You are impotent against the likes of powerful men. But still you will act.

Yes.

Which is an answer: a commitment, a moral judgement.

To you. To me, what happens happens.

No, Harsent. You can choose: to destroy or to preserve. The world is as it is. But in it you will be praised or blamed.

Harsent shifted to ease his posture yet was still bowed by the pounding across his head and the words that would drown him. Daupus smiled, and the gesture bore no compassion.

There are things begun, Harsent, which are not finished.

Which are?

I should not have to tell you.

Daupus lounged again upon the bed. He blew smoke towards the ceiling.

Things begun, Harsent: the passage of our lives and the deeds we must commit.

Daupus crushed the cigar into a plate. Looked full at Harsent until the other raised his glance.

Admit it, Harsent. You are contracted, my friend. You have no power to avenge, except at others' behest.

And Harsent felt the truth of it and his impotence. He closed his eyes, seeing in that privacy strange lighted shapes against the blackness which floated there unattached to the sadness of his thoughts. He sighed. And would leave to look elsewhere for the continuance of his life, but could not go.

Then in the passage were voices, and steps approached them with quick purpose which stopped outside. Someone knocked. Harsent stood, made nervous by the strangeness of the place and his inadequacy in it. Daupus gestured him to sit again.

Wait, he said. Hear this first.

The door opened on two men: the one Joe Silver; the other in cleric's collar, named Thorne at the introduction. He was darkly bearded and severe, his clothes likewise and all musty with the smell of mice. Only his eyes held colour: a sharp blue which did not blink. He regarded Daupus in silence; Silver, too.

You are Daupus, he said.

Yes, came the response.

You were described differently, as a military man. I had expected such.

Daupus laughed: I do not deceive you, reverend. I am the man you need.

Very well. Let me tell you of my circumstances.

Thorne stood contemplating, then with sudden resolve waved Silver towards the door who backed out, obsequious and grinning.

Please excuse me, he said. This is a private matter.

The door latched closed. In the quiet Silver's steps receded.

Now, Mr Daupus, said Thorne, have you heard tell of marauding hordes laying waste the northern regions?

Daupus nodded: I have.

Thorne sucked at his beard, considered the lounging man before him.

I am told they will soon swerve on my mission. I am also told to expect no assistance from the army. In consequence I must form a private force. I am no general, Mr Daupus. Nor am I a banker. My resources are limited, but I have no choice. You have been recommended. For your service I can guarantee some payment. My society has advanced a small amount towards it and I shall raise a similar figure. I believe you will find it adequate, even given the circumstances.

Thorne stopped and into the silence rose the voice of Madame Blanche and faintly the piano. Daupus lay still upon the bed, his eyes closed, yet he was not asleep. Thorne rocked and balanced on his heels, hands clasped behind. He stared down at Daupus, waiting. Where he sat Harsent traced the patterns on the carpet with his eye, and they were all that was invested in his mind. Below the singing ended. There sounded some applause and calls of Bravo!

### Harsent drunk

Harsent was drunk again. The liquor now light in him, his mood changed utterly to songs and whistling. He went careless from Villa Sylvio at a late hour, stumbling upon the steps, bowing to invisible figures in deep flourishes, his hand extended fluttering to imitate a French cavalier. He stood to sing, to bellow rude verses of fornication. And laughed, raucous laughter, uncontrolled. In this way he passed down the street where those awake smiled at his intoxication; those woken cursed him. At the town's edge he danced, lay down his jacket upon the dust and danced. Went round in complicated steps, not stumbling, not hesitant, so neat. Then breathless, humming, he moved on.

163

*Amid accounts of historic violences and a massacre where hundreds are slain, the true nature of Thorne's intentions is manifested. Through it all resounds the women's howl of lament.*

## Prayers, and the distribution of rifles

ON THE FOLLOWING DAY THEY LEFT THE SQUALOR, going north over the hills. They were Harsent and Podumo and Clarence and December and Ruyter. On the rise none looked back but went into the ravines glad to have ended this time of lassitude. They progressed down in a damp silence without birdcall or the scuttling of rodents in the undergrowth. The bush grew dense and arched overhead. Each felt menaced, glanced constantly about. Yet soon they came out on to grasslands and wooded reaches of tree-protea that held no threat. They rode in file towards a buttress crowned with cliffs from which rose vultures on the early thermals, spiralling up. To no one had Harsent spoken of their venture, nor did any appear bothered to know. Only Clarence was curious, called out if they were hired.

Yes, said Harsent, turning on his saddle.

By Daupus?

You will see, he replied, and spurred his horse until it cantered.

At this pace they continued round the buttress, crossing upwards of a farm: those in the fields stopped to watch, held their hoes like weapons while the horsemen passed. Ruyter yelled, waving. The farmers ignored his gesture, did not cease from their vigilance until the band was gone. The land afterwards was uninhabited, sloping towards a stream. They slowed, until beneath willows Harsent had them dismount, and here they waited.

There came before noon two wagons, and Daupus on a pale horse. The men stood watching the approach: none raised a hand in greeting, but kept in the shade, most nonchalant. Daupus acknowledged each and called the men about. From the front wagon came Thorne, unsmiling, who was introduced. He stared at each one as if he would read their souls. The men scuffed, shifting uneasily throughout his inspection. Daupus looked on.

Then Thorne told of his predicament and that he would hire each one for a sum already agreed. If any were unhappy, he said, then those should ride away, for who joined with him were truly Christian and blessed before God. Again he glared about, his mouth working in his beard, forming words left unspoken. None in the assembly moved, nor did one dare ask the price their service commanded. This way the matter was settled. And Thorne retrieved from the wagon an advance on their contract which he dispensed to each man as a gesture of his intent. The balance, he said, to be due on termination. Then he asked if all were agreed. The men mumbled their accord. And Harsent asked what would be done in the instance of those in the group killed. Thorne shrugged to suggest that was ill-luck. But Daupus interposed that their wage would be shared among those surviving. At which the men seemed satisfied.

Then Thorne asked them to bare their heads and kneel. The company obeyed. And the missionary prayed over them, thanking the Lord for His mercy and beseeching Him for His grace in the coming danger. All muttered, Amen. Now were rifles and ammunition distributed, and clothing supplied where it was needed, which was by every man.

## Through regions ever sparser

In the afternoon they traversed level reaches through a dry grass that stood as high as their horses' bellies. Across this country cut occasional swathes of reeds where the going was marshy and the teams of four strained to pull the wagons through. The outriders offered no help but stood their horses, grinning at the spectacle. For the rest they rode uneventfully even without seeing other men. And all that registered their passage were the plovers which rose screeching from their approach, or a bustard put up seemingly for their sport, yet none could shoot it down.

The order of the column was haphazard, redefining itself through- out, except where Harsent and Podumo rode in the fore beside the lead horses. They seemed regenerated characters in the cut of their new coats and the smartness of their hats. Over his left shoulder Harsent bore a single bandoleer of bullets and had his rifle holstered from the saddle, and Podumo likewise. Behind them came the wagons with Thorne sternly in the first, seated upon a cushion for the boards were uncovered. The wagoners were sullen tribesmen, ill-dressed, unlike those hired and now dapperly kitted. Beside the wagons rode Clarence who allowed his horse its head and held before him his battered book of verse to recite the poets. Ruyter laughed at him, as did December, from where they ambled behind. Daupus came at the rear, and stayed there.

Now was the grass reddened by the dropped sun and although the landscape still stood featureless it appeared a different country. Above them circled ibis, stark white against the darkening sky, about were antelope miraculously conjured from the earth. It was a peaceful time, sanguine and luminous. The men rode quietly, struck by this hour. Later Daupus called a halt.

This was not an auspicious place, marked only by a single acacia and some scattered rocks. Beneath the tree, charred debris of other travellers was heaped, on which the wagoners built their fire. Thorne walked off alone, the others squatted by; Daupus leant against a rock watching all in this quickly fading light.

Here they ate what Thorne provided. The wagoners sat separately in the dark; the men kept about the fire; and Daupus stayed where he had been, invisible in the shadow. The missionary allowed only a brief stop for he would have them journey throughout the night. The men accepted his wish, keeping private what opinions they had.

Daupus let them go. He sat upon the rock until their noise subsided: the creak and thudder of the wagons; the grate of a horseshoe against stone. In time these sounds ceased altogether, but the land stayed silent: neither insects called, nor owls, nor did distant jackals whimper. He was alone. About him the night was implacable: of a density that could have been stone and as hard. Only above was there light, yet it gave no illumination to the plain. He did not consider what was to be done or how or the consequences but knew there could be no undoing. Nor did he take resentment at his part in it or derive satisfaction from what was to come. But held it necessary. Eventually he rose and stamped down the fire, grinding the coals into small knobs of red heat beneath his boots. He drew from his possessions a cloak and fastened it about his shoulders and pulled up the cowl and set on that his hat. Then he rode after the others.

The men journeyed now in a knot behind the wagons, led by Daupus. A wind came up from the east and whistled in the grass like adders and the men had no option but to face into it. They drew their blankets about themselves and bent their heads. Yet the wind still cut in. Ruyter called to Daupus that they should stop but if Daupus replied none heard him, nor did Ruyter call again.

Fatigue ached in the men: sometimes they slept, their heads rolling upon their necks; sometimes in a dream one fell and woke to find he was almost slipped from the saddle. They rode on.

And where the plains sloped into a valley, mist enveloped them. The grass no longer whistled: all sound was dampened. In this they proceeded without sight of their fellows, trusting that the horses would keep constant, glimpsing occasionally a rider or a wagon. On their clothes formed pearls of dew; from their hats dripped a steady condensation. The going was hazardous and they sensed a sharp descent with possible chasms beside them or, equally, towering granite. Whatever their true circumstance, no one cared to discover it, and the mist kept its consistency.

Until they emerged where the land was devoid of all grass, dry, stony, being of stunted acacia and other white-thorn species, and seemed to step from the mist into this as phantoms would from a wall.

They rode into a region sparse and black, the trees like posted sentinels, yet unchallenging, and followed a track across it that belied the passage of other wagons. Here was the progress easier and the men dozed through a terrain become part of what they dreamt. At some time Harsent woke to find the hooded man beside him, and altered his pace, and when he woke again found Daupus had taken up on his other flank. He did not sleep thereafter.

Thus they journeyed, stopping only at dawn to water the horses in a drift of pools. Fish beat in the diminishing holes, gasped in a medium now mud: carp and bass and tilapia. These Ruyter speared; the others watched or lay asleep. Four carp he scaled and gutted and slit open to cook upon coals: the flesh was brown, tinged with sediment and redolent of rank water. On these they breakfasted, yet none relished the flesh. They went on with the taste of stagnation in their mouths.

All morning they rode and in the afternoon came on an arena of human bones. Here the soil was red, corrugated by the wind: the bones shining upon it. What vegetation grew grew in tufts, a withered yellow grass. Lizards seemed the only living creatures. No signs existed of human habitation, recent or historic, or of why these dead should be here. Or of how they had died. The landscape was as mute as it had always been. And through it Thorne's wagons continued, and the men would have done likewise, glancing about, unsettled, puzzled. Ruyter joked that perhaps the fish were more poisonous than they tasted, and some laughed.

But at this spectacle Daupus dismounted, going curiously among the remains. He shifted parts with his boot; some he retrieved for closer inspection then discarded these at the sight of others which seemed more pertinent. He stared into the sockets of various skulls, he pondered upon femurs and mandibles. Harsent had the wagons stop and the men gathered about. Thorne approached.

I have seen many sights like this, he said. In these regions all the tribes were slain by marauding warriors, men who showed no mercy, but killed everyone.

This was not a battle, said Daupus.

It was, confirmed Thorne. I know people who remember it.

Daupus held up a fist of bones.

These are unmarked, he said. Except from scavengers.

Thorne shrugged. When first I came here, spears still stuck between the ribs. I can tell you that in those days bleached bones lay everywhere about the veld. Testimony to unparalleled massacre. But that was years ago. Others have raided here since for the weapons. Elsewhere the bones have been covered over, the veld lies pristine again.

I would say these here were murdered, said Daupus. I would say each throat was slit without struggle, each small finger cut off to be redeemed in cash. Perhaps whoever held them captive preferred a lesser wage than slaves fetch!

You would be wrong, said Thorne. There is nothing sinister here except the savagery of war.

I did not say it was sinister.

Such you implied.

Not at all, said Daupus. All I meant was there were no cleaved skulls, no small metacarpals or phalanges. No signs of men run amok.

Thorne sucked on the hair below his lip.

There are strange things happen here, he said. Things no rational man can understand, or explain. Let me tell you this is a wild country of brutal people that are not like us, that do not aspire to the greater good. Theirs is a life without morality, they are brute souls like animals. Each one is condemned unless we bring the light. Hell's fury awaits them all.

He turned away. Daupus let the bones fall one by one on to the sand at his feet.

They make a good pattern, he said.

Ruyter sniggered.

Do you see some mystery here? asked Clarence.

No, said Daupus, this tells a story one way or the other.

Then he signalled that they should remount, and they did, and rode on.

### Arriving at the mission

Three days later they came across refugees fleeing the mission. These were women and children and dogs wandering without direction or purpose. Who at the sight of armed horsemen ran in blind pandemonium, forsaking all they carried, even babies, in a cry of abandonment. Only the aged waited with terror for what they considered certain death. The men drew up. Thorne stood in the wagon and spoke to the fugitives and they raised their heads in joy at his voice, crooning his given name, swaying before him in adoration. And those who had run away now ran back, collecting what had been dropped until they were gathered before him. Thorne blessed them and calmed them and assured there was no longer a need to fear.

Where are the men? he then asked.

And was told some had driven off the cattle to strongholds in the mountains; that others waited in defence.

Why are you not with them? he questioned.

And was told they had been dispersed where the marauders would not follow because it was reasoned the raiders sought livestock and slaves and that to flee in small groups was their only escape.

And he queried about the mood at the mission.

It was desperate, lamented the women. Each night they expected attack. Each night they lay awake: the men crazed with fear, the women in continual weeping.

Thorne chewed at his beard, his eyes fixed and unblinking, yet his hands shook. Then were plans discussed with Daupus. The men waited, stone-faced at the exchange.

How far is it still? Daupus asked.

A day's ride, said Thorne.

Daupus took reckoning of the sun.

We should rest and eat, he said. Perhaps ride again near midnight.

Impossible! argued Thorne.

Daupus looked away. He slapped a rein against his open palm.

That is my opinion, he said.

It is my purse, said Thorne.

Daupus shrugged: Then have your way.

Which Thorne did. The women he had provisioned and instructed to follow, ignoring their pleas not to be left unguarded. He had the men ride on with greater urgency through the day's remainder and through the night. They rode as hard as the teams would allow and sighted the mission at dawn.

In some low hills to the west Daupus had them stop. He drew from his possessions a fieldglass and climbed with Harsent to a vantage point. On the flats before them the settlement lay quiet without smoke or movement. Daupus examined it: saw four low structures of mud and grass that were the mission buildings and clustered apart small beehive huts. All were closed, perhaps deserted. The ground was barren about, except for withered maize patches beyond the huts. Between the dwellings stood marabous: some stabbed at offal, some waited on the roofs. He could see no sign of other life, man or beast. Yet even as he watched the storks took flight, unhurriedly circling, or strode out to an imaginary perimeter.

They smell death, said Harsent.

Daupus grunted neither in agreement nor in disagreement.

Now Daupus scanned among the dwellings and saw a man emerge, who stole forth, pausing often to listen. The marabous regarded him, those farthest out closing in. The man crept towards the huts and went among them and was lost in shadow. Daupus cursed. He looked back at the dwellings, which were as closed as before. From between them the man reappeared and Daupus fixed him in the glass: he was nonchalant now, swinging back towards the shelters. Soon some

twenty others stood in the early sun. Daupus lowered the glass, glanc__
at Harsent.

It seems we are not too late, said Harsent. Nor would have been
tonight.

Just so, said Daupus.

They descended, Daupus first, tall and black against the yellow
hill.

The group rode out of the hills towards the mission, the wagons
leading. Those among the huts watched their coming until the
distance lessened, then ran forward to greet the company. Behind,
the marabous bunched closer. Soon the defenders milled among the
horses and Daupus saw they were tribesmen bearing antique arms. At
their coming into the mission a man awaited them. He was Thorne's
subordinate, one Reverend Lightborn as they were introduced, though
he was no missionary in disposition or appearance, being deep-browed
and covert. He looked none in the eye for his gaze skittered about,
and his hands trembled. Nor had he information of the hordes, his
speech spluttered and stopped at Daupus's questioning. Afterwards
he kept away.

### Disgruntlement among Daupus's men
In the following days Thorne sent out for those who had fled, and
these gradually returned, bringing livestock. All spoke of the hordes,
yet none had seen them. They told of dreams and similar visions, of
the burning of villages, of the consumption of human flesh, of a swarm
of bees descending from the north. Daupus listened to their stories
without comment. Thorne likewise, making notes of all they said.

During this time the men grew unsettled: each day they patrolled
but encountered no hostile forces, nor even other people. And those
who guarded at night were startled by nothing other than marabous
which came to roost upon the dwellings. Among themselves the men
were of agreement: there was no enemy. They bought now of the
beer brewed by the women and were often drunk.

Only Thorne was content with such inactive days. For he not only
ministered to his congregation but studied, too, their anatomy. In
his records all were to be catalogued according to the size of their
heads and the number of their teeth and the measurement of their
limbs, and their features sketched. The men collected when he was
about these activities and asked him what he hoped to learn, and he
answered that until all possibilities were known there could be no
complete understanding.

Of what? Daupus inquired.

Of what was contained in the universe, he replied.

And then? said Daupus.

Then we shall be closer to God, said Thorne setting down his notations. And understand our place.

At which Daupus glanced at each and said the meaning and purpose of individual lives resided in their souls and that no science or measurements could determine it.

You are both right and wrong, said Thorne.

No, said Daupus. Not in this.

It was here Daupus told Thorne of his disgruntlement which the missionary heard in silence. He was for moving on, he said, and that cash settlement in full was his intention. He spoke reasonably, pointing out there was no enemy, nor any necessary defence, nor even a threat according to his estimation. He allowed that such might have been the situation but as he saw it these circumstances had altered.

Thorne chewed at the hairs tufted on his lower lip this while until his temper was enraged and uncontrollable. He stamped, the dust rising like smoke at his feet. He shouted at Daupus that this audacity was in violation of their contract, that they were scum and drunkards not worthy of his mission, not worth what he had paid let alone any additional recompense. But that he would not release them from their obligations. Not before his terms were met.

Daupus nodded, seemingly with full patience, abiding until the missionary had calmed. Then he warned Thorne that his attitudes were foolish. That men such as were here recruited could not be cowed by angry words, that words spoken thus were of little meaning to those armed.

Do not threaten me, Thorne hissed.

It is no threat, said Daupus, only fact. Then he demanded of Thorne what terms had not been met.

Terms of protection, Thorne responded, adamant that he would have the hordes vanquished before the contract was void.

How? Daupus interjected.

By your men and these my followers, said Thorne.

Daupus sniffed and hawked out the residue.

We have rifles, said Thorne. Most can shoot.

To kill a buck perhaps.

To kill a man.

As you will, said Daupus. When?

Tomorrow, he was told.

# Preparations for a massacre

For two days they rode south-east through a droughted region. They were Daupus's men and some twenty of Thorne's, and Lightborn and the missionary. Each wore bands of cartridges about his body and his waist, and four packhorses led behind were burdened with other ammunition. They rode steadily at a pace Daupus determined which would not exhaust them, either man or beast.

On the second evening they were stopped in a koppie's lee when scouts brought news of a tribe's settlement three miles out upon the plains beyond. They told of numbering some five hundred men and a like total of women and children. None seemed armed, except with spears. They had no horses. Daupus heard their information and in the dust had them sketch the attributes of the village and any surrounding features be they rises or gullies or outcrops of rock. These he studied in the failing light along with Thorne and Harsent.

Then Daupus described a scheme whereby they would lure the men from the village and surround them and shoot them, keeping always outside the reach of their spears. And he instructed the men to adopt a formation that would never be more curved than a sickle moon, which would scoop the heathen before it until all were annihilated. In the case of attack, none should stand and fight but ride out and from safety kill those in pursuit. This he insisted was their advantage against such numbers.

And Thorne added that he would countenance no rapine or murder of women and children and would watch expressly to prevent it. If any did he would have them hanged without ceremony. He said too that their queen should be captured and whosoever did this would receive financial reward. Despite all rumours of her magic and her powers, he vowed she was mortal and merely woman, and none should be afraid of her.

The men heard him out but among his followers there was consternation. Whereupon Daupus instructed that his outfit would apprehend the queen but all would share the prize. Which Ruyter protested; Daupus eyed him down. Then were they dispersed. At dusk Daupus ordered the fires extinguished whether a man's food was cooked or not and forbade the taking of spirit. Later, those posted to watch saw in the distance how the village fires flared, yet in that blackness may equally have been gazing at stars.

Harsent and Podumo settled on the group's extremity and were joined there by Ruyter and December, both liquored, and by Clarence. Ruyter offered a flask of gin and Harsent accepted, drinking hard. Podumo, too, at his turn. And Clarence. Podumo cleaned his knife and sat deeply engaged by this. Then the men watched how he bared his right forearm and slit the skin on the inside. Blood beaded on the cut which was no longer than a man's small finger, and welled into a tear. From a pouch Podumo took a pinch of powder and rubbed it into the wound. The bleeding stopped. The men watched him wipe the blade on his trousers and sheath it, and retie the pouch and pocket that. Thorne had come to stand before them.

Give me that, he said.

Podumo did not respond.

It is evil, said Thorne. Give it me.

Neither man moved, nor any in that circle. At which Daupus intervened.

From the darkness he said, I would leave him.

Thorne turned.

He has killed for that substance. Who knows what innocent child he cut for those parts, probably while it still lived. And doubtless drank its blood.

In their way, said Daupus, it is what Christians do.

Thorne chewed at his beard, his teeth appearing like those of a mouse. Gradually they slowed at their activity. He spoke quietly.

You blaspheme, Mr Daupus. I would thank you to honour the Lord's church.

Whom I honour is no concern of yours, said Daupus.

There is only one God.

So they say who would convert.

Then have him give me that.

No, said Daupus.

I will not tolerate superstition, said Thorne.

You have hired his service, said Daupus. Nothing more.

I have hired him for Christian work.

You may call it that, said Daupus, I will call it for what it is.

I shall . . . but Thorne's threat dangled, for Daupus pushed past into the night.

You are warned, shouted the missionary: They are scum, these men.

When he was gone each brooded on the nature of the substance Podumo held, its acquisition and its powers. Until Clarence broke their meditations. He asked of Podumo what was the powder and was informed it was medicine.

Against disease?

For protection, he was told.

Even against bullets?

Against all evil, Podumo said.

Yet we have not seen you use it before.

There was no need, Podumo replied.

Not even during the worst times?

I carried it then, which was enough.

But now it is different.

Yes, he answered.

They sat silent until December queried further if it was for the protection of others as well? Which Podumo confirmed, provided that such men had faith in it. And when asked what faith this would be, they were told it was faith in the properties of natural things and of the power within every living being which could be taken and used for greater potency. Then was it made from human parts? Clarence inquired. Podumo would not answer. Yet Ruyter did, saying it was of various organs: testicles, penises, liver, a breast, sometimes an eye, or vulva lips.

As the missionary said?

Just so.

Even the killing?

Even that.

Later, across the night that was cold and had covered each man with a white frost, came an eeriness striking fear into those sleepless and into those brought from the sanctuary of sleep. It was instant and hellish and echoed only in their minds. It was a cry both of lamentation and of hate that was not human yet was the ululation of women. It screeched in its intensity, it traversed cold through their blood as if those who howled were among them. And they imagined fierce hags, their mouths swart maws in which the yawl fluttered like crazed bats that escaped to rake at their throats and eyes. These women: anguished by mourning, by the violence of men. Their faces such horror, such rancour, their tongues at the ululate, shrill, piercing.

There were men who screamed and those who covered their heads and others such as December who rose petrified at the consternation to find the terror was within them. They stared about. Daupus and Thorne called to restore equanimity and the excitement quietened but no man would sleep again. They lay alert and terrified.

What was it? whispered December.

A cry women make, said Clarence. I have heard it many times, but not like that. These hills must magnify the sound.

Then they know we are here.

Most likely.

And of our intention?

Men at these co-ordinates have only one intention.

## A vast carnage

Silent and stiff with cold they waited for the dawn. And with its coming strapped on their ammunition and prepared their horses. They mounted; some were wrapped in blankets against the cold, some wore scarves across their faces. They did not talk. Daupus stood aside, a sabre hanging from his belt; and concealed beneath his coat a revolver. Thorne was unarmed, and Lightborn carried no obvious weapon. Then Daupus filed the column between the koppies; Harsent took up with Podumo in the rear.

The sun sat off the horizon and held yet no heat and they rode into it, their shadows thin and long across the veld. Before them the ground was frosted, a whiteness on which they left dark prints. Their going was at a walk, almost of reluctance. Whether they were observed or anticipated none could say, for their progress went unchallenged. Which fostered unease. They went on in greater caution.

Daupus squinted ahead but smoke from the fires obscured the village, lay over it like a mist that was contained and exact, and spread to no other part of the plain. Yet from out of it voices carried and the screech of fowls, and with their nearing dogs barked. Daupus raised his hand and the horsemen stopped and he gestured them to assume the commanded formation. They were but a short sprint from the village which ghosted now in the drifting smoke. The sun was well risen; acquiring warmth.

From the haze walked two men dressed in skirts and cloaks of skin who bore as weapons only knobbed ceremonial sticks. They came on without fear, glancing neither to left nor to right at the line of men, stopping but a few paces off. One called a greeting and Thorne responded, and the men turned to address him. They talked and the missionary listened and spoke in his turn. When he finished Daupus asked what had transpired.

Thorne said that they were invited into the village.

Like lambs, Daupus interjected.

I am no fool, sir, said Thorne, but he professes they do not want bloodshed.

Then have you asked them to leave?

I have.

And?

They say they cannot go back to their lands because there is no grazing for their cattle, the rivers are dry and the wells. They wish to settle here. They proclaim they mean no harm but just to share of fertile land.

Daupus shrugged: Then it seems a matter for negotiation.

Not at all, said Thorne. You do not negotiate with such as these.

Then the smoke thinned and they saw men armed with spears and shields massed on the village edge, waiting. The shields were a warrior's size and the spears greater than a man's length. Each held four or five of these lances; some bearing, too, axes or other clubs. Each was naked, yet adorned with strips of skins and fur.

Do you see? Thorne said.

Daupus grunted.

And these would have lured us in there. To certain death. It is as I said, these are savages.

Thorne pointed at this force and spoke to the men before him, deriding them for this prospective treachery, and even while he talked Lightborn reached into his coat and drew out the revolver he had holstered there, and sighted with sure expertise and fired. None noticed his actions until the gun discharged and the man nearest Thorne was hurled from his feet, a clot of gore sprayed from the shattering of his skull. Then the revolver jumped again and the second emissary collapsed with his head similarly destroyed. In this instant the men on the horses saw the warriors start forward and heard the call of their stampede. Before this they retreated, galloping back across the plain.

They dispersed widely; only about Daupus remained a group that were his men and some of Thorne's. The missionaries, too, were with him. They rode furiously until Daupus brought them up. He ordered each to dismount and they stood ready beside their horses while the horde closed upon them. At this there were some who shot wildly and without effect, who then fled, but the rest kept discipline, firing within range: tribesmen fell; yet the charge was not arrested. Daupus's group beat away.

From a distance they watched the warriors collect their dead, give aid to the wounded. Most set back for the village but a band remained which advanced towards them. The party was again complete, with those who had panicked now rejoined. Daupus wasted no words on them but Thorne reproached these for their cowardice. On the flats the band crept closer, yet Daupus waited.

How many? questioned Thorne.

Some thirty, Daupus replied, putting away the fieldglass. To the men he shouted: We will do with them as described.

Then they rode out towards the warriors and dismounted before them in the form of a sickle moon. Daupus and the two missionaries stood behind. Each chose him he would kill though the shield of his adversary revealed no body parts except the feet.

Let them come, called Daupus. They must open to throw their spears.

And they did as he predicted, the lances lofting up, the men exposed in the action. And the rifles retorted: each witnessing what he had anticipated come to pass. Each bit at a cartridge and recharged, aware of the tumult about him, and of warriors coming on.

Now Daupus raised his revolver and fired into the shield that was nearest. It fell away and a warrior stood before him spouting blood from his chest as it was pumped out. Daupus reloaded, eyeing the man this while who neither attacked nor sought to stop his wounds. Daupus shot again and the man was bent backwards at the impact, going down, but did not die, but agonised and writhed upon the ground. Soon that stopped. Daupus stared about for the first time at the scene: spears littered among them, yet not one of their number was wounded, nor the horses. The warriors lay dead or dying.

Then the group went after those upon the flats and enacted a vast carnage. They used the tactics Daupus had decreed and believed themselves immune to wounds or death for none were cut down. They were blackened about their mouths and their teeth, and had mutilated corpses for oddments which they wore as charms. There was about them little recognisable as those who had followed Daupus in the morning, for everyone was grimed and blooded now with this business. And the plain lay strewn with bodies yet the warriors still milled and wheeled towards them with each onslaught. Again and yet again Daupus's men came riding to within range, dismounted, fired, escaped away with high yells of triumph before the warriors could surge upon them. And it built a fury in the tribesmen that this enemy was untouchable, causing decimation among them with such impunity. They cursed against this plight, even inviting the bullets, standing unshielded in defiance. Thus were they slaughtered.

Yet in this a raider was speared who was taken from his horse with the force of the thrown lance. But came to his feet, the long shaft trailing from out his back, and ran. The warriors gave chase, taunting him, closing about to spit and jeer, pulling free the lance. The man fell: his back and his trousers dark-stained, the blood leaking through his shoes. He was face-down and clutched at the dirt and wailed, and at his wailing they laughed. Then they set him up and he staggered on. Throughout they whooped and whistled. Behind, the one who had withdrawn the spear, who wore bands of fur about his arms and chest but was otherwise naked, prepared himself: reached back his arm, paused in the balancing of the lance, and pitched it. The raider was impaled, the blade passing out his chest. He reached for this with both hands, and held the metal and was holding it even when he fell. At which the warriors yelled their revenge, and the first among them ripped open the man's bowels. He cut out the liver, brandishing this, dancing with it aloft, while another chopped away the head, his blows inaccurate, his axe blunt. At this activity both were shot down, for none had noticed the approach of Daupus's men. Others died, too, in the retaliation, only a few escaping.

Then Daupus surveyed the devastation caused by his strategies and among it the knots of warriors still defiant. With deliberation he scanned these through the fieldglass: they were scattered about the plain, bloodied and weary and watchful. He called his men and in the sand demonstrated a plan of attack to quell these last remnants, then divided his force into groups and sent them out. They rode as he had commanded in an action of perfect choreography and seemed to pass over the veld with utmost dispassion, the tribesmen wilting before them. And some of these rose in their wake only to fall again in the return sweep and lie finally still.

### The boiling of the skulls

At the end of the afternoon the massacre was completed: the village burnt; the women and children had fled. Cattle wandered among the fires and among the corpses on the plain where those wounded still groaned. Elsewhere the raiders looted for food and beer.

On the plain a group of silhouettes walked slowly among the dead. They seemed to come from out the sun that hung now bloodshot above the western rim and in their semblance were raptorial. Sometimes they stooped like marabous to examine the corpses, and gathered round in a circle to perform their deeds as storks do. And sometimes they handed up an object to the one who rode, who dropped it in a sack of similar objects which hung tied from the saddlehorn. Then they moved on, making their way purposefully. No words were spoken between them, the one leading merely selecting the mementoes by gesture. So they came on towards the gutted village.

And occasionally their progress was distracted when dying men rose to challenge them: ferocious men desperate with death who expected no mercy. These they dispatched summarily, marvelling at the fight left in such wounded men. For one reared up on his knees, his lower legs broken, lunging at them with axe and spear. They shot him. Another they stuck with three spears who was already wounded in the chest, but their casts were poor and the spears hung from the man's thighs and abdomen. They stood about him in curiosity and the man snarled at them and bellowed. Then he wrenched the spears from his thigh and flung them back, which scattered the group. All laughed. They shot him, firing in turns. Clarence performed the decapitation. The last to confront them was one-armed, his other hanging by tendons and strapped to prevent its loss. He ran at them with a levelled lance which he drove through the horse's chest before they meted out his death. The beast fell yet Daupus jumped clear. They went on more quickly as the twilight deepened.

That night they sat before a fire and had set on it a large pot scavenged from among the village ruins, that they filled with water to boil. About them were other groups and the smell was thick of cooked meat, and the noise of laughter and feasting. They too were replete and had beer yet were of more sober intent: fatigued, not exhilarated in the aftermath. Even Ruyter was subdued, declining the hands of cards the others played. Except for the calls, they did not speak. Often one stood to feed the fire. When the water boiled Clarence dragged up the sack, and December took its end, tilting it over the cauldron and the heads fell out, ten of them. They swirled in the turmoil: rising and sinking on the current, some open-mouthed, all staring fixedly. Clarence took a branch and stirred; the others gathered to watch. And Podumo asked how long it would take and was told all night. Then they collected more wood and decided on their watches. Those drawn later prepared to sleep.

Towards the end of Clarence's time, Daupus appeared who stopped to warm himself yet drew back at the wafts of stink. He moved upwind beside Clarence and lit a torch and peered through the steam and the scum that frothed upon the surface at the shapes rolling below. Taking the paddle he trapped one against the side, raising it: the eyes had boiled out, the flesh tore where the stick caught it. He released the head; returned the paddle to Clarence.

Clarence nodded and would have spoken but already the figure had gone back into the night. Thereafter he woke Ruyter and throughout the hours each took his shift troubled by the moans of jackals upon the plain and the bark of hunting dogs. Nor were their dreams free of these terrors and all slept fitfully.

In the morning they saw the process was complete. From the vat's surface Clarence scooped a yellow gluten and hooked out each skull which he put to dry in the sun. The mandibles, too, he retrieved, although on some a slime of flesh still adhered. These were laid out likewise. By this activity the curious were aroused and came to wonder at the display: at the bones which yesterday had called for their very deaths. Some joked at this, but most were perturbed, and soon moved away.

When later Daupus's group rode off, each had tied two skulls from his belt.

### In pursuit of women and children
At Thorne's command, the raiders went now in pursuit of the women and children and found some hidden in caves about the koppies, who hurled rocks upon them and chided them with imprecations. This stirred laughter among the men and they responded in jest, firing to frighten, struggling upwards against the missiles. Yet found they faced great resistance and were bruised and cut in the ensuing discord. Even so they subdued the women: fastened them with rope from neck to neck and tied their hands before them, and started for the mission. Of the children they gave no heed, dashed out the brains of babies, left the rest to follow as they could.

And out upon the plains fleeing east towards the mountains they found others. These were small groups who scattered as the horsemen rode upon them but were rounded up like cattle, being driven by gunshot and whips and the wild whoops of the men. The young fell beneath the horses and were trampled, their mothers herded away until they too went down with exhaustion. Then were they bound with rope and led from Podumo's horse. Those with child were left, and young children similarly.

And although Daupus's outfit scoured the region the queen was not found nor any of her retinue. Nor would the captured women speak of her either to acknowledge her life or to reveal the path of her escape. Even when Harsent threatened death, raised his gun to a woman's head, the others stayed mute. And he was forced to lower it cursing their obduracy.

Perhaps she does not exist, said Daupus.

She does, vowed Thorne. It is you who let her escape.

No, said Daupus. She is your demon.

He turned aside. And Thorne did not stop him or say anything in contradiction.

They marched their captives for five days before reaching the mission. And in that time some women died and their corpses were left upon the veld. And in that time many children gave up and fell behind and were not seen again.

# CHAPTER TWELVE

*Melville, a government agent, the banker Friedland, and Nunez, a slave trader, haggle over the price of the captured. A compromise is reached. Daupus and his men are further contracted.*

### The price of slaves

AT THE MISSION WAITED THE GOVERNMENT AGENT and the banker Friedland, and one called Nunez. The first had been longest there and were apprehensive, unnerved by the people and the constant marabous, questioning on the second day the wisdom of their waiting. Then had Nunez ridden in. Each was acquainted, yet the agent Melville offered no greeting and Friedland fanned at his nose to move the smell of the newcomer. Nunez dismounted.

Boa tarde, senhores.

The others nodded. He came up with outstretched hand.

Senhor Melville, Senhor Friedland, it is a pleasure.

But his hand was ignored and slowly he withdrew it and sank it into the pocket of his high-buttoned coat. His face was fixed in its smile of decayed teeth.

Ah, senhores, it has been a long time.

He looked from one to the other, his eyes quick upon their faces.

Do you have tobacco?

Melville offered him this, which he took wadding it between his palms into a ball, his eyes still shifting between them. Then he raised the plug to his mouth and chewed hard on it until a yellow juice glistened at the corners of his lips.

Where is the money? asked Melville.

Ah senhor, who would ride alone in this waste with so much money?

You.

He sniggered: Then that is the answer to your question.

Let me see it.

No, no. When the reverend comes we can do business. But now we must wait.

They sat out a day more, scanning hourly the horizon, cursing at the delay and the grinning Nunez. On the following morning he called them at the sight of a dust-billow that heralded the raiders' return and estimated their arrival for three hours hence. And as he had predicted the advance came in with Thorne and Lightborn and Daupus among them.

And before anything the missionary took aside the agent and the banker telling of a furious battle born of the treachery of the hordes. And of the viciousness of their fighting and their refusal to surrender. He said that it seemed yet a fantasy, unreal in the experience and in the reporting. However he said he was history's recorder and would bear true witness.

Then was there a commotion outside and they left the hut to find Harsent had arrived with the captive women who were taken to an enclosure and freed of the ropes but manacled with ankle chains supplied from the government wagons. This Nunez supervised, counting the captives and the young of suitable age and assessing the health of each. He grinned throughout; chewed on tobacco, looked well-pleased at his prospects.

Thorne said, They are not all in the price, Mr Nunez.

Não, senhor! frowned Nunez. He looked at Melville: That is not what we agreed.

No, said Melville, it is not what we agreed.

You will set another price?

No, said Melville. There is no need for that. You have more than we thought.

You should have said this first.

Melville waved the slaver aside.

It is just a small favour, Nunez, between friends.

Then he and Friedland and Thorne chose women that were young and suitable for household service and domestication. These were tagged for later separation.

Afterwards the three withdrew and remained at a distance with Daupus and Lightborn where in due course the others approached yet waited on the periphery in anticipation.

Thorne said, You have done well, Mr Daupus. You have our appreciation.

It is not to be thanked that these men have gathered, said Daupus. But for their money.

Thorne nodded.

You will get that, Mr Daupus, said Melville, but we have other propositions for you.

We have finished our dealings with you, said Daupus.

I think not, said Melville. The Portuguese is in need of your service . . .

For what?

To take the women to the coast. And I seek protection on the journey.

Consider it, said Friedland. Others would not spurn such opportunity.

Daupus turned to the men but they were of no fixed opinion: some shrugged, others gestured emptily.

Then came up Nunez who stood grinning from man to man. He spoke to Daupus: Are they agreed, senhor?

Not yet.

Come, my friend, I am honourable. I will offer you more money.

No, said Friedland.

It is a pity, senhor, but what is the alternative? The escravos are here, the ships are waiting, this thing cannot be delayed. Senhor –

he faced Daupus – will you do this thing for my wage and a taking from them? For the protection.

Yes, said Daupus.

Thank you, senhor. You will be rich men for it.

You cannot, said Melville. That was not our understanding.

No, said Nunez. But you will pay.

Do I have an option?

No, grinned Nunez. None.

And the men considered this good fortune and in the afternoon became drunk where they sat beside a hut, warmed by the westing sun. Now they adorned themselves with oddments previously cut from the dead warriors: skins, fur, beads, amulets and strange bags bearing shrunken parts unrecognisable as human, yet, Podumo vowed, were such, and powerful medicine. Most discarded these, except December who strung four about his waist beside the skulls. The other pickings they pinned to their garments and around their hats, unmindful that most were bloodstained. Ruyter had, too, loinskins which he fastened about him and at the men's chaffing pulled off his trousers and posed savagely before them. He drew the skins like a curtain from his genitals and ran about exposed, until Harsent called him down. Yet he said that was the way men should go dressed, at every moment prepared to do ravishment. Nevertheless again drew on his trousers keeping the skins over them, for the sun had lost its heat.

Then Daupus squatted among them and looked from one to another: at the dishevelment of them, at the wildness in their guise and demeanour. They shifted uneasily and none would acknowledge him. Except Harsent who glanced up and saw the charm tooth still hung about his neck and how Daupus fingered it. For long moments no one spoke.

At last Daupus said. It is for this exactly. For nothing but this exactly.

# CHAPTER THIRTEEN

*On the slave route to the coast occur further scenes of degradation and
hopelessness. Another massacre is witnessed and the aftermath described.*

### The slave route

THEY WERE TRULY WRETCHED. They
were without hope. They walked in pairs and were manacled at the
wrists and chained together and about them rode the men, uninter-
ested. They ached in their degradation and could no longer sing and

could not talk and their faces held a single expression that was of no describable emotion. Their skin was ulcered by the irons and would not heal; this pain became of their lives as it was of their freedom that had ended. Each morning they were lashed into motion and in the day's march could not stop to pass stools or water and consequently some were fouled on their legs and some leaked menstrual blood. And when they were halted each shat where she squatted and pissed there and was forbidden to move from her turds or those of her sisters. So were they also bitten and pestered by flies. And only in fording rivers were they cleansed. They were naked mostly, although a few wore skins. In the beginning their number was one hundred and thirteen.

About them, walking freely, were those of their children with the strength to abide who knew that if they did not they would die but could not conceive that what awaited them was worse. These were prepubescents on whom Nunez could place no value. Nor could he beat them off; nor could the men. At first the women urged them away, wailing at their stubbornness until one ran off who could be seen following and was chased farther out by Podumo but later rejoined them. Then the women stopped their pleading. The children continued with them as they could, sharing of their food and bringing what nourishment they unearthed upon the veld. Even so their lives were tenuous: the prey of all things animal and disease. Consequently it happened that a girl was found strangled and abused. And later two similar deaths occurred. Daupus saw the corpses as they were left splayed in perversity, and he shook his head, and rode on without comment or recrimination. Nunez gazed on them, too, and from curiosity would know who it was. But Daupus would not tell him. Then Nunez suggested, grinning, perhaps it was Daupus himself, and Daupus looked once at him and the slaver desisted. Which women mourned for their daughters did so in their hearts.

Thus they progressed towards the mountains. Each night there was meat newly shot and similarly were they fed in the morning. In this Nunez was unsparing. Yet there were deaths. Even on the second day one collapsed and was unmanacled and helped on by the children but she could not and they were forced to leave her. At their going she neither cried out to them, nor knew her circumstances. It was this way with the old and the weak: they died on the march or in the night cold. But this attrition caused Nunez no concern. He considered those that remained and was content. They numbered now ninety-seven.

And for sport Nunez had a young woman unshackled and he called the men to form a circle about her. Behind were the captives fearful at this new enterprise. Then Nunez jiggled in a dance, gesturing at the woman to perform in imitation. But she would not: she fell in the dust, crying up at him a wail. The men laughed at this and at Nunez how he bowed and beseeched in mock charade. He took the woman's hand and would raise her but she clung about his ankles and he stood as king above her nodding kindly. Now he called on the captives for their encouragement, speaking in an argot of his own devising which none could understand although they interpreted his manner and shouted back at the woman, laughing. Some even mimicked the steps Nunez had danced; others joked and pointed where the girl crouched. She looked up at all who grinned with this amusement. Nunez bowed in courtly fashion, even sweeping off his hat. Daupus's men slapped their thighs: hooted and catcalled and japed. Again the slaver jigged about the frightened girl, stirring the dust in his motion. And he tapped her with his whip, stroked this upon her back while the men whistled and the women behind shrilled at the funniness. And slowly the girl rose obedient and shuffled beside Nunez. Then the captives shrieked wildly with delight. Nunez waltzed and did other formal steps whirling his exuberance while the woman staggered in their circle. She was naked and her movements roused the men's lust: Ruyter howled, jerking a loose fist at his crotch. And the men shouted for her to leap and jump and cracked their whips about her feet until she did. Which occasioned more laughter from the captives. Yet she could not sustain this and fell and lay heaving there beneath lashes which bit and stung. And Nunez would lash her into further exhibition, and the women goaded her, but she would not move. The men jeered at the slaver's defeat and turned from the sport. Nunez cursed their fickleness and their bad attitude; dragged the girl back to the chains.

On the eleventh day they went into the mountains which rose in granite buttresses before them, snowbound and seemingly impassable. Here was the cold intense, blown about the amphitheatres and the knolls with ice. The women trembled at it, pulling tufts of long grass to hold against their nakedness which was no protection. Nunez forced them on: faster, cursing their trudge. The going was broken: of shale and loose sandstone and acacia thorn; and the women wore down, were beaten, but still endured, up and yet up a path trodden by others so captive and their traders. They were filed now singly and led by Nunez and Harsent with the men flanking and behind Melville and Podumo and afterwards Daupus, alone.

On the higher slopes San watched them who crouched among the rocks with ready bows, and the men, unnerved, slung out their rifles, walked their horses as shields. The women, too, were afraid, raising their chained hands towards the hunters, pointing. And Daupus called out that no man should shoot in provocation and they passed through unharmed. In the day's last hours they entered a gorge that rose steeply towards the summit and climbed above the snowline but no farther. Here they built fires and cooked saltmeat and waited out the night, those sleeping who could. And in the morning the dead were unshackled and the column climbed on to the summit that stretched flat and frozen and empty towards the sky. This they crossed, their feet cold-numbed and bleeding in the thick snow. Some fell and rose, and some fell and did not, and these were set free in this white kingdom. But most continued in the chain-gang with the horsemen about them.

On the second day they came out of the snow. They numbered seventy-four, and no children. They went on as they were driven, for their hearts were beyond feeling and they lived only in their misery, remembering no previous time, nor could a future be imagined. And now the mountain rolled below them and the going was easier, descending on a pass well-used and gentle with the cliffs receded behind them. Down this they went, unseeing.

On the escarpment Nunez brought them to a cave which was an overhang of rock constantly used by traders and littered with their evidence. In this he allowed them to rest. Then he called Daupus and Melville aside and described the terrors of the country beyond: the savagery of the tribes and the viciousness of bandits which operated there in the procurement of slaves. All would know of their coming and be in waiting, he said. At which Melville suggested another route but the Portuguese grinned that all routes were as dangerous.

This is a difficult business, senhor, said Nunez.

Daupus did not reply but moved away, going beyond where Ruyter and Podumo butchered their hunt, to an elevated place at the cave-mouth. He looked down on the captured women and the hired men and considered this was equal to where they were not.

### The fright of attack

They went into a broken country, pitted and ravined, convulsed, the guts of bedrock bent up in primary spasms, exposed still. Through this cut deep-eroded rivers that coursed into rapids and falls or lay seemingly placid. Everywhere swarmed all manner of beasts: crocodile and hippopotamus and elephant. The vegetation was dense being of aloe and euphorbia that loomed forth like alien warriors, many-armed or in spiked headdress. Here the heat crushed them: more women fell. And Nunez cursed their debility; in his grinning rage had them drag even those who were dead for he was now, every moment, consumed by fear.

They are here, he said to Daupus.

And Daupus looked about and knew they may have been but could see nothing in the bush.

And often they disturbed unknown animals that crashed away through the thickets. Then the Portuguese dropped from his horse, cowered beside it, wild with the fright in him. They waited, the chains clinking in the sudden stillness; and the heat settled about them and there was no other sound but the cicadas.

And at night he had Daupus's men take watches and himself slept with two primed rifles in full readiness.

Is it always like this? questioned Melville.

Sim, grinned Nunez.

They have attacked you before?

Once.

Just that?

It was enough.

You beat them off?

Yes. But the next time will not be so easy, senhor. Now they are angry. They will want some retribution.

And the fear took in the men: in Melville whose bowels forced a frequent voiding; in Ruyter most obviously who would wreak it among the women and was not checked. In the others more quietly, etching in their faces a gauntness, sinking their eyes in shadow. Clarence no longer read; Podumo mixed nightly in his blood further medicine. As did December that which he had taken from the warriors. Harsent tended his rifle, seemed careless of this fear; nor did it touch Daupus.

But it was also in the women who broke once in strident ululation that was instant and pitched, that curdled in the men's blood the fright of attack and some shot madly into the aloes in the terror of this noise. Which would not cease even under the whips but mounted and held, only fading down of its own accord when fatigue overcame them. There the women stopped and could not be moved and the men sat about them in like despondency through the afternoon and into the night.

They are here, said Nunez.

So you say, said Daupus.

In the next day they will attack.

Yes!

Sim, senhor, I know it.

Perhaps.

Not perhaps, Senhor Daupus. This is certain.

Nor would Nunez proceed in the morning until the way was scouted, which Melville supported, although Daupus refused to send out on such a mission. There was no call, he said, no sign that they were threatened or that men lurked in this vicinity. But Nunez stuck insistent. Nor would either party alter his position. And in the following hours the men grew restive at this impasse until Podumo mounted, went out ignoring Daupus's wishes. For three hours they sat expectant, before Daupus took Harsent and Clarence and December in search of him.

They found him naked and still turbanned at no great distance from their stopping place. His horse grazed near by on clumpgrass. The four kept mounted, silent before this brutality. Podumo's horse came towards them and December leant over to take the reins. Daupus looked about: at red earth scored with footprints; at the aloes, grotesque, their great thorned leaves held out like arms in mockery. Among them nothing moved. They sat to listen; the bush gave back its hum that was constant and unvaried and of insects without any sound of men. Then Harsent swung down and paused beside his horse but there was no interruption to the monotony.

They cannot be far, said Clarence.

No, said Daupus, his voice thick from his unspeaking.

Harsent stepped towards Podumo and the horses rinnicked in sudden unison, concerned with what the men could neither hear nor smell. Harsent crouched; the others milled and skewered in their saddles. So the moments passed without change.

Then he moved again to where Podumo hung impaled. He glanced up once at the body thus displayed but did not see it or how it was scored, saw only the spears, at which he pulled, fiercely, savagely, snapping the hafts in his violence. He threw down these sticks and drew out the third which came free quickly and Harsent staggered back. The body slid down until it sat like a man asleep against the stem. And in this motion the head lolled forward and the turban rolled away and the jaws slackened and disgorged a penis.

Jesus, said Harsent and spat, the bile risen in his throat.

Then he hoisted Podumo's body on to the horse and slung it there face-down. They rode back with Daupus leading this and the others close behind.

191

Daupus stopped before Nunez. He dismounted. Stood averted, let drop the reins of Podumo's horse.

Do you see this, he said at the Portuguese.

Nunez grinned without mirth.

Do you see this!

Daupus pulled down the corpse and laid it out, then raised his eyes to Nunez.

Come here, he said.

But Nunez edged backwards at the man's approach.

Come here!

And Daupus reached for him and bunched his fist in the slaver's jacket and held him and made him confront the body of Podumo that still bore the iron spearheads punctured out its back and showed him each inflicted mutilation.

This is because of you, he said.

Nunez gagged and was released and staggered away, choking: Now you will believe me. They are here. They will come in the morning before it is light. We must go on. Now. We must go. Quickly, quickly.

He dragged at the chains of the women, beat at them, cursing, and they swayed up and forward, but Daupus ignored him.

We must go, Nunez demanded. Now, now.

He looked to the men but they also ignored him, stood about the body of Podumo, self-absorbed and quiet.

Senhor Daupus, tell these men we must go. You have seen what has happened. Now it will happen to us each one. Please, senhor, we cannot waste time.

But Daupus said nothing, did not even acknowledge that he had heard.

Then Nunez turned to Melville.

Do you see, senhor, this is what they do. We must go. Now. Tell them we must go.

And Melville began but Daupus stopped him even before his words were formed, stopped him with no more than a raised hand. Melville desisted. As did Nunez, let fall the whip and his rifle. Behind him the captured women sank again upon the dirt.

They watched Daupus and the others collect dry grass and underwood and the fallen husks of giant aloe which they piled upon the body to the height of a man's chest. When they had done, the men gathered round; this pyre Daupus lit. It burnt quickly in a conflagration of tall standing flames and dark smoke, the men shifting back from its heat. Yet it was not enough. For when it had died and was ashes there could still be discerned the form that had been Podumo, now rendered of no man. Daupus turned away, and mounted and they went on although the light was failing.

And in the dark were forced to stop without any idea of how they were surrounded except of the archaic vegetation looming in what light the stars provided. Among the men none slept that night and from the women there issued a sustained moan that was like the wind over stones but also was not. Nor would they stop at Nunez's threatening and groaned this way throughout the hours.

Each man found what shelter he could, be it rocks or anthill or the stems of aloes, and waited, not knowing from which direction he would be assailed, but knowing it would occur. Clarence recited in a mumble from the poets and was sometimes still for long moments and at others intoned the stanzas in the manner of prayer. December and Ruyter could hear him from where they arranged a small fortification and dug in as much as they were able.

You will need more than those poets, called out Ruyter. More than their rhymes.

Undoubtedly, said Clarence, but now they offer some comfort.

Then they were silent until Ruyter spoke across the blackness again: Hey Portuguese! Senhor Nunez!

Nunez did not reply.

Mister senhor.

Enough, Ruyter, said Daupus.

Mister senhor why do you not give them the slaves? We do not want to die for such bitches.

You won't die for them, said Melville, but for the money.

The money does not matter.

No, said Daupus. The money does not matter. Not before. Not now.

So we should go.

But Daupus did not respond.

We're just going to sit here? questioned Ruyter.

Yes, said Daupus.


### At dawn

They waited on, listening to the night that held their destiny but offered no portent of what this would be, neither in the screech of nightjars nor in the sudden alarm of insects. Each could feel what was coming but did not think of who would die or how or who would live, if any.

At the first greying came a caterwaul that was of no man or beast

193

yet was of those who attacked who rose from the earth like a horde of nightmare forms made of that substance and blood and bones and feathers. They came from all quarters. And those who confronted them could not believe them human in any manner, or of their time. Some bore rifles, but most were armed with spear and axe, and leapt towards them in a vicious noise. Nor could they be distinguished from the shadows and seemed as flighted, more the horrors of apocalypse than men of humankind.

Then Daupus's men fired and the smoke drifted from their weapons into the whitened dawn obscuring for a moment those barbarous shapes which came on and did not stop their dinning or their yowl. Daupus pulled the revolver from his belt and discharged it deliberately and slowly and with great accuracy. Now were their positions breached and horses reared and plunged to snap their tethers and the chained women set up a screech that was added to the whistles and puling. In this dust and dimness a face leered at Daupus that seemed as much of bone as it was of flesh and was gone, leaving a spear pinioned through his coat. He tore free and threw out the lance. Everywhere figures ran and as he refilled the chambers he saw one with drawn blade slice down on Harsent's shoulder and sever his arm, and he saw December speared in the stomach and the chest and dragged from behind his protection and his fingers amputated. Simultaneously too exploded Ruyter's head and disappeared. Daupus shot again and as he sighted for the third time he saw Nunez emerge from the mêlée who carried in his hands the yards of his entrails and wore in his skull an axe. Slowly he knelt and in this tottered, letting go what he carried, staying on all fours like a dog and even raised his head but his eyes had turned up. The yammer of the savages had not ceased, nor the lament of the women which rose now in greater fear as the raiders raped among them, calling each to each in their frenzy. Daupus saw men advance on woman after woman in this violence, falling upon them, beating at their breasts and faces; and he lowered his gun. Throughout this time no one saw him and he was a witness to their deeds. Finally he watched the women led off to the chant of the men driving them.

And when it was still he walked about the ground that was stained and stank: the only bodies visible were of Nunez and December, both disembowelled, and of Harsent stabbed to death in a mess of savagery, and of Ruyter headless. Of the horses three were dead and partly butchered, the others missing. He found Clarence propped against an aloe stem and in his guts a spear which he held there firmly. Daupus squatted before him. At the scrape of his boots the hoods of Clarence's eyes flickered and stayed open, the pupils were whited like marble.

Who is it? said Clarence. Daupus?

The same.

Clarence moaned at the effort of his speech and at the movement of the iron in his wound. Yet he asked after the others. Daupus glanced back at the bodies and the horses.

Dead.

Clarence breathed red bubbles and coughed and groaned.

Water, he rasped. Some water.

Daupus unclipped from his belt a canteen partly filled and held it to the man's lips yet much of the water dribbled away. Again Clarence coughed and moaned at the pain it brought. For a while he was still, nor did Daupus say anything. A spasm of pain passed through Clarence that seemed wracked to kill him but he opened his stone eyes again at where he thought Daupus stood.

I will die soon.

Daupus did not respond except he drew his revolver and Clarence heard the action of the hammer drawn back.

There is no need for that, he wheezed.

But Daupus followed a movement he saw among the brush.

Then do it, said Clarence.

Daupus hissed at him for quiet. Now Clarence seemed to listen, too.

What was in the brush made no secret of its presence, then was silent, then came on again. A face appeared at the farther edge of the clearing and Daupus saw it was Melville. He eased down the hammer; fitted the revolver back into his belt.

Melville called. And again. Slowly he dragged himself across the dirt: Daupus stared down at him and Melville looked pleading back, whimpered in his breathing like a dog. He bled from the shoulder and at the knees where his legs had been smashed.

He gasped, but the sounds were inarticulate.

What? said Daupus.

Melville stammered, They left me to die.

Yes, replied Daupus.

Melville beat at the dust.

Help me, he said.

You ran, said Daupus. When they took Nunez, you ran.

Help me, Melville whined.

He asked for water but Daupus denied it, merely shaking his head.

There is not enough, he said.

And Melville lay crying on the ground.

Clarence sighed some earnest recitation that was subsumed in his agony yet he persisted and some words were uttered but most were not. Afterwards he seemed unconscious or in earnest meditation and held the spear tightly. Melville quietened with the gathering heat. Before them sat Daupus in a thin shade, his eyes closed yet he did not sleep. Thus they stayed as the sun shifted blurred across its zenith in a sky burnt white. No air moved to bring them relief and they were beset by a myriad of flies.

Later Daupus searched among their remains for ammunition, finding little. Melville watched him at this, marked his preparations, begged not to be abandoned, promising rewards of gold and like enticements of debentures and other investments and finally that none deserved the death that would be his in that place. Daupus heard it all without heed. As did Clarence who opened his marbled eyes at the sound and followed blindly where Daupus moved.

He left in the shadowed hours: went among the towering aloes that were black and inflamed and leant together. About him seethed the bush from the day's heat and the passage of insects, nor did it cease at his passing but rose to a new stridency. He walked into this, going back the way he had come, and he walked without fear or hesitation. He was alone; he was sufficient: his coat was dusted and stained and he wore at his belt two skulls which danced there white at each stride. In the clearing he had left sat one with bowed head holding a spear who was not dead yet, and beside him one who wept. And where they had been killed the corpses of others. From this he went; and about gathered the marabous and the vultures large and patient in the trees. They did not lift at his appearance, but waited as he need not. He went through them, and on.